VARIOUS STATES
OF
DECAY

MATT HAYWARD

POLTERGEIST PRESS

POLTERGEIST PRESS

ISBN: 978-1-913138-18-9

Intercepting Aisle Nine originally appeared in Freedom of Screech, edited by Craig Spector. Crossroads Press, 2019; *Where The Wild Winds Blow* originally appeared in Lost Highways, edited by D. Alexander Ward. Crystal Lake Publishing, 2018; *Rodent In The Red Room* originally appeared in Tales from The Lake Vol. 3, edited by Monique Snyman. Crystal Lake Publishing, 2016; *Comes With The Rain* originally appeared in the limited hardback edition of What Do Monsters Fear? Thunderstorm Books, 2018; *She Sells Seashells* originally appeared in Dark Moon Digest Issue 32/33, edited by Lori Michelle. Perpetual Motion Machine Publishing, 2018; *I'd Rather Go Blind* originally appeared in Letters From The Grave, edited by Bob Stevens. Orbannin Books, 2019; *Dark Stage* originally appeared in Welcome To The Show, edited by Doug Murano. Crystal Lake Publishing, 2018; *An Unusual Pet* originally appeared in Hidden Menagerie Vol 1, edited by Michael Cieslak. Dragon's Roost Press, 2018; *In The Pines* originally appeared in The Horror Zine Spring 2017, edited by Jeani Rector. Haunted Computer Productions, 2016; *Bangers And Mash* originally appeared in Clickers Forever, edited by Brian Keene. Deadite Press/Thunderstorm Books, 2018; *Father's Day* originally appeared in the limited hardback edition of What Do Monsters Fear? Thunderstorm Books, 2018

www.poltergeistpress.com

For Jessica.
Thanks for unknowingly giving me this title.

ACKNOWLEDGEMENTS

Special thanks to Anna Hayward, Bob Ford, Melissa & Fionnuala Hayward, Kelli Owen, Paul Michael Anderson, Edward Lee, Bryan and Jennifer Smith, Brian Keene, Os Andres, Cooper Gordon (RIP), Ivan Byrne, Rachel Autumn Deering, Aaron Dries, Patrick Lacey, Mark McNally, Paul Goblirsch, Don Noble, and Tim Meyer

TABLE OF CONTENTS

Matt Fucking Hayward

ROCK STAR, PROFESSIONAL IRISH GUY, TWISTER OF WORDS, CONVEYOR BELT MAN

by Kelli Owen

I MET MATT at the Scares That Care convention several years ago in Williamsburg, Virginia. I hadn't read anything. I hadn't heard anything. I didn't *know* anything about Matt Hayward. He seemed to be polite, with a soft-spoken accent that belied his excitable nature, and as our conversation floated across the genre and writing, I quickly grew to enjoy chatting with him.

Then I read his fiction.

While reading through *this* collection I made up a new term and caught myself mumbling it several times: conveyor belt story. It describes the kind of tale that pulls you forward naturally, and not just within the words, but physically as well. Your posture changes from a relaxed position to sitting up, then scooting to the edge of your seat, and finally you find yourself hunching over the pages. You literally *lean* into the story.

That's one hell of a trick, and one Matt Hayward pulls off several times here.

Among these pages you'll find an eclectic collection of short works that don't seem to be connected on the surface, yet feel related by the ghost of an undertone. One example is the smooth and subtle way a waterfront tale *mentioning* the sadness of a lost pet naturally flows into another story, where the pet in question is *itself* the question. These stories don't follow each other directly, but the first one sat and stewed in the back of my mind enough that when I reached the second I paused to reflect on the other stories, to try and decide how many *other* pieces fit together with jagged edges and sneaky themes. This phenomenon is partially due to choosing the right stories to include, but also in designing the order of their appearance, and it's done as well as the stories themselves.

Writing is more than the idea, it's the execution, and Matt has successfully bridged the chasm between. Beyond theme, Matt's use of setting is a force to be dealt with, and nowhere is safe, or sacred, from the twists of his internal set director. And be it wind, rain, fog, or forest, even the weather seems to be a character. His ability to create malaise and wonder will have you shrinking from grief and cheering for cannibals. Your eyes will widen, your brows furrow, and your lips curl, as you are dragged, willingly, across a gamut of emotions and expressions you can't help but let escape with gasps and sighs.

Unassuming as he may be, kind and honest as he comes across, the way Matt slaps words on the page makes you question the darkness of his imagination, and will definitely make you believe he'd been doing this much longer than he has. Perhaps it's a type of magic borrowed from being a musician for years before turning to writing. Or maybe he's just got that internal spark and understands how to twist the words just so, to make a little kernel better, stronger, and turn a simple idea into a conveyor belt story. I'm leaning toward the second, and sitting a little forward in my chair since I finished reading this collection.

If you've never read Matt, this is a solid place to start. If you've read him before, you'll be glad you added this to your collection. And while I for one, will be looking forward to his next offering, this one will cause me to pause before digging for the remote or other lost items in my own couch cushions...

Kelli Owen
Destination, PA
October 2019

A Brief
Introduction

WE BOTH KNOW fear.

See, fear, unlike love, is universal. It's been with us since that first human banged rocks together over a pile of sticks to keep the warmth in his bones and the shadows at bay. And it comes in all shapes and sizes.

Recently, I got married. I have a partner who stands by me and who has opened a whole new world of possibilities when she said, "I do," but fear, of course, came along for the ride. A fear I'd never known. What if I lose her? What if she goes to work one morning (after a quick coffee and a peck on the cheek) and never returns? I've seen it happen before, after all, and to one of my best friends. Speaking of friends, that conversation you just had with a certain someone will be terrifying in retrospect, I'm just warning you now. Because *things happen*. And then those final words haunt; become a worm in the apple. Again, I've had it happen many times.

And you? You know fear. You know it as well as I, both the terrifying and the mundane. Sometimes it's hard to distinguish the two. You're broke and it's two weeks to Christmas. You've just dropped little Mittens off at the vet for the night and she was looking a little weak, wasn't she? Your partner is somewhere without you. Feel your gut churning? Heart rate going up? Because what if *something happens*?

Find me someone who has nothing to fear and I'll show you Pinocchio's long-lost cousin. Usually it's the same person to ask me, "Why do you write this kinda thing?" and the type to ask you, "Why do you read it?" And our answer, of course, should always be, "Why *don't* you?" Why *not* face The Big Scary? Repeat exposure, like the old psychologists say. And with fiction, with movies, what better way is there? It's safe. You can put the book down at any time, you can turn off the TV. You're in control.

When I wrote my first novel, *What Do Monsters Fear?*, I poured a lot of myself onto the page. The novel itself personifies facing The Big Scary. But still, it terrified me to know people would read it. What if they saw through the fiction and saw the *real me*? I lost sleep because of it. But then something strange happened—people did read it. They enjoyed it. No one laughed, no one scoffed. It won a nomination for a Bram Stoker Award, and for a brief time, was under consideration for a major movie adaption. Trust me, good things come when we give the middle finger to fear. It's cathartic. Refreshing.

And let me let you in on a secret. This foreword? Frightening to write. I'm a reserved person at the best of times, so to open up and talk to you like this? Petrifying.

VARIOUS STATES OF DECAY

But I faced it, and I wrote it, and here you are reading it. So we've both made the first step, and for that, I trust you. Because you know fear as well as I.

So get comfy. Maybe even grab a drink (or does the mention of alcohol make The Big Scary raise its ugly head?) but whatever you do, don't be afraid. I've walked the bridge you're about to set foot on before. I built it, after all. The first step's a little creaky, sure, but I'm telling you—it won't break. You're in safe hands here.

But I might be lying.

You could fall...plunge into darkness and never return. That *could* happen...but are you willing to find out?

I dare you.

Matt Hayward
November 2018

VARIOUS STATES
OF
DECAY

INTERCEPTING
AISLE NINE

"WHAT IN THE world is a *Squiggly* bar?"

Ronald glanced around the supermarket to make sure no one had heard his muttering. Seven or eight customers shuffled about the Supersave, each looking lost and sedated. A large man of undeterminable age waddled up the aisle with a basket in-hand.

"That the new Squiggly?" he asked.

Ronald placed the bar back on the shelf with the others and tried to look preoccupied with his search. "Fucked if I know."

Ronald didn't want to talk to anyone at three in the morning. God knows who they might be. Serial killers, junkies, weirdos, what other kind of person would be up shopping at this hour?

Me, Ronald thought. *I am.*

"Heard they're awesome." The large man scooped a bar from the shelf before wandering off with a smile.

Ronald watched him go before turning back to the Squigglys, squinting at their wrappers. He'd lied to the fat man. He *did* know the Squiggly to be a new product. Only he hadn't seen it advertised on a television commercial, in a magazine, or on the side of a bus. He'd seen it in a dream.

19

Ronald had woken at two-thirty, same as every night. He'd been asleep for less than twenty minutes, and even though every cell in his body had screamed for more rest, he'd known waiting for sleep would be a fool's errand. Insomnia was one hell of a curse.

So, instead, Ronald had crawled out of bed, slipped into a tracksuit, taken the elevator down to the first floor and gone across the street to the Supersave to shop—all on account of a phantom craving left lingering from a dream, one for a nougat-filled chocolate bar called a Squiggly.

In his dream, short as it'd been, he'd been having dinner with Mary-Ann, his friend of five years from the apartment downstairs. The two had laughed and reconnected, having a very merry time while waiting for their meal in an upper-class restaurant. Beside their table stood a waiter with a pearly white, shit-eating grin and a face that demanded a punch.

Arms behind his back and in a voice perfect for radio, the waiter announced, "Don't let kids hog *all* the fun. Grown-ups can enjoy desserts, too!"

Then he ripped free his blazer to reveal a tie-dye t-shirt reading *SQUIGGLY!* across the chest.

"New from Carpco.," he continued. "A chocolate bar that's just *bursting* with soft and squishy nougat, the Squiggly!"

Silence followed while the waiter looked frozen in time. Mary-Ann lifted her knife and fork and cut into the chocolate bar on her plate as if nothing out of the ordinary had taken place. Ronald pushed himself from the table and smiled to the waiter. "Sounded like you were going to pee yourself you got so excited there, kid. You eat it. It looks like shit, anyway."

Then an ambulance had screamed by the apartment, bursting the bubble of the dream and leaving him confused and staring at the ceiling.

"Can I help you, sir?"

The question made Ronald jump. A friendly, square-faced man with a crop of curly brown hair approached. His nametag read "Pierce."

"Um, no thanks, that's okay. I'm not really sure what I'm looking for."

Pierce squinted. "Well, I believe it's a Squiggly you're after, right?" He plucked a bar from the shelf and presented it to Ronald in an open palm. Then his voice dropped in volume, his expression soured. "Only you're not so sure *why* you want it, am I correct?"

Ronald tried to speak but couldn't find his voice.

"Look, don't be so frightened," Pierce said, speaking from the side of his mouth. "This is all explainable, trust me. Will you follow me to the till and let me ring this up? I'll tell you more on the way. Just act natural. I'm Pierce, by the way. Pierce Tiernan."

Ronald said, "I'm still dreaming." But he followed the young man, all the same.

They passed an old woman with a basket full of shaving foam, a middle-aged businessman who looked out of place, a fat woman in running gear who stared at the baked goods, and a person whose gender was as confusing as what they wore.

"Here we are." Pierce got behind the checkout and beeped through the Squiggly. "That's fifty-eight cent, please."

Ronald handed over a Euro coin and took his change with a smile and a thank you, the everyday task still demanding a token of graciousness even though there were more important matters at hand. Confusing matters.

Ronald leaned into the checkout so as not to be overheard. "Look, Pierce, how in the world did I know about this...*thing?*" He waggled the bar like a flaccid penis.

"I hate all chocolate to begin with, why would I...why would I crave it and know it exists, all because of a...*dream?*"

Pierce gave a tight smile. "Marketing and advertising, my friend. The scum of the earth."

Someone in a far-off aisle sneezed. Ronald stared at the cashier; aware his mouth had dropped open. *Catching flies*, his father would have said.

"Ronald, don't be so surprised."

"How in the *world* do you know my name?"

Sighing, Pierce leaned forward, giving Ronald a whiff of his cologne. "*OneWave.* Ring a bell?"

"Certainly does."

Ronald had attended what the company OneWave called "Sleep Studies" for the past month, along with three or four other insomniacs. The position was sought after by many unemployed, sleepless citizens across Dublin city. Especially since Ireland's recession, when many folks were so worried that they couldn't sleep. Why not get paid for it?

"What have they done to me?" Ronald's voice shook.

Pierce indicated with his eyes to be quiet as a hunched lady shuffled by. Once she passed, he spoke low. "Oh, they're doing their studies, all right. Just not the type they're telling you. They're not trying to cure insomnia, Ronald. They're creating an algorithm to influence the subconscious mind."

Ronald wheezed a laugh. *It's a setup*, he thought. *Got to be.* "Look, Pierce, I don't know who's in on this or how you've done it, but that's amazing. Seriously. You would've had me if you didn't start sounding like Bill Hicks on crack."

Pierce's expression dulled. "Sure, okay. Hey, do me a favor. When you start having advertisements in your dreams for more products you've never heard of, come and see me, okay?"

Ronald's face fell.

"Listen. I'm an intern at OneWave. I've seen you come and go. I know you live around these parts. I *needed* to talk to you."

"What's in it for you to expose them?"

Pierce spoke through his teeth, "I just hate the bastards."

"Then why intern with them?"

"Look."

Pierce nodded to the side where a car turned in the carpark, its headlights briefly glaring off the front window in the Supersave. Ronald watched until the vehicle indicated and left the lot.

"Was that a black SUV?"

"No." Ronald squinted out the glass, but the vehicle had already gone. "I think it was just a hatchback."

Pierce sighed, as if relieved. "Ron, they've got arms that reach far, know what I'm saying? If a black SUV came by, a Mercedes, a Land Rover, a *Pilote de Terre*, I'd be in trouble. Thank God."

Ronald had never heard of a *Pilote de Terre*, but he got the message. "Answer my question, Pierce. Why would you intern at OneWave, if they are, as you put it, the scum of the earth?"

"*To be on the inside.* Don't you get it? How else could I prove what they're doing? I needed definitive evidence, and I've got it now. The CCTV footage has all four of you insomniacs coming in here at all hours of the night to grab a Squiggly, something you could *never* have possibly known about because there's been no advertising for the product. That's *proof.*"

"Couldn't it have been coincidence? Maybe the wrapping attracted us?"

"Oh, please. Look at this." Pierce grabbed the Squiggly from Ronald's hands and held it up in the light. "This is about as appealing as a brick. White packaging with one black word. Squiggly. That's *purposely* done, Ronald. They *made* it unattractive so that no one else would ever buy it within the first twenty-four hours of its release besides the insomniacs who were experimented on. And it's worked. You were the last one I was expecting to stop by."

"That big guy, the one who bought one just before me, he's...?"

"Another test subject? Bingo."

"Jesus."

Ronald pushed himself from the counter and rubbed at his forehead, the room seeming to spin. He'd suffered from insomnia as a young man, but the condition had slipped away over the years, only coming back full force when he'd been let go from his job as a bookkeeper for a law firm, a job he'd held down for almost thirty years. Then insomnia had moved back in like a headstrong ex-partner.

"Why would somebody do that to me? *How* would they do that?" Ronald asked.

The rate at which modern technology improved and advanced dumbfounded him almost daily. He remembered buying a bargain set of encyclopedias back in the mid-eighties and had always enjoyed flicking through the pages to the amusement of his friends. Now his nephew could know the capital of Zimbabwe at the touch of a button. Ronald wasn't *completely* in the blue, though; in fact, he now owned a smart phone, but getting used to the quick paced world still took time. As far as zapping advertisements directly to sleepers went, it didn't sound *completely* farfetched to him.

Pierce glanced around before speaking. "The Japanese set the foundation back in the early 2010s with that fMRI scanning. It measured brain activity based on blood flow. The method, even back then, was able to produce recorded images of dreams with *fifty-percent* accuracy. Pretty cool, huh?"

Ronald nodded. "I agree, it is pretty interesting."

"They would wait until the sleeper reached REM inside the scanner, monitoring the EEG, then wake them and ask what they dreamt about. See, certain parts of the brain work while thinking about certain things, like cats, dogs, SUVs, whatever. It's all about patterns."

"So," Ronald said. "We're up to a point where we can translate a person's dreams onto a screen, like a TV show, right? What then?"

"Right. What always happens is *what then*. Some fat-cats wanted to know how they could capitalize on the technology. They patented part of the process and developed it further, learning how to *influence* those patterns."

"For the purpose of making money?"

"Of course. You'd hardly think they'd use it to cure nightmares or something, did you? They want it to make money to return their investment and start turning profit. And what's the easiest way to do that? Advertising. Always, advertising. Bid off to new companies seeking to broadcast their products and see who'll pay the most. Could you imagine having your product in a new market, one that isn't saturated with competitors? If it worked, your merchandise would be seen by every single person sleeping, all at the same time. How much would you pay for that slot? Makes something like an advert at the Superbowl in the US look like child's play. Am I right?"

A businessman approached the checkout and Ronald stepped back to allow him to pay. Pierce managed the transaction with a smile, but Ronald noticed the young man's hands shaking. Talking about OneWave really riled him up.

"Have a good night," Pierce shouted after the man, then turned back to Ronald. The smile slid from his face.

Ronald scooted closer. "Those *cunts*."

"Damn right, those cunts. But now I've got a case against them, I can try shut them down. But I don't know if it'll work."

"What do you mean?"

"These aren't the type of guys you'd like to go up against in a legal fight. They've got deep pockets. Every media outlet on earth is probably on their side with the advantage they'd get. You can only imagine the potential, and then you'll see why no one would want it stopped. At least, no one in the capital world."

"But you've got evidence now, right? And you'll have my testimony." Ronald's heart raced. "I'll stand up and say exactly what I can remember from the tests. With the CCTV footage of this place, they can't deny it, right?"

"Let's hope. It's the only reason I took this shitty job, so I could get that security footage. Send the intern, they thought. Little piece of advice, Ronald, never trust a smiling businessman."

The woman in the running gear approached with a three-cake pile in her arms. "Is this a get-together or is this a fucking shop?" she asked. "Move it, come on."

"Jesus, lady." Ronald turned back to Pierce. "I guess I'll let you get back to work."

"Right, no worries. Go home and get some sleep, Ronald. I'll be in touch tomorrow. I've got your number."

Get some sleep, sure. Like that's going to happen.

Ronald gave a quick smile. "Call me tomorrow. Please."

On his way back to the apartment, he realized he still held the Squiggly. Unwrapping it, he took a small nibble and rolled it about his tongue. The chocolate tasted like gooey wall-plaster, the nougat like sadness.

This can't possibly sell well...

Unless, Ronald thought, you hi-jack people's dreams and implant an artificial craving. Jesus, soon enough the entire planet would all eat the same, dress the same, watch the same shows, have the same hopes and desires, all because it would be coming from an outside source. All because the entire population would be *told* what to like without even realizing.

A thought came to Ronald then, and his stomach lurched—What if a politician paid for an advertising campaign that way? Manipulated the population into thinking he was *their guy*? Could that be allowed?

At a nearby rubbish bin, Ronald tossed the Squiggly and wiped his hands on his jeans. He doubted even a rat would touch that crap.

"You're...you're just throwing it away?"

Ronald turned to the voice and jumped out of the way as a homeless man barged past. He dipped inside the bin, threw a used burger box, and came out clutching the candy like a Faberge egg.

"You know how hard it is for me to get one of these, mister?"

"I'm..." Ronald swallowed, his throat dry. "I'm sorry, I didn't think."

Wait, Ronald thought, *how would you know about the Squiggly?*

Before he could ask, the man shredded the wrapping and slammed the chocolate into his face with shaking hands. His neck bulged as he swallowed.

"You're wearing *those*?"

"Excuse me?"

Ronald followed the man's pointed finger to his black store-brand shoes.

"Why aren't you in line for a pair of CloudAirs?"

He sounded genuinely confused, as if Ronald had agreed upon an appointment and let him down.

"I don't know what you're..."

Ronald's brow creased as, over the hobo's shoulder, one man slammed another's head into the side of a building. The crack rang out.

"Jesus!"

Ronald took off, intent on breaking up the fight before the victim's head turned to pizza. Behind, the homeless man called out, "I don't think you'll get a pair, man, folks have been lining up all night!"

"Hey! Hey, stop that!"

Ronald reached the two just as the first man dropped the second like a bag of wet clothes. The aggressor panted and wiped his bloody hands on his jeans.

"Know how long I was waiting?" he asked, wheezing. Ronald shook his head.

"Two. Fucking. *Hours*." He punctuated each word with a kick to the unconscious man's ribs. "And. This. Fucker. Wants. To. Skip. The...*queue*!"

Something snapped and the victim groaned. Ronald backed off, his heart slamming—and banged into a couple cradling a box between them like a newborn.

The man snarled. "Fuck off, Grandpa! Want a pair, then go get in line like the rest of 'em!"

Ronald stuttered for an answer, but the pair raced off. When they rounded a corner, he heard a hollow knock, and then the girl screamed. A crimson trail trickled into sight. Followed by a shirtless egg of a man dragging a baseball bat.

"Wha-what the hell?"

Ronald took off, his entire body shaking as his apartment complex bobbed into view. Behind, people screamed and yelled. A gunshot barked in the distance. He entered the passcode to the building and climbed the stairs, muffled voices booming from behind each closed door. A few words cut through. *"New shoes, Helen. Want me to be seen in these another fucking day?"* Then, *"Can't expect me to watch it without 3D, you cocksucker?"* And, *"If you don't move, I'll fucking make you move, Marty!"*

He unlocked his door, the key missing its target twice. Once inside, he slammed the door, double-checked the lock, and took a shuddering breath. The outside world had turned a dark and sinister place, with greed's teeth deep and empathy but a memory. Indoors, he could at least *pretend* all was okay. Until he slept, of course. Then he'd be invaded and violated against his will, just like the others.

But how? How did OneWave get to them all? Unless of course this wasn't their handiwork...

"A competitor?"

Despite the excitement of the night, Ronald's eyes stung with the need for sleep. He wanted to call the police, but of course, all lines would be clogged now. It'd been days since he'd slept for more than a three-hour stint, and his entire body hummed in a telltale way, making him head for bed. He'd hear all about the chaos in the morning. Hell, if the cops weren't quick, it might still be happening. Besides, being awake only meant stress with a topping of worry, both of which could lead to a heart attack at this stage in his life. He needed to take advantage of such depleted energy while the going was good.

After undressing, he eased into bed, the fresh sheets hugging him and sending a shiver of comfort through his body. The pillow sunk beneath his cheek, cool and soft. He drifted off almost instantly.

In his dream, a desert spread out before him in all directions. A high wind blew, making waves of the sand and rearranging the barren landscape. He stood on a dislocated highway, the tarmac beneath his feet fresh and dark. A road rarely traveled.

It's a lucid *dream*, Ronald thought. *I'm self-aware.*

Music suddenly boomed all around, coming from nowhere and everywhere all at once, like giant speakers built into the ground. A Western soundtrack played, Spanish guitars rhythmically picking a flamenco style. Ronald squinted to the horizon, where a watery heat wave danced and swayed.

Something approached, taking shape out there—a black dot in the barren wasteland. As it came closer, the purr of an engine increased. He made out the shape more clearly now. A black SUV.

A disembodied voice filled the air, the voice of a whiskey drinking, clichéd cowboy. *"Taking yourself where you need to be, isn't that what life is all about? Freedom. Living how you want to live. Going where you want to go. And it all starts by taking the road less traveled, partner. I've only got one question. Where will it take you?"*

The SUV broke to a smooth stop directly before him, forcing Ronald to guard his eyes against the sand. He flinched as light glared off the high-polished chrome hood-ornament, a symbol he didn't recognize—A horse on its hind legs with elegant text below. *Pilote de Terre.*

The driver's door opened with a satisfying pop and out stepped a man, dressed like a Spaghetti Western hero.

"Need an iron horse to take you where you need to be?"

Ronald recognized him instantly. Despite the large black Stetson perched on top of his head, his boyish features were too distinct. If the get-up was meant to make him more manly, it didn't work. It only gave the impression that Pierce Tiernan had dressed for a Halloween party.

"You son-of-a-bitch." Ronald gritted his teeth. "You're not trying to take these bastards down, you're *in* on it. People are *dying* because of this!"

Pierce continued his pitch as if Ronald's words blew through him. "*Pilote de Terre* would like to hand *you* the keys to the future. Take it. Fire up *your Iron Horse.*"

Ronald swung a punch but the dream dissipated, puffing out of existence like an unplugged TV. He burst awake, caked in sweat and panting. The bedside clock read 4:30 AM. He wiped at his face before scooping aside the bedcovers. Then he sat for a moment, head in his hands. Outside, sirens wailed.

Pierce's smug face floated about Ronald's third eye, mocking and laughing. "The bastard's a competitor..."

But if Pierce Tiernan was some kind of entrepreneur taking an internship at OneWave, how did he get in the door without them catching on? Unless he'd given them a false name. Unless he had the money and the means to fabricate a false background.

These people have deep pockets, Pierce had said. *These aren't the type of guys you'd like to go up against in a legal fight. Never trust a smiling businessman.*

But then why give his real name to Ronald? Why not develop the research in secret?

"Because the research is already complete and ready to go," Ronald said. The peach-fuzz on the back of his neck stood. "He was *gloating.* Because he knows he's sitting on gold and no one can take him down...he's untouchable. Robbed all he could from OneWave and started a rival business...and now...*that cunt!*"

Somewhere out in the city, a chainsaw roared to life. Ronald pounded the mattress with his fists. He had an idea to confirm his suspicions. His nostrils flared as he pulled his pajamas on and scuttled to the living room, firing up the laptop and taking a seat.

The only difference between OneWave and Pierce Tiernan, Ronald knew, was that Pierce had finished his technology and OneWave were still plodding along in development. OneWave was still testing, and Ronald had seen not only Pierce's first official advertisement, but the power they could unleash, too. The image of a French SUV flashed before his eyes, followed by a flutter in his chest. A craving.

Pilote de Terre...

"It can't be true. It can't be."

After launching his browser, Ronald typed, *Pierce Tiernan Advertising* into his search engine.

The browser took a moment, then displayed the results. The first hit made his stomach drop.

"No," he moaned. "Don't let it be true."

He clicked the website and waited for the homepage to appear. Then he read the text.

Pierce Tiernan Inc. We make dreams a reality. Company website launching soon.

Screams filled the city.

WHERE THE WILD WINDS BLOW

THE DYNA'S HEADLIGHT spluttered, strobing the mountain road like a bad disco. Tony gripped the handlebars and relaxed the bike to a steady twenty, unable to navigate the flickering. He rolled to a stop and kicked the stand before easing himself from the seat with a grunt. The bike purred, and he tapped the tank for good luck. If the night could get any worse, this was it.

"Baby, don't do this..."

He kneeled and knocked the malfunctioning light with his knuckle. It blinked once, twice...died.

"You givin' up on me, too? Fine."

His dry mouth tasted of stale booze and too many cigarettes. He worked up some saliva and managed to swallow as he got to his feet, the only glow now coming from the city through the matting of spruce on his right. His jeans sagged and he tightened his buckle a notch, unfazed by the past week's shed weight. Colliding with a vagrant at fifty caused all kinds of side-effects.

Tony clicked his tongue, squinting further up the mountain road and gauging the danger. Twenty-odd miles to go, the left side an abrupt plummet and the right nothing but pines. The trip home could be made. In the dark. If he was careful.

"And if I keep from seein' double long enough."

That, too, he thought. Like smacking a homeless man head-on, downing a bottle of whiskey also had its effects on the body and mind. He thought of Lisa back home, pacing the living room in her robe and chain-smoking a pack of Luckies for the sixth night in a row. He'd taken off with the Dyna for three-day stints before, sure, but not in the last decade. The fight this time, what little he could remember, ended with him getting the bottom of a bottle in the right eye socket. Now the bruised skin was still tender to the touch, but healing.

Lisa'd promised to stay sober with him, and goddamn it, if she caved then he had a fucking right to hit the town, too. Sure, he might've gone overboard with a week— and a fifty-worth a night in Jeff's Juke only paid back in a sore head—but the *principle* mattered. Now, at the end of this all-time low, he could return home and stitch it all back together.

Except, Wednesday night'd ended in a hit and run...Boy, have you fucked the puppy.

He planted his hands on his hips and scanned the road, waiting for his eyes to adjust to the gloom. The wind hissed through the trees. He could make it home... praying, of course, that Lisa hadn't already set fire to the place and shat in his Corvette. A seventy-thirty chance at this point. Either way, he needed to go back, if not for her then to gather his things and hit the road. Before the local rednecks slipped into gear and caught up to him for killing ol' Homeless Harry.

Unlikely, seeing as Tony'd dragged the hobo's body to an alleyway and left him in a sleeping position. Bums died all the time, who'd waste their evening with an autopsy?

Right after, with his nerves shot, his hands trembling, and his leg screaming—the top layer of skin left somewhere on the street—Tony'd hobbled back to his bike and taken off, leaving the body behind a buzzing trash can. A three-minute ordeal tops.

"Better safe than sorry." Tony shook away his swaying vision and shuffled back to the bike, his thigh burning with each step. He'd doused the leg with whiskey the night of the crash while watching a rerun of *The Price Is Right* in a motel off the highway. So far, the wound stayed clean but he'd need proper bandages once home.

He lifted the leg across the seat and eased himself back on the Dyna. She rocked in response. Once satisfied he could see at least ten feet head, he kicked the stand off and pushed forward, keeping a stable fifteen at first. The Dyna growled, a metallic panther chewing up road.

Tony shivered in the night chill, the thought of coming home and clicking on the heater in the living room giving his chest a flutter. He could curl up on the couch and drift off for the night, what little was left of it, deal with the inevitable argument and severe hangover after he'd caught at least a little shut-eye.

"Daddy's comin', sweetheart. Don't go just yet..."

As he slipped up to twenty, his confidence rose along with the speed. An urge to gun the bike—to thirty, forty, fifty—kicked in. That very urge, last time, ended with him skidding from the Juke's lot at three AM and smacking a vagrant from his shoes. Still, his stomach tickled with excitement. The steep drop to his left teased him to try. Or better yet, close his eyes and count to ten, see where he ended up...for *The Thrill.*

His knuckles whitened as his lids fought to shut but his brain refused, still having enough sense to know the consequences of wrecking the bike on the mountain. Hitching back to his and Lisa's didn't appeal, not when only the odd trucker took this route to grab breakfast at the diner in the hills or grab a beer in town before hitting the highway.

"Just get home...you've had your fun. Just get home."

But Lisa *had drank*. And after *promising* him to stay clean, too.

She'd *let him down*.

And you'd only be letting yourself down by getting into more trouble. You're done, Kid.

"...But the night ain't over yet."

Tony crept the bike to twenty-five, the speedometer jittering. Wind lifted his hair from his shoulders and the sensation curled his lips. He could go further.

The whiskey seemed to agree.

Into thirty, his heart nudged his ribs like an old high school buddy—*That all you got, Pussy? Come on. Where's the Tony Williams the ladies gush for, eh?*

Touching fifty now, Tony surprised himself with a laugh and leaned forward, adrenaline thrumming through his veins in a good hit. He took a corner and his left hand refused to brake, the tire skidding and spitting rubble from the cliff edge. The sheer drop came into view for a split second—a chunk of dark pines separating the mountain from the town bathed in blue moonlight—and Tony had a brief impulse to leap from his seat and drop. Surely it'd last at least eleven seconds? And what a fuck load of fun that'd be! But then the bike took off again, back on course, pulling both him and his death wish away by its own accord.

He licked his lips with a chuckle and returned his stinging eyes to the road.

A fog lay ahead.

Thick as cotton, swallowing the path.

Slow swirls like beckoning fingers called Tony to gun the bike and slam right on in. Penetrate the unknown... for *The Thrill*.

The ball of anticipation in his guts turned to a rock of fear and Tony's hand eased back the accelerator. He slowed to a stop just before the wall of white, something in the back of his brain screaming a warning. The air was warmer here, moist.

The wall of fog reached for him, curling out and dissipating, never spilling over its invisible threshold.

He glanced back the way he'd come, a good fifteen miles from town. Nocturnal creatures chittered in the thicket, but other than them, he was alone here. He could make it through the fog if he cut the crap and took it slow, eased himself along and tried not to think of the damn otherworldly warmth oozing from the stuff. He'd call round to Henry's in the morning, explain what he saw and get an answer. Henry knew plenty of trivial things, kept him king at the local pub quizzes.

"And you better have an answer for me, Henry, because this shit's givin' me the creeps."

Tony rolled the Dyna forward, and the fog enveloped him.

The sudden increase in temperature sent a shiver through him and Tony's teeth chattered. Not at all unpleasant, and that in itself was somehow...unpleasant. *Unnatural, more like*, he thought. *But how could it be unnatural? There ain't no factory belchin' shit out here, no one burnin' nothin' or I'd smell it, no swamps...just woods.*

The fog eased back a touch, revealing a sliver of road before his front tire, dishing out just enough to lead him forward. The road steepened, calling Tony to give a little more power, and the Dyna roared to take on the challenge. He imagined a sudden bend, one that sneaked out of the white and caught him off guard, and imagined the unexpected plunge through the icy night air...suddenly *The Thrill* had turned to fear, his adrenaline congealed to sickness. And what about a sneaky rock or downed tree in the path? Those would send him off into the unknown, too. Anything could if he wasn't careful.

He blinked, clearing his vision, the fog in his head competing with the fog on the road. He shouldn't have drank today. He knew better. Knew Lisa would smash his teeth in at the whiff of booze.

A scream cut through the fog, high and shrill. Tony's arm hair rose to attention. He eased on the brake and slowed to a stop, his breath visibly disrupting the thick mist before his face.

"*He's dead!*" The voice screamed. A woman. "*There's blood everywhere, Carl! Someone's killed him!*"

Tony arched an eyebrow. "Carl?"

He remembered the bartender, a burly bloke with two sleeves of tattoos and a face like a puckered arsehole. And a nametag to the right of his shirt. One that read Carl.

No, but I'm out of town? No way I'd hear someone finding that bum? Not out...here...

"It was that bastard on the bike," Carl said. His voice whipped left and right like some studio effect. Tony turned his head, trying to discern the source. "*I'm tellin' ya, I was just waiting for him to slip up. Get Pat on the phone, have him come out. I'll close up inside.*"

The rolling fog slipped away on the right and the sudden clearing made Tony yell. A young woman crouched over a body, her face scrunched in fear, and as Tony dismounted the bike and jogged to her, the fog reclaimed her. He reached out where he'd seen her, but his fingers clasped only on thick air, his hand slamming in an empty fist.

"Hello?" he said. "Where are you?"

No one replied.

Tony turned and back-pedaled to the motorbike, his heart racing. The fog cloaked everything, licking his face, slithering into his clothes.

The bike! What if I can't find her?

Tony grunted as his stomach collided with the tank, sending the Dyna crashing to the gravel. His boots skidded in the dirt as he gripped the frame and pulled the Dyna back up. Once on the seat, his lungs burning, he wiped sweat from his forehead and grimaced as more fog slipped down his throat. The taste of rotted meat clung to the back of his mouth.

He batted his face, as if wiping the fog away could help. The ghostly figures stayed branded in his mind's eye, though, the bourbon in his stomach half-heartedly claiming responsibility for the sight. His innards roiled, a lack of food adding to his conclusion.

Tony shook the thought as he began to move, the Dyna's growl reassuring his nerves. With a nod to further steel his courage, he kept a steady eye on the road as the heavy mist dished out five-foot rolls. A bend came from nowhere and Tony balked as he whipped the handlebars right, narrowly avoiding the edge. Then a wind kicked, and the hollow gust sounded like guttural laughter. Tony's skin prickled.

"*Hey, buddy.*"

The voice came from everywhere and nowhere, from inside his head and all around, an all too familiar toothless rasp. He eased on the brake but didn't stop, the Dyna rumbling. He whipped his head left and right, but the curtain of fog kept everything hidden.

"*Spare me some change? Know I gots to get inside tonight. Lost a toe last winter. Can't lose another. Just a dollar, two if you got it.*"

"Oh, fuck this..."

The Dyna roared as the speedometer jittered, the wheels chewing up the gravel. Tony kept the engine gunned and fought to keep from slowing. No thrill came from the danger now, instead his stomach threatened to empty its contents and he gritted his teeth to keep steady.

"Come on, come on. End, you sonofabitch!"

The road blurred, a never-ending path of dirt, and then a figure appeared. Tony slammed the brake. The man smiled. Tony hit the dirt face first.

His breath whooshed from his lungs as pain bloomed around his nose and cheeks. Pressing his hands to the gravel, Tony pushed himself upright and gasped for air, winded. Warmth trickled down the left side of his face. He whipped around but the smoke-screen filled the road like soil collapsing back into a hole. The Dyna groaned from beside him and Tony righted the bike with a grunt, sniffling back fresh blood. Then his skin prickled as a presence came up from behind.

In his left ear, someone whispered, "Spare a dollar?"

The smell of stale whiskey attacked his nostrils and Tony leaped onto the bike with a yell. He took off as the back tire spat pebbles and smoke, fighting the urge to look back. Things just beyond the veil of white crawled and swayed all around him, shapes never quite close enough to discern. He swore he saw something slither along the ditch.

Then the fog broke.

Tony burst into a clearing, the fresh night and sudden cold making him gasp. He braked and spread his legs, the bike rocking like a bad carnival ride. A horn honked, and headlights blinded him as he veered left, back towards the guardrail, letting out a yell as chrome crushed chrome.

He landed with a thump, back screaming as air gushed from his lungs and his spine arched to breaking point.

His skin burned as he clamored to his feet and watched the taillights of a hatchback disappear down the interstate. The stench of petrol sent alarm bells ringing and he spun to see puddles of brown splashing from the Dyna's tank. The petrol seeped into the forest floor and pooled across the road.

"Shit! Not tonight, not tonight..."

The bent handlebars sent a devastating punch to his heart and his legs almost gave up. With a sniffle, he brushed debris from his clothes, ignoring the stinging in his hands. The Dyna was dead, that much was clear, but a forest fire looked more than likely if he didn't intervene. A cigarette out the window of a passing car was all it would take.

A car honked as it sped past, and Tony waved but the driver kept moving. He gave the bastard the single-fingered salute and got another honk in response. Across the way, a warm glow from the windows of Benjamin's Breakroom beckoned, a single building in the middle of nowhere that promised safety, comfort, and a much-needed payphone. Two calls needed making—one to the police for the crash (he'd be long gone before the blue and red started flashing and could claim the bike back tomorrow. "Had to rush to the hospital, officer, treat my wounds. Alcohol? No, sir, not a drop.")

The second call would be to Lisa. At this rate, he wouldn't get home for God knows how long, and her chances of leaving skyrocketed by the second. The realization that he didn't know her number forced his eyes wide and he stomped the ground, pulling at his hair.

"Fuck! Why tonight, huh? Why?"

Her mother's place. At the very least, he could show up on the doorstep bandaged and bruised and bike-less in the AM. Worth a shot.

"Hell, it's my *only* shot."

He glanced at his wristwatch. Close to four in the morning. At this hour, the all-night diner was most likely empty, but a single red Globetrotter truck said otherwise. It rumbled in the parking lot beneath a lone, dim streetlight, the driver-side door open.

The prospect of a conversation with someone, an act so simple and normal, turned Tony's stomach. He took off, limping through the intersection like an undead ghoul. At the lot, the truck driver came into view. He sat by a tire of his vehicle, hugging his knees.

Tony fished his Luckies and Zippo free from his shirt pocket and lit a cigarette, left leg throbbing from the fall. He sucked smoke deep into his lungs, relishing the burn and the nicotine hit. The sudden silence, the cold night air, felt surreal in its normality after what he'd just been through. He worried this could be another hallucination, something shown to him by the fog just like the voices, but he pushed the thought from his mind, chalking it up to nerves. He crossed to the trucker, taking another pull from his smoke.

"I need a phone. Just trashed my bike. You got a... everything all right?"

The man, mid-fifties with a John Deere baseball cap, raised his head. His sunken eyes vibrated in their sockets, his skin ashen. His throat bobbed as he made to speak.

"I saw my kid," he said, a voice like sandpaper.

What little heat and strength Tony had left drained from his body.

The man sniffled. "I saw the rope Richie used to hang himself, swayin' off the overpass. Saw it and him and...Jesus, I can't stop shaking, I...worst night of my life, pushed in my face and I couldn't look away."

Tony's mouth dried. He tried speaking but his throat refused to open, and instead, he eased himself to the road. They sat in silence a moment, Tony unable to meet the trucker's gaze. The bike and Lisa took second place to the implications of this man's word.

A soft rain patted the pavement, then hissed all around. Tony flicked away his cigarette, the cocktail of nicotine and adrenaline in his system leaving him ill.

Finally, the man spoke. "You saw it, too, didn't you?"

Tony didn't answer.

"What'd it show you? Tell me."

Tony swallowed. He wiped dried blood from his upper lip.

"Took me over along the highway, you know. Lasted 'bout three minutes. That's how long, I think. Been sittin' here piecing it together. Just...couldn't see anything, man. Only white. All white."

Tony faced the trucker now, needing to see his eyes. See if he saw his own fears reflected. "It passed through the woods," he said. "Caught me on the trail."

The man nodded. "I know. I saw it slip down that way."

"What is it?"

"I have no idea. Something no one should ever see, that's all I know. But then again, I..."

"You what?" Tony skittered forward. "Tell me. You what?"

"Maybe it's something I *should've* saw, after all. Things I couldn't let to the surface before, things I kept bottled... popped into my face, made me look. That's what I saw."

Tony thought of the vagrant, the sound of the crash that night, the lack of emotion as he'd dragged the body off-road...

"I do know one thing."

"What's that?" Tony asked.

"It's blowing south, past the mountain...and God help that town when it hits."

ALISHA

"**YOU'VE TIED UP** a girl, I'm hearing you right?"

Rachel eased herself onto the couch without removing her gaze from her friend. Dan stood in the doorway, a hand propped against the frame, panting. Fresh snow dusted his shoulders. "You just need to see this, all right? I'm not crazy, Rach. But, honestly, I can't explain it."

Rachel nodded and mouthed she understood but no words came. She cleared her throat. "Robby?"

Her boyfriend stirred in the next room, the mattress creaking as he rolled out of bed. That man could sleep through a banshee wailing.

"Good," Daniel said, and clapped his hands. "Bring Robby, bring everyone."

"Just…" Rachel sighed and squeezed the bridge of her nose. "You've got a girl tied up, and you want us to come see. I'm not misunderstanding this?"

"You're not. And I've called the Gardaí on my way here, it's okay, they're already on their way." Rachel doubted very much that things were 'okay', but she allowed him to continue. "Said it could take a while with the roads the way they are but they're coming. Rach, it's *why* I have her tied up that you need to see."

"Right."

Rachel calculated the distance to the equestrian center through the snow, a fifteen-minute ordeal if they moved at a good clip. The police should arrive soon after—and if Dan had tripped a wire in his think-jelly, both she and Robby should be safe. *If he's telling the truth. About the police* or *the girl.*

Robby shimmied past Dan into the living room as he pulled his nightgown across his midsection. His puffed eyes found Rachel as he nodded, his hair a rat's nest. "What's goin' on, Dan?"

He leaned over and kissed Rachel's head before sniffling and sitting beside her.

"Dan's got a girl tied up," Rachel said. "He wants us to see."

Robby jolted as if splashed by ice-water. "Excuse me?"

"Well," Daniel said, palms forward as a nervous laugh escaped his lips. "It's not like it sounds, man. You just need to see this, *please.*"

For the first time, Rachel eyed her friend up and down, taking note of his pockets and belt-line—seeking a weapon. He appeared clean.

"Dan, did you take anything tonight?" Robby asked.

"No!" Another laugh. "Guys, please. You've known me, what, five years? You ever think I would do something to harm anyone? Rob, I've walked Rachel home more times than I can count, I've never laid a hand on a woman and you both know that. *Please*, we need to get out there, okay? Can you just come, can ye?"

When Robby gave no response, Rachel nodded. "We'll come, fine, but—and I'm not saying this to hurt you, Dan— but Robby's taking a knife, understand?"

Surprisingly, Dan sighed with relief. "Good. Place it to me fuckin' neck the whole way, yeah? *I don't care*, can we just go now?"

"Right." Robby stood with a grunt before shuffling to the kitchen. He pulled a steak knife from the wooden holder above the stove. "This is crazy. Dan, wait in the hall while I get dressed, okay? Then Rachel gets dressed and I keep an eye on you." Then, almost as an afterthought, "The fuck is going on."

"Fine."

"I can't fucking believe I'm holding a knife right now. This is a goddamn dream or a joke and I don't care which, I just want it to be over with so I can go back asleep."

As Robby dressed, Rachel kept an eye on her friend through the open door with the knife now in her hands. Daniel tapped his boot, arms folded. "Feel strange having that in your lap when it's me you're worried about?"

"Dan, you've brought this on yourself. You can't just show up here in the middle of the night telling us you've got some girl tied up and not expect us to be edgy."

"Right. How's the work hunt goin'?"

Rachel cocked her head. "Sorry?"

"Said you were still lookin' for something local. Get any offers?"

"Dan, I don't think it's time to be talking about work."
Or lack thereof.

"Sorry, just makin' small-talk while my pals hold me at knife-point."

"Because you've got a prisoner."

"Point taken. Just worried about you, said you were feeling lost and all. Making sure you're okay."

More like I'm no longer the main character in the movie of 'My Life', Dan. But there's more important things to think about here.

Still, the genuine concern eased Rachel's fears some. *This* was the man she and Robby called a friend, and his lucidity meant he wasn't *completely* nuts. Or so she hoped. She'd read psychopaths hid that kinda thing all too well.

"Rach, go on and get dressed." Robby appeared wearing his sports-coat and woolen hat as he pulled on a pair of thick gloves. He slipped the knife from Rachel's grasp and pointed to Daniel. "You stay."

"Ah, for fuck sake, man, you think I'd try anything with both of you like that? Just hurry up, will ye?"

Rachel passed them both and quickly climbed into her winter gear, pulling a scarf over half of her face. When ready, she allowed Daniel to lead the way, Robby close behind with the knife to the small of the man's back, and by the looks of it, more for appearance than out of actual fear. "Lead on," he said, and walked Dan outside.

The cold snap hit Rachel as she locked the door, and her breath streamed away in a pillar. She followed the two men down the drive, careful of her footing as snow crunched beneath her heels.

Dan sniffled. "It's really just something else, guys. You've never seen anything like this."

"Lead on, man."

They clomped through town, their breath blowing away in fat clouds. White clumps swelled on rooftops, cars, and foliage. The few other residencies of the estate sat in total darkness. Mitch and Jess would be fast asleep by now (the couple rarely made it past eleven), and the three other homes belonged to secluded older couples Rachel and Robby only knew on a grunt n' nod basis. A crescent moon hung overhead, surrounded by twinkling stars, and the perfect night only furthered the sense of dislocation, as if Rachel were watching the start of a horror movie cliché. "Got your phone, babe?" she called, suddenly hit by the recurring thought that this could be a setup, no longer feeling bad for her distrust. It wasn't *their* fault he knocked the door at one in the morning raving about a tied-up girl; let the consequences fall on *his* head.

"Yup," Robby called back. "You okay?"

"Doing fine."

Daniel chuckled. "Lads, this is like something you'd see in a movie, it's just insane. If we just find a rope in the snow, I'll be the first to commit myself to a loony bin, I promise, but you're not gonna believe it. I can't wait to see your faces."

"Just what is this, Dan? Tell us."

"*You just need to see it.* We're almost there."

For the next ten minutes, the trio trekked without a word through the icy terrain, their silence only broken by the occasional sniffle or cough. At the equestrian center, they passed the wooden welcome sign and stalked up to the house, a home big enough to fit five other houses. Two horse statues sat to either side of the snow-covered porch, and Daniel's Ford was nothing more than a white lump from the weather.

Rachel often wondered how Dan could ever feel safe working in such a vast, empty mansion, but then she'd never known the luxury of a big home. And now, with no work, she wondered if she ever would. Living day to day was bad enough, but now, without knowing where the next paycheck could come from, she felt aloof and disconnected in ways she never had. Daniel's call only served to further that sensation.

"Just around the corner. Here we go."

Rachel's arms fell to her sides. "Oh, sweet Holy Jesus."

Her mouth lolled open. Beside her, Robby let out an unintentional sound, not even a real word. And Daniel, with a smile, motioned to the sight.

"What did I tell you? Are you believing me now, yeah? Want to put that knife away? The Gardaí won't take kindly to you wagglin' a steak knife about the place, and, because I'm actually a good friend, I'll say nothin'."

"This is unbelievable."

The young girl, perhaps all of sixteen, floated at least two feet from the ground. Gooseflesh rippled across Rachel's skin.

"This isn't right."

If it weren't for the horse rope around her left ankle, Rachel imagined the girl just might float up and up and never be seen again except by a keen-eyed astronaut.

"It's a magic trick," Rachel breathed, "I'm dreaming. Robby, wake me up, please."

She grabbed his forearm but Robby simply shook his head.

"Did I fucking tell you?" Daniel pointed a finger. "I mean, *what the fuck*, guys? What the hell is this? Look."

He clomped across the lawn and stood before her, head back. The girl faced the heavens, mouth agape and eyes closed. Her limbs appeared limp, her auburn hair cascading down the back of her blue pajamas. With a tug of the rope, Daniel brought her to ground level, then, released it. She drifted up again, bobbing as the rope tightened. "Now, if this isn't the strangest thing you've ever seen then I'll eat my own excrement."

"*Daniel*," Rachel scorned, but shuffled closer. Robby pulled his phone and jabbed on the light, illuminating the bizarre scene in a glare. The harsh light only furthered the sense of a movie scene. The young girl appeared to be in good health, no abrasions or bruises, no blood. Her chest rose and fell with each breath, evenly paced and relaxed. "She's sleeping. Like a human balloon."

"That's what I thought."

"How did you find her?" Robby said. He pocketed his knife as nervous excitement seeped into his voice. "Tell us *everything*."

ALISHA

"It's just..." Daniel shook his head. "Oh, man. Right, so I was washin' my hands by the side window there, and I look out and catch some movement. So, I see it's a girl, but—*but her legs aren't moving*. I know, I know. She's just floatin' across the lawn like the wind was blowin' her away, like she weighed as much as a bad fart. So I rush out still in me slippers, fall across the snow, shouting 'hey, hey' and all, but she doesn't hear me, doesn't change direction, doesn't rush off, *just keeps floating*. So, I place a hand on her shoulder but there's a *force*, like an invisible person is trying to take her, so I grab hold of her shoulders and shake her but she's not waking up. She's not cold either, seriously, feel her ankle, warm as a cuppa. So I drag her over to Sally's post and take the rope and get it around her ankle so she doesn't bob away and drift off onto a road and get smacked by a truck or something, and I run inside and call the police, but you know with this weather, up on the hill is a mess, so they say they're gonna be a while."

"So you called us."

"So I called you guys, yeah. And, here we fuckin' are and I'm still just as freaked out." He sniffled. "Now, here's my question—what the actual fuck do we do with her?"

Rachel pulled the glove from her right hand and reached out, poking the girl's ankle. The warm flesh sent a shiver down her back. She refitted the glove and eyed Robby a question, not knowing what to ask in words. He simply nodded in response. Then he removed his glove and pressed his index to her calf. "How is she warm out in this?" He asked the question more to himself. "It's bitter as a witch's tit."

Daniel laughed humorlessly. "How is she fucking *floating* is what I want to know."

"Obvious question."

Rachel reached out and tugged on the girl's pajama top–also warm. "Excuse me," she said, and Daniel snorted a laugh.

"Expecting a 'yes'? A 'sorry I floated into your lives, I'm trying to find my way back to my home planet, any directions?'"

"Fuck off, Dan," Rachel said, and tugged again. "Can you hear me?"

They fell silent and watched the stranger, breathing through their mouths.

"Excuse–"

The girl gasped and Rachel yelped, tripping and landing on her ass in the snow.

"Sweet Jesus!"

The girl blinked frantically, her features cast in shadow from the light of Robby's phone, and her forehead creased with confusion.

"Rachel?" she said.

"I'm, I'm...what?"

"Rach," the girl repeated, and a sincere smile lit up her face. "What are you doing out in the snow?" Then her eyes fell to her ankle. "Why am I tied up?"

"How do you know my name?" The question came as hardly a whisper as Rachel's heart punched and punched.

"You serious?"

"Yes, of course."

"Um–you're my sister?"

"I'm not your sister, I have no sister."

"What the hell is going on here, why am I tied up?" She asked this as if the situation amused her rather than frightened. "Dan, was this you?"

Now it was Daniel's turn to be stunned. He stuttered. "How do you know my name?"

"You're my teacher. English. I gave you the horse plushy just last week, it was your birthday."

"No it wasn't and no I'm not. I can hardly speak English, let alone teach it. I work here in the equestrian center for Eoin Fleming. I've tended horses for over a damn decade."

"Hah!" The girl shook a smile from her face. "No, you don't. You don't even live here in town."

"And where do you live?" Rachel asked.

"Right here."

"What's your name?" Robby said, and Rachel noted he had withdrawn his knife. Her stomach somersaulted. "Where do you come from?"

"*Where do you come from?*" The girl repeated, mocking Robby's serious, deep tone, still taking no note of the knife. "Let me guess, you're not my uncle, either."

"Of course I'm not. What the hell are you talking about?"

"You're uncle Robby, you're Mum's brother, but you're younger than you actually are. I've seen photos of you this age, though."

"Younger than I actually am," Robby repeated, "What does that even mean?"

She sighed. "This is a clearly a very vivid dream. Obviously."

"You seem awful lucid to be dreaming," Rachel said, her words now coming by their own accord. "What's your name?"

"Can't believe *you're* asking me my name, Rach. *Alisha.* I'm your fucking sister."

"I don't have a sister."

Alisha mulled this over. "Ouch. I have to admit, all this is vivid as hell, but I've been having vivid dreams for a while. So fucking *lucid.* Could've been the pain meds. I've been dying of the flu for a damn week, sweating like a fat man in a sauna." Then she repeated, "So, so vivid."

"That's because it's real," Rachel said. "We're not a part of some fucking dream."

But how would I know?

"Then explain how I'm floating, smart-ass."

"I—I can't."

Alisha's lips curled upward. "Amazing. *You just seem so real.*" Then she asked something that sent waves of terror through Rachel. "What happens to you when I'm done dreaming? When I leave and wake up?"

Rachel's fear was mirrored in both Dan and Robby's eyes. What *did* happen to dream-folk when their creators ceased to sleep?

Rachel grabbed her own arm, sank her nails into the flesh as pain bloomed instantly. She felt it. She *knew* she felt it. This was real, all of it...It had to be.

"I feel this," she said.

"Of course you'd say that," Alisha said. "It's what I think you'd say."

Explain the floating lady who knows your name, Rachel. Explain that.

Thoughts of her recent disconnection from the word drifted to mind, but then...

"What do I work as?" Rachel asked, and did not direct the question at Alisha. Robby opened his mouth but gave no answer, and alarm bells blared in Rachel's mind. "Robby, what did I work as? Answer me."

"I—I don't know."

"Robby, please!"

"Rachel, I don't know."

"I guess that's because I don't know," said Alisha, and laughed. "We haven't spoken in a month and you got fired."

Anger boiled in Rachel. "Shut the fuck up, you little mutant! You're not...*we're not* in a dream!"

"I could make the grass purple if I wished."

"You could not because this is not in your mind."

"But it is."

"Then do it."

"Fine."

Alisha scrunched her nose, clearly enjoying the fear in her sister's—*she's not my sister!*—eyes.

"*Poof!*" Alisha clapped her hands. "Done."

Rachel eyed the grounds, but the snow concealed any evidence of the trick. Robby and Dan looked, too.

"This is all crazy and fun," Alisha said, "But I have to wake up now."

Fear punched Rachel's chest. "W-what happens to us if you're right?"

"You said I wasn't."

"I know, but..."

"But, but, but. I guess we'll just have to find out."

"Rach, I'm terrified." The lack of color in Dan's face gave her chills. "I don't know what's going on anymore."

A hiss made Rachel scream, she leaped and grabbed at her chest, controlling her erratic heartbeat. The rope lay like a dead snake in the snow.

"Where's she gone?" Robby screamed. "Where is she?"

Daniel grabbed the rope as if *needing* to feel something that wasn't quite there. The word 'no' fell from his lips over and over...

"Can't be." Rachel laughed now, her mind slipping like melted butter. "This isn't how it...this isn't how things are supposed to work."

She fell to her knees and dug her gloves into the snow, shoveling away pile after pile. "This isn't real. This isn't real. *This isn't real.*"

Slowly, blades of grass emerged, easing upright in the night air. In the moon's glow, Rachel struggled to discern the color. Then an engine rumbled in the distance.

"The police," Robby said. "They're coming. What in the world do we tell them?"

And how did they travel through such thick snow, Rachel? It's impossible. You know it.

Rachel ignored Robby's question and fought for better sight of the grass. She plucked a handful, ripping icy clumps free before getting to her feet. A dozen blades lay beside specks of snow on her shaking mitts. And as the police car approached, light blinded her for a moment, but soon, the car bobbed across the lawn and came to rest a few feet away.

"Don't tell me," Daniel said. "Do not tell me that the grass is fucking purple."

Rachel's brow creased as she opened her hand and light from the police car spilled across her glove. No. She wouldn't tell Dan. She didn't need to.

Because the things crawling from the police car said it all.

MORE WILL FOLLOW

WHEN THE KNOCK came, David quit stirring the beans and clenched his teeth. The wind rattled the cabin's bones, and the door bucked as another knock followed—wisps of snow dancing around the frame.

"Anybody home?"

A young man, David noted. Confident. Dangerous.

He wrapped a towel around his hands before removing the pot, then crossed the cabin, taking his time. With a grunt, he settled the pot on the table. He took a deep breath before stalking to the door and cracking it ajar— just a sliver.

"You want?" he growled.

The young man smiled, wiped frozen snot from his moustache. *Just a caterpillar on the lip,* David thought. *Recently shaved. Nearby camp. Either his own, or taken by force.*

"Thank God, old man. Freezin' to death out here."

"And?"

The man's smile faltered. "Seriously? You're one of *them*?" As he followed David's gaze up and down his body, he shook his head. "I *am* carrying, if you're gonna ask. Most everyone is these days, ain't a sign of nothin'."

One arm raised palm-forward, he brushed aside his overcoat and fished about in his belt, then added, "Easy, now. Just passin' it your way."

Clean jeans, David noted. Few days in the outdoors, maybe less.

"There." The man extended a Glock by the barrel. "Just a meal and a bed, one night. Think you can spare that? Then I'm gone, I promise. I won't overstay my welcome."

David accepted the man's weapon and slipped it inside his pants next to his own before stepping aside. "One wrong move, boy. Just one."

The stranger exhaled and tension melted from his shoulders. "Saving my life, man. I'm William, by the way."

"David."

"David," he repeated, and extended a hand that David shook. A firm grip, and tightening.

Kid's gauging my strength.

"Just beans," David said. "Some canned meat, too, fresh off the stove."

"Every person's diet these days, buddy. Weren't expectin' much else."

"Good."

David closed the door and led him to the table where a pot steamed in the center. The fire cast long shadows on the walls, though outdoors there was no way to tell, as David taped black bags over the front windows a long time ago. He pulled a spare bowl from the cupboard (one of three), and grabbed them both a spoon before returning. The man eased himself down at the table, as if in his own home. He shivered. "*Nice* in here, old man. Saw the smoke driftin' above the pines 'bout a mile off. Wanna be careful with such things."

He accepted a spoon with thanks and David ladled out a helping of food, his mouth watering instantly. "Here."

"Much obliged." William pulled the bowl under his nose and took a deep breath. "First meal of two days. One of the luckiest men alive."

David sat as the man shoveled food, his open mouth giving a clear view of the chewed up goods, all etiquette lost with the arrival of the bad times. He gorged like a homeless mutt on a steak. "Where were you?"

"Huh?"

"When The Times started, I mean." The man sniffled. "Where *were* you?"

"Outside Seattle."

"Ah. Portland, myself. Trekked north for the better part of two months. Gonna see a lot more folks up this way now that the pirate station put out the report."

David's brow creased. "What report's that?"

"Ain't got a radio up here? Dangerous move, old man."

"It's David. I already told you. You gonna show no respect after I give you food and heat?"

"Sorry, old...David. Just don't look like a *David*, y'know? Burnin' eyes and skin like leather, you the outdoors type that were *built* for these kinda situations. Ain't no *David*, that's for sure."

Again, David asked, "What report?"

"Yeah, um, some guy outta Fairbanks, broadcastin' for the past two weeks. Says he ain't seen none of the Eaters for days, not with the snow."

"They don't get far in the cold."

"Exactly."

"That what they're callin' 'em now? Eaters?"

"Seems to have stuck, yeah. Seen any 'round here?"

"Couple. Dead and covered by now."

"Right." The young man cocked his head and licked his spoon. "You live out here before the Times?"

David shook his head. "As I said, Seattle. Cabin here for getaways with the missus past fifteen years."

"And where she at?"

"Digestin' in the belly of a beast, same as most everyone."

"Damn..."

"And you, your accent, you're not from Canada, that's for sure."

"Kentucky, originally. Visiting a girl when Hell came to poop the party. She didn't make it."

"Most didn't."

"That's right." The man released his spoon and pushed back from the table, tapping his stomach before giving a hearty belch. "Most didn't make it, but I'll tell ya one thing, the meek shall inherit the Earth? Bullshit."

"That right?"

"Saw me enough to know, that's for sure." His eyes drifted to scenes unknown to David before flashing back. "Not sayin' your lady was meek, just folks I know. You see much up here?"

"People or...*Eaters*?"

"Either."

David took a breath. "Couple of folks on their way further north. Now I know why."

"Yup. Most'll be tryin' to make it to Barrow. Most won't. People regressed *way* back when shit splashed the wall, eh?"

"Damn right about that."

"Saw me a little girl, 'bout eight, crackin' a boy's head off a curb, over and over, until she held onto nothin' but *mush*. All over a shopping bag full o' candy. Believe that shit? Man's head just popped off his shoulders right beside me back in Canada, too, some crackhead on a rooftop with a sniper rifle took 'em out. Those times stick with me more than seein' the Eaters go to work, ain't that funny?"

David grunted indifferently. The man leaned forward. "See, the Eaters, wherever the hell they come from, are workin' off *instinct*, ain't that right? Just followin' biology, doin' what their bodies tell 'em to do, eat, shit, repeat, but people? Man, we're supposed to be *civilized*, like we've evolved beyond that senselessness. But soon as the safety net gets pulled from 'neath our asses, holy shit do we belong right beside the Eaters."

"Amen to that."

William gave a sad smile and bean sauce glistened on his mustache. "But, hey, here you are, up a goddamn mountain with a cabin, sittin' pretty and maintainin' your manners. It's a sight, old man. It's a sight."

David's heart began to speed, but he took a deep, slow breath and hid the shakes. He noted William's tense body language. Then he counted to three before letting the strain slide from his limbs. "Glad to hear it," he said.

"Somethin' wrong?"

"Huh?"

"I asked—something wrong?"

"All good."

William grinned, showing too white teeth. "No one else with me if that's where your mind's goin'."

"It's not."

"Well, all right, then."

The wind picked up outside, making the flames in the stove dance like passionate lovers as the wood creaked. "Floor do you good for tonight?"

"Floor does me fine."

"And where were you before here?"

William's eye twitched. "Coldfoot. Hunkered down in a restaurant. Only two people livin' down there now. Had me eggs and canned shit, then trucked on up here to Brooks Range. Not a soul from here to there."

"And why not just stay there?"

William clicked his tongue. "As I said...people just as bad as the Eaters these days. Just as powerful when they got a pistol, too. With everyone makin' their way north, I ain't sittin' pretty like an apocalyptic king until some pack travel through and paint the ceilin' with my think jelly. Need someplace quieter, more outta the way."

"Like here."

William chuckled, eyes never leaving David. "Ain't like that, man, I promise. I'll find me somewheres alone. World needs sense these days, so I ain't gonna blow yours all over the wall. It'd be a waste."

David's eyes flashed to the window as something shifted in the blizzard. He quickly looked back to the man.

"Spot somethin'?"

"Snow playin' tricks, I guess."

William nodded. "Happens. Thought I saw me a few Eaters on the way up here, just trees and the light playin' my paranoia."

Soon, David thought. *Soon...*

William leaned forward, shook his head in disbelief. "Look, you got my gun, man. I ain't gonna try nothin' stupid. What separates us from the Eaters is our civility. And I aim to keep mine. You gonna throw me out?"

"No. You get to stay the night. One night. And that's it."

"Hey, I agree."

Another shadow shifted out in the snow—a quick dart from left to right amidst the pines. Too nimble for an Eater, and too cold, too. Only people moved with such purpose.

"Got a blanket I could use for the night?"

David cleared his throat, reminding himself not to check the window again. Appearance was the only leverage he had, after all. "Got a quilt I bought down in Deadhorse you're welcome to. Long as I get it back."

William laughed. "Ain't plan on takin' shit, man. Won't even know I'd been here."

Soon as the safety net gets pulled from 'neath our asses, holy shit do we belong right beside the Eaters...

"So," David said, "How's a guy like you make it up this far alone? You gotta have done some bad things."

"I live with what I done," William said, and clicked his tongue. "That's the way it's gotta be. I don't have to like it. Survival is king now, out there among the bastards. And I don't mean the Eaters."

"I agree. You do what you gotta do."

"Amen, brother."

William leaned back in his chair, sighing as he patted his stomach again. Three taps of the hand, evenly spaced.

That sure ain't Batman you're signaling, you bastard...

The snap forced William's eyes wide but David whipped the gun as his legs hit the floor.

"Easy, now, easy."

"The fuck was that, man?"

Genuine terror now, all bugging eyes and beads of sweat. Exactly as David wanted.

"Back down now, y'hear? Stay the fuck seated."

"A-alright, I ain't movin' none."

"How many?"

"Huh?"

David aimed low and squeezed the trigger. The gun *kicked*. William screamed and toppled, clutching his bleeding ankle. David lowered the pistol and popped his ears while rotating his jaw. No time left for foolery—the shot would draw more.

"Now, you're gonna speak before you lose the other, y'hear? I asked you—how many. How many of you are out there. A number."

Scrunching his face, William hissed, "Three."

"Including you? Boy, listen to me. Does that include you?"

"Yes!"

"Guns?"

"Another pistol, on Avery."

"Well Avery ain't gonna be usin' it any time soon, that's for sure."

"Please, what's going on?"

"I'm just about to find out. You stay put now."

He kept the pistol gripped and crossed the cabin. He took a breather by the door before stepping from the cabin, head low against the unforgiving wind. Through the white noise of the chaotic outdoors, he spied footprints, *almost* covered. The group had been sneaky, that's for sure. He'd expected them much earlier. After all, he'd heard the gunshot two hours ago. Most likely a buck carcass stashed someplace close by, but not worth his time in the blizzard.

All he needed lay in the bottom of the pit around back.

The sliver of light spilling from the cabin's back window pointed directly into six feet of hollowed-out ground. Two minutes ago, that patch appeared complete, with a mesh of thin branches holding the snow in place and disguising the fall. The boys had crept to the window to look inside, just like David planned for. The curious nature of men like William became predictable in The Times; always the same. They'd raced right to that square of light like moths to a porch, and that familiar snap never failed to give him a rush. *Always the same.*

He'd chop more branches come morning, reset the trap for another day. The cellar couldn't hold much more, but he'd stack and use what he could. A prosperous age for his type.

In the pit, the men lay wriggling on sharpened pikes. David clasped his coat tightly and shook hair free from his face, wanting a better view. He cocked his head, and enjoyed the sight.

The first had been pierced through the gut, a good clean shot that now gushed steaming crimson through a thick woolen overcoat. David's mouth flooded with saliva, but like his mother always said, "No use cryin' over spilt milk." He'd get plenty from the flesh and the clothes. The second had taken a stake through the neck, already dead and blue and empty, but with as much blubber as a fine baby whale. A goddamn jackpot. And as his stomach growled, David closed his eyes and listened as the first man's organs failed. The man wheezed out a splutter that devolved to winded gasps, slowing and shallow, until...

"That's two."

The ladder waited in the cellar, but with a good meal already prepared, David decided to wait until after supper. Besides, he still had the dumb sonofabitch leaking in the cabin. Too many resources to go to waste from standing around. The weather would keep the meat. He made his way back to the cabin.

"Back, asshole!"

"Ah, you're up."

William whimpered at David's return. He hobbled around the house clutching a chair, legs-out for defense. His eyes sat sunken in ashen, sweaty skin; a time-bomb ready to pop. Ammunition was rare as hen's teeth around these parts, and with a fresh Glock, David didn't plan on wasting a single bullet. If he played it smart, his current inventory could last him a month. But there'd be more, of course. There always was.

"Blindspots overtakin' your sight yet?"

William didn't answer, his knuckles white on the chair. As he spoke, spittle flew from his lips. "The hell are you, old man? I've seen me more Eaters than you can imagine, but you? You're somethin' else."

Something else, David thought. "That's what we've all become, though, huh? Somethin' else. We've adapted. Same as we always do."

Keep talking...that's it, bleed out. Get the ol' heart racin'.

"You still haven't caught on yet, have you?"

William lowered the chair, from lack of energy or submission of defeat, David couldn't tell. Nor did he care. But he did feel he owed the man an explanation.

"Listen, I'm just following biology, like you said, son. Can't be mad at nature. The meek have certainly not inherited the earth, you're right about that. And, William, you're gonna love this, hold on."

He crossed to the cupboard and snatched the walkie-talkie, bringing it to his mouth. "Jerry, you got a minute? Over."

He waited, excited for the final puzzle piece to drop in William's fading mind.

The device crackled. "What's the latest, geezer?"

"Got a fan of yours here. Wants to say hi. Can you give him a shout-out? Name's William, or so he tells me. Don't matter."

William shook his head from side to side, mouthing something unheard.

Jerry's laughter came distorted through the mouth-piece, and David couldn't help but smile. "Well, howdy, listeners. You're through to the only station in town. You recognizing my voice yet, Willy? Gotta get to Barrow, huh? Best way through is Brooks Ridge, but wait till Sunday because a damn fine storm's kickin' out there, and we've heard tell of a group of Eaters bravin' the cold to chance snaggin' a meal on the trail, riskin' their lives for a snack." He took a beat. "Or, y'know, ol' big, tall n' ugly there was still hackin' the last few up and we needed time to reset before I sent the next group through."

David chuckled. "All right, Funnyman. Take a break. I'll be through to you soon. This one's goin' down for the count. Think you're boring him to death."

"Ain't you the comedian."

"Damn straight. All right. Over and out, Jerry."

David pocketed the radio and spread his arms, for a moment actually expecting genuine admiration on the boy's face. But his shuddering eyelids told David he'd checked out a while ago, just waiting for his body to catch up.

"Makes you feel any better," David said, "Most don't stick around long enough to get a message from Jerry. Most pop around back and go whoopsies while spyin' in the window and don't bother to knock. You're one of only five I can think of right off that's done the same. And you got a meal out of it, how 'bout that? That was Peter we had with the beans, by the way. Knocker number four. Fat wife, took three stakes through the abdomen before she finally stopped screaming."

And with that, William collapsed.

"Shame," David muttered. "Getting used to havin' company again."

He seated himself with a sigh and grabbed his spoon, digging into supper before getting to work. The beans and meat had cooled some, but any warmth felt like a godsend right now. After eating, he'd retrieve the carcasses from the pit and store them with the rest in the cellar. Then he'd hack up William and get his limbs preserved for the crew's arrival in the morning. He'd heard the town had enough meat for everyone now, and David couldn't wait to switch posts with someone else and enjoy some time off back with the others. He still had an unfinished game of chess with Jerry, and Elsa promised a new jacket once she got more leather. Excitement fizzled in his gut and David pushed from his chair before placing the empty dishes in the sink. Then he grabbed the walkie.

"Jerry, you still there? Over."

"I'm here, big man, I'm here. What's the status?"

"Three of 'em, all young. One big 'un, has a pistol. Got a Glock off of the mess currently on my floor, too. So that's two pistols, tell Tim to add 'em to inventory. I'll check back with an ammo count."

"Right on. And time frame for the next wave?"

"Give me...two days. Collection in the morning, seven-thirty. I'll have 'em stacked by the front door. I'm keeping a carcass for myself, but you can take fatty and the fresh one. I know the kids were craving a stew, you've got plenty for stock now, let me tell ya. They'll be as excited as the Old Times on Christmas mornin'."

"Amen to that. Alright, geezer, you get to it. I'll put out another message. Be ready in two days. I'll see you back at camp when your shift's done. Gotta finish this chess someday, huh?"

"I'll kick your ass come two weeks' time. Over and out."

David sighed and shook out his limbs, ready for a long night of work. He made a mental note to sharpen the axe tomorrow; that last crew'd blunted the blade something fierce. He eyed lean arms on the dead man and thought he would've made a good addition to the crew. Such a waste, but not to worry. More would follow. They always did.

HAPPINESS INC.

"THE WALLPAPER CHANGED color."

Her smile didn't falter, frozen like a default setting. "Sweetie, you're talking nonsense."

Kevin placed his palm on the paper. "It was blue. Same color as our old room on Third."

The floral pattern on the red paper turned his stomach, each print so familiar yet somehow alien. Even that mark from pushing the dresser remained, like a scar in the crimson now.

"Baby, you're being paranoid. Explain how someone would get in here and redo our wallpaper, the *same* wallpaper, just in a different color. It's ridiculous. You know it is."

"Our wallpaper's blue. Always has been."

Standing there in his pajamas, Kevin couldn't deny the paranoia creeping through his core. The preposterous notion they had a 'wallpaper burglar' almost made him laugh—if not for the immutable fact the walls had *always* been blue. He'd papered them himself, for God's sake.

"I'm not crazy," he said with a laugh. "You think I have something wrong with my eyes?"

"You're getting your colors mixed up? Makes a little more sense than a wallpaper prankster."

"Jesus." He ran a palm across his face. "I don't mean to scare you, honey. But I know the color of our damn bedroom...this is messed up."

Then an anchor of fear dropped in his stomach as he spotted the painting above the bed. "It's a ship."

Laura's perfectly plucked eyebrow arched. "Yeah?"

"Laura? We have a painting of the lake. *You* painted it."

She chuckled. "I did paint it—I painted a *ship*, Kevin. Not a lake."

His face fell. "This isn't funny now. What the hell's goin' on." He climbed atop the bed and traced a finger across the artwork, each brushstroke raising the hair on his arms. The ship, a generic transporter with port-holed doors, brought an odd sense of déjà vu. "I...I need to sit down."

He eased himself down on the edge of the bed and cradled his head in his hands. "Laura, are you messing with me?"

"Excuse me?"

"Is this a prank? You need to tell me if it is, because I'm seriously freaked out, okay? Look at my arms, hair's standing up like crazy, got gooseflesh everywhere. I'm not joking, *the walls are blue, and you painted a lake.*" The sentence trailed with unintended laughter. "You did."

She smiled. "But I didn't, Kevin. I painted a boat. And our bedroom is red...what? Why are you looking at me like that?"

He rose, cocking his head as his heartbeat quickened. "Your face."

"What about it?"

"Why are you wearing makeup before bed?"

"*What?*"

"You're...you're wearing..." He laughed again as utter disbelief wracked his system. "That's the same light red you wore on our wedding day. You always went dark, but that day you said it matched the dress and you were nervous it didn't suit you. You never wore that lipstick again. Why are you wearing it now?"

Her smile remained. "You said you liked it."

"It's not a question of if I *like* it, honey, it's that you were *not* wearing makeup ten minutes ago and *now* you are!"

Her dress. She'd been wearing the purple bathrobe not five minutes ago. *The dress*, the goodwill bargain she'd showed off for the weekend that they'd road-tripped to Bobby and Anne's party.

"What's happening?" he asked, and all traces of humor vanished. "Laura, what's going on? We were getting ready for bed. You're in a dress, wearing makeup, and the walls are red and that painting is wrong."

Wrong. The word suited the entire night.

"Honey, I think I should call a doctor."

Something thumped in the kitchen and Kevin's body tightened. "What was that?"

"What was what?"

"You're joking now. You didn't hear that?"

She shook her head, confusion marring her features.

Kevin grabbed the photograph on the bedside, clutching it sideways to use the frame as a weapon.

"Stay here."

"Honey, I didn't hear anything?"

He crept from the room as sweat beading his forehead, his face tight in concentration. A light glowed from around the living room doorframe. He'd switched everything off before bed.

Passing the bookshelf, titles grabbed his attention—*The Last Call* by Herbert Shrewman. *To Save The Day* by Frank Carpenter. He'd never heard of a single one. At the living room, he took a breath before barging in with the photograph raised and found—*nothing.*

The clock ticked above the sink. The fire still crackled, down to only embers, and atop the mantle sat a photograph with strangers.

"What the hell is going on here?" The sentence came as a moan, words dripping with anxiety, and vomit roiled in his guts. "*Honey*, get in here."

Laura appeared, heels tapping the hardwood, dressed better than he'd ever seen. Her hair was now wrapped in curlers.

"What?"

"Who are those people?" He pointed to the photo, still eyeing her up and down, his breathing fast.

"It's...us...Kevin."

"That is not us." He lifted the picture and caught his own reflection in the glass—red hair and a thick beard—nothing like the clean-cut, bald man in the photograph. The smiling brunette in his arms was a total stranger. Same went for the photo he'd swiped from the bedside.

"Honey," Laura said, and gingerly lifted the two frames from his grasp before setting them on the mantle. "Sit down. I'm calling a doctor. Try and relax, okay?"

Her words soothed him like a balm, same as always. Something had clearly snapped in the hard-drive of his brain, a misfire that needed maintenance ASAP. Laura'd called a doctor. Good. He'd sit and wait, and try not to vomit.

"I don't know what's going on," he muttered. "I'm so sorry if I'm scaring you, I just...I don't know what's happening."

"It's all right," she said with a smile, but Kevin paid her no attention. Behind her, a prime steak sizzled in a pan. She hadn't so much as opened the fridge. A smoky scent blossomed and his mouth salivated instantly as another wash of déjà vu took hold. Kevin's nerves sang.

"I'm so fucking scared," he muttered into his palms, "I wanna wake up. Feel like it's all a dream. It's gotta be."

When he removed his hands, Laura presented him with his favorite dinner—a full plate of prime steak, mashed potatoes, and coleslaw. All of ten seconds had passed since he'd spied the steak on the pan, yet displayed before him was the perfect dinner, ready and waiting. Laura's immaculate makeup made his eyes widen, her early-forties skin replaced by a mask re-capturing her mid-twenties self. That dress, that damned bargain she loved now frightened him for reasons he could not articulate.

"It's like you're an alien," he said.

"Excuse me?" Laura set the dinner on the coffee table and stepped back, arms folded. She grinned, and—*yes!*—he'd seen that *exact* grin before, almost like a photograph superimposed—the day he'd suggested they adopt a puppy. That very line now skirting her lifted lip caused a shiver. "What's going on here?"

Movement from the window. Kevin jumped to his feet.

"Honey, sit back down, it's probably the doctor."

"No. Something's wrong here."

Kevin stalked from the room, pulled the door open, barged outside and—froze where he stood.

The strange neighborhood stood in total silence.

A perfect summer's night hung overhead with stars twinkling around a crescent moon. Carbon-copy and alien homes sat in total silence, most looking brand new. Flowers peppered most of the yards, roses and tulips, and for the life of him, Kevin could not recall ever seeing such a place. He lived in Portland, Maine, in a cabin by the national park. He fished on weekends with Henry and the boys, and his nearest neighbors were the Williams. None of this made any sense.

In the driveway sat his car, and something about that tugged his brain, something *off* that he couldn't quite comprehend...

"I'm losing my mind."

Alzheimer's. It's fucking Alzheimer's.

"Bullshit."

Then again—he would say that, wouldn't he?

Before he could think further, something toppled in the backyard. His chest tightened as he rushed back through the house.

"What now?" Laura asked. Kevin ignored the fact she now wore red high-heels from their third anniversary.

He whipped open the back door and fell out onto a perfectly manicured lawn, sprinklers set evenly apart on uniform grass. He stood alone, no sign of anyone else within the confines of the white picket fence, yet...an overturned flowerpot lay beneath the bedroom window.

"Someone's out here." He returned inside, locked the door, and glared at his wife. "Laura, where are we?"

"We're home."

"We're not."

A possible answer floated to the front of his mind, and he hated himself for thinking such a thing, yet he asked, "Are you having an affair? Is this *his* house? Did you *drug* me?"

It answered some questions, like the strangers in the photograph, his own car in the drive, the odd neighborhood, yet did not account for the lapses in time, Laura's magic dinner-making skills, her clothing tricks, or the fact that the bedroom was *almost* right. Save for the color of the wallpaper and that painting. Besides, they'd been getting into bed when all this started. *Nothing made sense.*

"I am not having an affair, Kevin." Laura's look of betrayal hurt as much as a punch. "I've called the doctor, okay? Now sit down and wait."

"Someone's sneaking around outside. Now I don't know what's going on, but there's someone else around here and I *know* I'm not imagining that. There's an overturned flowerpot outside and I *heard* it crash. I'm *not* imagining anything. I'm not crazy."

There's that cliché line again, nut-bag, the one they all *say...*

Then Laura said something that made his skin grow cold. She looked him dead in the eye, flashed that winning smile, and said, "We'll call him Fred."

The out-of-context statement rang a bell, yet still, Kevin could not place it. But something about it gripped his stomach.

"Excuse me?"

"Fred, it's an excellent name, I like it. I had a Labrador named Fred, remember? It'd be a nice homage."

Back to dog adoption. But he'd never spoken that memory aloud. How did she know he'd been thinking it? Every word from her mouth once again brought about zaps of déjà vu.

"Honey...what are you talking about?"

"I'm just so happy," she said. "A dog! Look, since Felix ran off, I didn't want to say anything, but I did miss having an animal around. It was so nice when you were at work to have her curled up purring on the couch while I painted. A dog would be lovely."

"We've had this conversation." Kevin's head spun as realization dawned. "We've had this *very* conversation. Next, you'll tell me—"

"—I can take a trip out to Doc Kelly's and send you back photos of any I see that I think you'd like, just don't want an—"

"—'Ankle dog'," Kevin completed. And in unison, they said, "They're not *real* dogs, 'ankle dogs', more like wind-up, yapping toys."

Then she simply smiled at him, a smile that once again caused his head to swim with the strangest notion he'd seen all of this before, a callback to better days. Was he not happy lately?

Something bad happened...

The walls were white.

"What's—what's going on now?"

"How do you mean?" she asked, following his line of sight but apparently finding nothing out of place.

"The paint on the walls is gone. They're bare."

"They're not," she said, and shook her head as if to say, 'oh, my big silly Kevin...'

Then someone knocked the door.

Kevin went to the sound like a man in a dream, merely *floating* through the hall until his hand discovered the handle.

"Um, Mister Peters?"

"Yes?"

"Can I come inside, please?"

Kevin stepped aside as recognition sparked but refused to catch. He knew this man. Knew him well. Only, he couldn't place from where. The bushy moustache and horn-rimmed glasses invoked *some* recollection, but the memory struggled to ignite. The man made for the living room as if he himself lived here, and Kevin thought that was entirely possible. Hell, anything was possible now, it seemed.

"What color are the walls?" he asked, and Kevin followed. He pulled a tablet and tapped the keys before sniffling, as if he'd asked something mundane and routine as '*how long has it been leaking?*'

"Are you the doctor?"

He smiled. "Something like that, yes. The walls, Kevin?"

"They're bare. White."

"I see." He jotted that down before beelining for the oven as if on house-inspection. "You made dinner, I see?"

"My wife, she..."

Where was she?

"Laura?" he called.

The man cocked his head, muttered, and noted that, too.

"W-were you in the backyard?" Kevin asked, and his voice sounded someplace far away.

The doctor—if he was a doctor—sighed and asked, "The bedroom was giving you issues?"

"The bedroom's not right. The picture isn't right."

An anchor of gloom plummeted in Kevin's guts then, though he could not place why.

The man, doctor, whatever he was, pulled his phone. "Okay, Tony, you can pull it."

"Pull what?" Kevin asked.

"Mister Peters, I'd like you to have a seat for this, please."

Kevin fell to the couch as the stranger seated himself with a sigh. He unzipped his sports-coat and blew a breath, as if to say, '*hot as a forest fire tonight, eh?*' then gave another sniffle. "Mister Peters, what do you remember about being here?"

"Here?" Kevin looked around. "My wife said it's our house, but it's not...not exactly. It's *similar*, but *off*, in a way. She's not here. She was here, but now she's not and I have pieces of time missing and I don't know what the hell is going on. And I'm frightened."

"Right. Things are going to come back to you slowly now, okay? I will need you to stay seated."

"What's happening?" Fresh tears stung his eyes and a sorrowful, hollow ball swelled inside him, his body two steps ahead of his brain with some forgotten pain.

The man noted his expression, those calculated eyes magnified behind the frames. He leaned forward. "Mister Peters, is it coming back yet?"

"I-I don't know."

"Peters, my name is Harold Sizemore, and I work for OneWave. We've met many times before. Does my name or my company ring any bells? *OneWave*."

"She's dead."

The statement slopped from his mouth. A blanket of misery cloaked his mind. "Laura's dead."

"You live here in Lavender Meadows, remember?"

"No. Yes. I don't know. What's...what's happening?"

"Kevin," Harold whispered before licking his lips. "Your wife passed away six months ago. You live in Lavender Meadows. You're a beta tester for OneWave."

Laura's dead. She totaled the car on the way to get photos at the vet's and got slingshotted through the windshield and the life-support (beep-beep-fucking-beep!) and the breakdown and the—

"No!"

Kevin fell to his knees and ripped at his hair as a primal wail exploded from his lungs.

"We're getting you back online, Kevin, please stay still."

The door rattled as someone barged inside. A hand grasped Kevin's collar and ripped his head from his hands before the blurry face of an older gentleman appeared, features set. "Just a mild sedative, Mister Peters, just a mild sedative."

"I don't want this! Let me go!"

"Now, now, Kevin, please try and relax."

"I couldn't even blame the weather!"

Something sharp pricked his neck and Kevin balked, whipping his head back before dragging himself away. The two men stood before him as if he were a feral dog.

"You saw your wife?" Harold asked.

Kevin shook his head.

"Visual receptors are online," Harold noted. "No damage. Just a software glitch." Then, to Kevin, "You touched her?" He waggled his fingers in demonstration.

"Y-yes."

Harold, again to himself, "Sensory pads are fine..." He settled his phone between his shoulder and cheek. "Any confirmation on that software glitch, Jennings? Fine, all good. Another minute? Sure thing. Client is sedated, waiting for him to relax."

Client. OneWave.

Visions of Laura's open casket finally broke from the flotsam of his brain, her porcelain-like features forever frozen in sleep, never to smile again. The blue-red-blue-red of the lights that afternoon swimming through their living room curtains. The officer with his hat in his hands as he delivered the news, perhaps thinking of his own partner at home, consoling Kevin as he collapsed and yelled and cussed and cried and...OneWave.

He cried now, and the release surprised him, a gush of anguish finally escaping, one he hadn't felt for some time.

"I want out," he yelled. "This isn't right, I need this out of my system, all of it!"

Whether he meant the implants or emotions, Kevin didn't know.

"I need it all out, it's not right! It's not right! It needs to come out!"

"Coming back online," said Harold. "Nothing but a good hard reset."

"No! It's not right!"

Needle-man simply shook his head in pity, sighing before folding his arms and leaving the room. From the hallway, he called, "Got another in 03, wife, mid-forties. Same deal as here. Whole damn system musta bugged out. Catch up when you can, man. Poker still on for tonight?"

"Yup." As the door closed, Harold crouched before Kevin.

"It's all right," he said, and the bastard actually smiled. "This isn't your first rodeo, but you'd hardly believe me. Just a couple of hiccups before the system's on its feet for good. Way things are going, this'll never happen again. You're paid up for the long haul, Mister Peters. Everything will be right as rain in just a few moments. Sit down and wait a spell, okay? Laura will be back before you know it."

"It's a lie," he mumbled, and an alien comfort invaded his thoughts, spreading..."I need to get it out, it's not right. Not right..."

Then the room *flashed*.

"Sweetheart, get off the damn floor."

She stood in that wonderful purple dress, pretty as a picture, and her voice brought a sea of joy. "Your dinner's going cold," she said. "I've made your favorite." And her smile—*that smile*—didn't so much as falter, frozen like a default setting.

RODENT IN THE
RED ROOM

"YOU SURE THIS is where you're meant to be?"

The man in the driver seat arched an eyebrow. "Seriously, I don't think this town has anything to offer besides O'Brien's Bar and peculiar looks. If I go back to the motorway, I can find you a bus stop back to town. People around here...they like to *keep it in the family*, if you know what I'm getting at?"

Ben forced a smile and said he did.

"All right, then. Just as long as you know where you are."

The wipers whined as they struggled to keep the heavy rain off the Toyota's windshield, weather the driver had described as *pissing* when he'd collected Ben nearly a half-hour ago. Now they'd reached Ben's destination, a small town named Rathdun.

Zipping his army jacket, Ben took his fisherman's hat from his lap and gave the driver a final, tight smile. "I really appreciate the lift."

The driver's face fell in concern, his hands fixed to the wheel. "Sure thing. Look, take my number, okay? The wife and I only live fifteen minutes from here and if you're stuck for a place to stay, we've got a room. It's no trouble."

"That's very kind, but I've got a friend here. Thanks again for the lift."

"Your decision, boss."

Ben closed the passenger door and gave the roof a tap as the driver took off, hazard lights flashing in response. Then the car disappeared down Rathdun's main street, slipping away under the heavy cloak of rain.

Closing his eyes, Ben lifted his face to the falling drops and let them beat his face. The constant migraine that accompanied these trips felt worse than ever today. Whatever lurked in Rathdun, whatever force had drawn him here, had to be very powerful. He wanted to get the job done and leave before sunset.

Wiping his face with his sleeve, Ben scanned the town. Rathdun sat on a summit in the Wicklow hills, little more than a street slithering between overgrown foliage. To his left stood a burned-out school, a *No Trespassing* sign stuck to its black iron gate. In front of the gate was a phone-box, and Ben sighed in relief. Phone-boxes were being decommissioned all over Ireland, replaced by more modern means of communication that made his job a lot harder. Luckily, backwoods towns like Rathdun weren't high priority for phone companies and Ben made his way towards the booth. Picking up the receiver, the familiar hum filled his ear. Still in service. He dialed.

"Burkley's Fish and Chips," the voice on the other end announced. "You want it fresh then go someplace else."

"Cut the crap, William." Ben grinned and leaned on the booth. "I'm here. Now, what's the deal?"

"Nice to hear your voice, too, Benjamin. All right, look, from what I know, a suit-and-tie man by the name of Richard Evans went missing there almost a week ago. JEM Entertainment founder, remember?"

"I remember. Just tell me where I need to go, my head is killing me."

"Poor baby. Okay, listen. My client says there's a brothel there called *Seomra Dearg*, but I think I've told you that already. Some fucked-up deal the town's got going with a so-called pimp. The locals get their pockets filled, keep their mouths shut, and everything stays hunky-dory. But listen, the whole place is in on it, so, needless to say, you need to be careful. Who, or *what*, is running this operation is just guesswork at this point, but that's why I have you, isn't it, old man?"

"William, please, this one is serious. My head feels like it's about to explode."

"All right, I'm sorry. There's a code to get in, a series of numbers. No ID allowed, they're very strict on that. My guess is that my client's partner, Richard Evans, did something to piss off the owner and got himself wasted. Now, normally, this would be a case for local law, but it's been kept out of the media. That's when it started to get suspicious. And after your headache began, I knew we had a live one here. I just don't know *what one*."

"I'll get the job done. Give me the numbers."

William listed them, and then added, "My client's name is Peter Jones, the J in JEM Entertainment, as you've probably already guessed. That's your new name. You'll be expected, I should think."

"Expect a call back from me tomorrow."

"Confident, huh?"

Ben sighed. "I've never let one slip by before, have I?"

"I guess not. But be careful, buddy. I mean that."

"I know."

Ben cradled the receiver and exited the phone-box. Starting up the street, he slung his rucksack over his right shoulder. Even if he hadn't been *called* here (because that's how he thought of it now, being *called*), he would have kept an eye on the place. It oozed bad mojo.

A sign to his left welcomed him to Rathdun, and before entering, Ben stashed his rucksack in a nearby ditch for safe-keepings. He'd collect it later, if later ever came.

The buildings to either side of Main Street seemed to lean inwards over the potholed road. He knew it to only be a trick of the eye because of how the road veered slightly to the left as it descended, but it gave a very claustrophobic vibe. Slick, bare plaster walls ran with rainwater, the occasional red brick popped through like a sore. If the right wind were to blow, the whole town could collapse.

"Y'all right there, lad?"

The voice caused Ben to jump. Scanning the rain-battered street, he spotted three men standing in the doorway of O'Brien's Bar. They huddled together in the small cubby, pints in hand, watching him with stupid grins splitting their faces. At two in the afternoon, drinking seemed to be the day's plan for these folk. The one in the middle stood just over five feet, bald-headed, and wearing a very clean tracksuit. Ben doubted the man was an athlete. Two tall men flanked him, both with faces uglier than the last.

Ben raised a hand in good-nature. "Hi there. I'm fine, thanks."

The small one, who Ben guessed to be the leader, nudged his friend on the right. "Goin' fishin', are ye?"

Fuck it, Ben thought. *The sooner I get this over with, the better.* Besides, he already knew that what he'd come looking for prowled behind the walls of O'Brien's Bar. The *feeling* pulled his brain like a magnet. That had to be where the brothel lay.

Ben started across the street. "Actually, I was hoping to come in."

The three men exchanged looks of fake-surprise before breaking out into laughter. Two sounded like donkeys, the other like a hyena. The bald *athlete* spilled a slop of beer while shuffling into the road, leaving a bare space between the two larger men.

"Go on in there, then. But you know it's not a barber shop, yeah? That's three doors down."

The tall, donkey-laugher's heads bobbed as the joke registered. *Good one*, Ben thought. *Small town yokels telling a guy with long hair to go and get it cut. How original.*

Speaking low and steady, Ben said, "You going to keep talking shit or am I going to make you?"

The laughter cut. Cheeks turning red, the small man's face fell. "What did you just say to me, lad?"

"You heard me. I'm not fond of repeating myself."

Nobody spoke. The white noise of rain continued, patting off car roofs and hissing down the tarmac.

"Go on inside," The bald man said, cocking a thumb over his shoulder. "Go on. I dare ye."

Ben pushed by the three without hesitation, catching them off-guard. One of the tall men's arms shot out and gripped him by the jacket, but Ben whipped his sleeve free and shoved the bar door open, not turning back.

As the door swung shut, one of the men shouted, "Fucking hippy."

Inside the dingy pub, heads turned. Ben spotted many identical faces, each with half-closed eyes and drooping mouths. *Inbreds.* He remembered an article he'd read online before coming here that declared Rathdun to be one of the most inbred towns in Europe. Not just Ireland, fucking Europe.

One of the tall idiots from the doorway shouted in, "You hear what this lad told to Davey Mac?"

Before anyone could respond, Ben stalked to the bar and said in a loud, clear voice, "I'm here for the *Seomra Dearg*. Do I need to call the boss and tell him I'm being mishandled?"

An almost tangible tension descended. *Seomra Dearg. The Red Room*, in Gaelic.

The bartender, an elderly man resembling a potato, scuttled from the far end of the pub, his face strained with fear. "No, no! No need for that. I'll just call up and let him know you're here, Mr...?"

"Jones."

"Mr. Jones. One minute."

Jones? The name had been Jones, Hadn't it? If not, then things were going to turn very ugly, very fast. Ben breathed slow and steady through his nose, trying to appear calm and collected. The headache messed with his brain, making it hard to recall details.

Numbers, he thought. *That's what comes next. He's going to ask me for the numbers.*

The bartender muttered on the phone, cradling the receiver to his face with his back turned. Then he nodded frantically, listening to the speaker. "Yes, sir. Yes, sir. I'll send him right up. Bye, bye, bye." Turning with a smile, the bartender clasped his hands behind his back and announced, "He's expecting you, Mr. Jones. I'm sorry for how you were treated outside."

Ben forced a smile, feeling it twitch his cheek like a hook on string. "That's okay. Thank you."

"I have to ask you for something. You know what it is, I'm sure."

Ben licked at his lips. "12," he said. His throat clicked. "6, 31, 42, 47..." His heart-rate quickened. Shit. Had the last number been a 9, or a 15? Definitely a multiple of 3. Or had that been something he'd told himself to remember the 6? "15." He guessed.

The bartender glanced slowly around the room, scanning his customers. Ben kept his eyes on him while slipping his hand into the pocket of his army jacket, wrapping his fingers around the grip of his pistol. His kept his expression neutral and steady. The bartender addressed the crowd. "This is Peter Jones, everybody. One of the owners in JEM Entertainment, so if you want to ever drink here again, you'll leave him be and treat him with some respect, understand? As for Davey Mac and the Rourke brothers, you're on your last warning. Boss won't stand for it again."

Ben shuddered with relief and released his grip on his pistol. He held a hand up to the bartender. "There's no need, it's all right. Simple misunderstanding, that's all."

Then the short man named Davey Mac strutted into the pub, doling out winks and nods. "Sorry, Mr. Jones. Shouldn't have all that long hair if you're a big important businessman, though, should ye?"

The bartender suddenly slammed the counter, making Ben's chest lurch. "Right! Davey, honest to God, last warning, do you hear me? You think you're high and mighty because of all the money, but where do you think it comes from? It comes from people like Mr. Jones." He pointed to Ben. "If I were you, I'd treat him as if he was your boss, because you could be put in the ground very soon if you don't, son."

Davey's smirk faltered, but only a little. "Fine."

The bartender sighed and rubbed at his forehead. "Look, sorry, Mr. Jones. Go straight up the stairs, it's the only door up there."

"Thank you."

Ben stepped toward the staircase, shuddering as the people of Rathdun eyed him closely with their mouths gawped. One of the men, Ben noticed, had a fly scurrying across his cheek.

"Have fun, lad," Davey Mac shouted. "See ye in a bit."

Ben started up the stairs and did not look back. The further he got, the chatter in the bar picked up like an agitated hive. If he'd stumbled over the numbers, he hated to think what might have happened. The man in the *Seomra Dearg* was sure to have supplied the townsfolk with plenty of weapons, Davey Mac wouldn't have been so bold and confident otherwise.

A thick mahogany door presented itself at the top of the stairs, and like the bartender had said, it was the only door up here. Ben crossed the landing and gave three quick knocks.

Footsteps approached from the other side and the door crept open a sliver, spilling a blade of dim light. A wiry woman with thinning hair peered out. Ben couldn't help but notice the bags beneath her eyes and the thick bruise that fattened her left cheek. "Mr. Jones, is it?" she asked, her voice raspy and shaking.

"Yes," Ben said.

"Come on in."

The wiry woman stood back while opening the door, revealing herself and the room behind. She was completely naked.

The walls of the *Seomra Dearg* were painted a strange red, a shade leaning towards orange. Dark and dirty bare wood covered the floor, and fog-like cigar smoke hung thick in the air. Somewhere in the room, a radio played a golden oldie.

"Come in, Jones, come in!"

Ben looked to the sound of the voice, and there, sitting in the corner on the only piece of furniture in the room, was a large man slumped in a chair. The chair looked like it'd been pulled from a dumpster a decade before; its stained upholstery fighting to keep in the stuffing. The man didn't look much better. He was naked, save for red boxer shorts and socks. Curly, black hair covered his meaty stomach, which spilled over his legs and glistened in the dim overhead light. A chubby cigar butt poked from his fishy lips.

"Close the door behind you, man. Don't want any of those poor fuckers stumbling up here by mistake, do we?"

"No." Ben said, and closed the door.

"Katherine." The fat man plucked the cigar from his mouth and clicked his fingers. "Fetch a Cuban for Mr. Jones, make yourself useful."

The naked woman quickly nodded and scuttled to the other exit in the room, a hole in the wall covered by beads. The beads swished as she passed through, and Ben gave a quick glance, hoping to catch what lay beyond. He did. More women. All naked.

"Ah, there's plenty of time for them, Jones, you can relax."

Ben blushed and looked to the fat man, trying to smile but only managing to twitch his lip. He wanted to vomit.

The fat man scratched at his bloated midsection. "Look, no hard feelings about Evans, okay? We need to get that in the open first."

"No," Ben said. "No hard feelings."

"I run a smooth operation here, all right?" The fat man shifted his position with a grunt. "Big men like you come down to the country side, pay me my share, and you have at all the lovely hick girls you could ask for. I still don't understand why you'd like a country gal when you've got all those preppy little things back in the city, but who am I to judge, right? Supply and demand, that's what I say."

Except they're not product, Ben thought. *They're people, you shithead.*

The fat man seemed to notice Ben's mood change. His forehead creased. "Hey, if you're worried that these ladies don't want to be here, you can chill. Their families get paid handsomely for this. Shit, even their kids have some pocket money. We're putting this town on the map, baby."

And then all the men go and drink those earnings up, Ben thought. *Just like you know they do. That's why you came here. Because it's an inbred town far away from prying eyes. One you can nest in and remain unnoticed.*

"Ah, Katherine," The fat man said with a laugh. "Thanks, doll."

The naked, wiry woman approached Ben and held out a cigar and a box of matches. Ben noticed the twitch of her smile and the wild look in her eyes. For the first time, he also saw the scattered burns across her upper right thigh. Cigar burns.

A whooshing noise filled the room, followed by a sharp *crack.*

The woman wailed and fell forward as if slammed from behind, dropping the cigar and matches. Ben looked beyond her to the fat man, his heart jackhammering his chest. The man held a whip.

"Don't help her up, you moron. She's meant to light your damn cigar, not hand you the matches. She gets off on shit like this. You know how this works, Mr. Jones, don't make me think less of you, now."

Ben squeezed his shaking hands in and out of fists, hating that he couldn't help the woman, knowing she didn't want to be helped. He watched her scramble to her feet and fumble with the cigar, eventually getting a match lit. Ben took the smoking cigar without a word, knowing he had to. His stomach knotted.

What the hell is this place?

He couldn't use the gun in his pocket, not yet. He needed a name first. Names were everything. In his younger days, when he'd been faster and braver, he might have kicked down the door and shot the man between the tits. Asked for a name while the bastard bled out. To hell with the inbreds downstairs, too, he'd have had a ball with them one at a time. These days, though, his draw was slow. He hadn't noticed the man's whip, either. He could have any number of things at arm's reach.

"Now, how about we get down to business, shall we?"

"Sure."

The fat man clapped his hands, jiggling his fleshy arms, and three women sauntered into the room. They stood between the two men, dumb smiles lifting their faces that mirrored the male counterparts downstairs. The one on the left had matted blonde hair, her face caked in a comical amount of makeup. Her large, sagging breasts spilled over her stomach, her legs covered in scratches and bite marks.

The second woman, the one in the middle, looked like little more than skin stretched over bone. Her thin lips pealed back in a smile, revealing filthy, bucked teeth. Her eyes stared off in opposite directions.

The third woman was pregnant.

A neon green wig sat on her head, looking as if it'd come from a cheap child's costume. Her chubby legs were checked in bruises and Ben put her to be in her mid-thirties, but guessing age was near impossible with any of them. Smoke drifted from a cigarette in her left hand.

"I love this part," the first lady said. "Feels like we're models waiting to be picked for a show or somethin'."

The fat man chuckled. "And you like it, don't you? Tell our client how much you like it."

"We love it," The boney girl answered with a smile. "All those downstairs, did you see them? They're uglier than piles of shite, and they're broke, too. We get exec...ex..."

"*Executive,*" The fat man corrected.

"*Executive* treatment up here. We're posh now. So don't be shy or anything, pick one."

Ben swallowed back the ball of nerves trying to crawl up his throat. "I see you've already helped yourself to one?" he asked.

The fat man smiled. "Oh, yeah. Mrs. Keogh here is one of my favorites, ain't you, sweetie? She's a proper sub, if you're into that kinda thing. Let me shave her head, spit in her peehole, stick it where the sun-don't-shine, you name it, she does it. And ol' Willy Keogh downstairs, and little Mercedes back home get a nice pocketful of change each and every day for it. Makes for one big happy family, don't it?"

Mrs. Keogh honked a laugh. "Money keeps Will *drinkin'*, and that keeps him happy, and that makes *me* happy, and Mercedes got food, so we're all good. Especially now that we've got little Redmond on the way."

As she rubbed her bloated stomach, Ben's chest lurched. She'd said *Redmond*. Now he had an idea who, or what, the fat man might really be. He should have guessed from the beginning. After encountering tales of the *Fear Dearg* in other towns, Ben knew that the name translated to English as the *Red Man*. A giant rat who took human form, one that littered Celtic Mythology but hadn't made any recent stories. From personal experience, he knew that mythological creatures basked in their legends like rock stars. It's all they had, after all, and he guessed that if the fat man really was the *Fear Dearg*, it probably couldn't help but give the surname Redmond to the unborn child.

Cheeky sonofabitch.

Still, Ben couldn't chance it just yet. He couldn't risk getting the name wrong and blowing his cover. He'd have to keep playing it cool for the moment and strike first chance.

RODENT IN THE RED ROOM

He cleared his throat. "Mrs. Keogh, you sound like a lot of fun." He hoped he sounded sincere, because his stomach roiled at the words. "Mr. Redmond, you don't mind if that's my choice, do you?"

Redmond laughed, scratching at his bloated stomach. "Wouldn't have brought her out here if I did, Jones. Mrs. Keogh, you going to show our guest here what you can do?"

The pregnant woman smiled, then began to touch herself. "I'll take your breath away, Jones."

I highly doubt that, Ben thought.

He looked to Redmond. "Since we've had a minor hiccup, Mr. Redmond, one that I'm willing to forget, how about I get a clean room for my time? I can't stand dirt."

A smirk slithered across Redmond's face. "A clean room for the dirty, I like it. There's one out back, Jones. Keogh will take you there. I promise, not a spec of dirt or your money back. Speaking of which, being the good man that I am, you can pay me after. Deal?"

"Deal." Ben made a point of looking about the room. "But I can't help but think you might be lying."

Redmond's smile never faltered. "*This* room might be dirty, but I don't mind a little filth."

"It's not dirt that I mind. I just can't get rid of the idea that a building like this might have...rats."

Now Redmond's face changed. His cheeks bloomed red and he plucked the cigar from his mouth like a dead slug.

Good, Ben thought. *Keep it going.* "I see signs of one being here."

The words hit Redmond like a slap to the face. He grunted and shuffled from his chair, his hair covered belly jiggling. He stood to full height, his eyes little more than razor slits. "You want to do this, Mr. Jones? You think you know what you're up against?"

Ben pulled the pistol from his pocket. "Oh, I know exactly what I'm up against, *Fear Dearg*. Do you?"

Redmond yelled at the mention of his real name, falling to his knees as if he'd been tazed. He clutched at his head, his knuckles turning white. His teeth clacked as if electricity jolted through his body. The three women screamed, pushing each other out of the way as they broke for the beaded doorway, running as much from the sight of the gun as from Redmond, who had begun sprouting clumps of dirty hair all over his glistening body.

"You dirty little bastard," Redmond spat. His voice sounded like a drainpipe clogged with soggy leaves. Drool spilled down his beetroot chin. *"Who are you?"*

"That's for me to know."

Then it happened. Exactly as Ben had planned. Redmond exploded.

Chunks of flesh and innards hurled around the room and Ben winced as something hot and wet smacked him in the stomach. He stumbled back and gagged as the stench hit. It reeked of dead fish in a sewer.

The body of Redmond covered the orange walls, and something sat where he'd been, squirming in a soup of innards.

A rat. A *giant* rat.

The creature looked at least four feet tall, its chunky, fur covered body every bit as disgusting as Redmond's had been. Its greasy hair glistened from fluids like a newborn baby. Its thick, leathery tail smacked the floor like a whip, and that's when Ben realized—Redmond had never *had* a whip.

Ben raised the pistol and squeezed off two rounds, the gun bucking in his hand.

The rat squealed. Dark crimson sprayed the floor behind it in a cloud. Then the creature began scuttling towards him.

Ben backed up, hitting the wall. The rat leaped.

Weight pressed his chest, cold, wet fur drenching his clothes. The rat squealed, high and sharp, and then bared its fangs. Its claws pierced Ben's skin as easy as needle points. He gasped.

The creature brought its face forward, its wet nose coming within inches of his own. This close, Ben could see large ticks scuttle within its fur. "Tell me, Mr. Fisherman," it spoke. "Who are you, really?"

Blindspots bloomed in Ben's vision, the pain increasing in his chest. Somewhere in the back of his mind, he cursed his old age. But there was one thing the creature had overlooked, one thing they always did. Deities or not, they were still ancient, and weapons had come a long way since their time.

"I'm the man with the gun," Ben said, and with a shaking hand, he pushed the pistol beneath the creature's jaw, and pulled the trigger.

A deafening bang ripped through the room as the rat's brains splattered the roof. The body fell limp against him, the weight unbearable. Warm liquid gushed from its ruined head and soaked Ben like a dysfunctional tap. He grunted and pushed the beast's lifeless form to the dusty floorboards as it continued to spew a stinking mess. Ben worked his jaw, trying to pop his ears from the gunshots. Through the beaded doorway came the sound of the woman yelling.

Ben stepped over the dead rat, stopping to pluck a shred of the ruined red boxer shorts from the floor. A memento, same as always. Pulling a fishhook from his hat, Ben ran it through the red material and then back through the hat, securing it in place. Satisfied, he returned the hat to his head and lurched towards the doorway, wincing at the stinging in his chest. He'd need to disinfect the cuts soon, or risk them going septic.

"Come on out," he yelled, leaning against the doorframe for support. "Now."

The women filed through, four in total, pale and terrified. They looked to him like frightened children. The wiry woman who'd given him a cigar caught sight of the dead rat and passed out, two others catching her before she hit the floor.

"See that?" he asked. He pointed to the creature with the barrel of his pistol. "Mrs. Keogh, if I were you, I'd go to England to *see a musical*, as they say. I can't imagine what's growing inside of you right now. Good luck with that."

Mrs. Keogh screamed, and Ben left.

Quietly closing the door to the *Seomra Dearg*, he took a moment on the landing to catch his breath. His torso stung, his head swam, and the stench of wet rat clogged his nose. But his headache was gone. The creature had been defeated.

Still, he needed to haul ass before one of his wounds became septic.

Clutching the pistol in both hands, Ben made his way down the staircase, back to the bar.

The people of Rathdun stared with wide-eyes, sitting as they had been, not daring to move. The TV over the bar played a football match, the volume turned low. The gunshots might have riled them, but it seemed no one had dared come and protect the new town entrepreneur.

"What happened?" The bartender asked.

"Exterminated one hell of a rat," Ben said. He hoped he sounded confident because he shook with exhaustion. "Go see for yourself. But listen to me. This is your mess, not mine. You clean it up. And in future, don't make deals with devils, you got that?"

Some of the folk nodded stupidly, whether they actually understood or were simply agreeing Ben didn't care. He wanted to get out of there. Besides, one person had drawn his attention, a man with a smug smile on his face. A man named Davey Mac.

Davey stood in the doorway, leaning casually against the wall with the Rourke brothers flanking him. "Who do ye think ye are?" he asked. "Comin' here, taking away our way of making money? The ladies love it, we're fine with it. Why don't ye feck off and mind yer own business?"

If he were a movie hero, or a character in a novel, this would be the point he'd explain why he felt the town's deal with the *Fear Dearg* was unjust and corrupt. Instead, he was an old man, and he was tired. Besides, he had a low tolerance for assholes.

"Shut the fuck up, please."

Ben raised the pistol and shot Davey Mac square in the face.

The people of Rathdun screamed and scampered about, hiding behind chairs and tables while Ben took a deep breath and began towards the front door. He said in a tired voice, "Anybody else got something to say? Because I'm just about out of patience and want to take a long, hot bath. Anybody?" It appeared nobody did. "Good," he said, and left.

Outside, the rain continued smacking down. Ben removed his hat and let the water run down his face, washing away some of the stink and mess. He had a clean change of clothes in his rucksack, and he made his way to the ditch where he'd stashed it.

By the welcome sign, he removed a fresh jumper and raincoat from the bag and got dressed.

With the rucksack slung over his shoulder, Ben limped down the street and started towards the hills, leaving the town of Rathdun in his wake. He'd stick out his thumb once he reached a safe distance, and when a lift came by, he'd move on to a better place.

He'd stay there until the headache returned, and called him away, once again.

THINGS FOUND
IN COUCHES

THE UNMARKED TRUCK hissed to a stop outside Re-Home Decor as the driver waved over William Kelly. The young worker stuffed his hands inside his jacket.

"Cold as a nun's gaze, isn't it?"

"I sign for this?"

The driver rummaged about inside the cab before climbing out and handing Kelly an electronic scanner. He eyed the early-morning Wicklow street as a handful of cold and flu infested workers begrudgingly dragged themselves to office buildings. "Least I have heating in my cab," the driver said, "Poor fuckers. Bit of fresh air and a smoke when I need it."

William grunted a response before scribbling his name on the LCD screen and returning the device.

The driver checked it over. "Pretty good, actually. Never saw the use in this thing. At least with paper, it's a signature. Never met anyone who could write anything that looked like a name on one of these things. Like an Etch-A-Sketch. Might as well have just drawn a squiggly line myself."

"Right." William blew a white pillar and shivered. "What do we have here, anyway?"

The driver looked to the red-painted awning and back down at William. "Well, being a second-hand furniture shop, I'd assume second-hand furniture, wouldn't you?"

Cheeky fecker. Haven't even had coffee yet.

"We usually drive out for collections ourselves," William said. "If someone's delivering, it's usually a set. Want to know how long I'm going to shiver my balls off."

"Well, I'm not helping you carry it in, so that depends on how hard a worker you are. Here's the invoice."

Eoin kicked open the door and pulled a cigarette, popped it in the corner of his mouth. He caught sight of William and the driver before his eyes widened and he made to turn.

"Ah-ah," William shouted. "Get the fuck back here. I'm not doing this alone."

Eoin's shoulders slumped. He yanked the smoke from his lip before stuffing it in his jacket. "Fuckin' knew I should've used the back door for a break. Shite."

"You've only been in work for twenty minutes, Eoin. Give us a hand with this."

The driver rounded the truck and unlocked the trailer. The back door rolled up with a clang before he pulled down a metal ramp that thumped on the tarmac. Then he popped his back and nodded to William. "I'm going for a piss before my bladder bursts. You two have fun with this yolk."

He sauntered into the shop, leaving William and Eoin on the footpath. William rubbed away the tension behind his eyes, a carry-on from three cheap beers.

"Swear I'm quitting tomorrow," Eoin said, shifting from foot to foot. "This is a load of bollocks."

"Two months to Christmas," William said. "Really going to put Karen through that? Baby on the way?"

"Ah, don't start, man. You hardly like it yourself."

"But I wouldn't be stupid enough to quit with a paycheck coming. Let's just get this stuff inside before the driver marks all of our sofas with piss."

As they climbed the ramp into the back of the truck, an odd, fishy odor attacked William's nose. Eoin covered his face and balked. "That coming from George's down the road? Doesn't usually make it all the way up here."

William coughed and pinched his nostrils. "No. I think it's *that*."

A single couch sat off to the right, tied down by frayed chords. The green suede upholstery reminded William of his grandfather's centerpiece, a three-cushioned beast that ate up half the dining room. Brown stains peppered the backrest, and the cushions themselves still contained indentations of use. "This all?" William asked. "Just one couch?"

"Here, it makes our morning easier." Eoin stalked to the seat and began unbuckling the chords, whistling as he worked.

William folded his arms. "Yeah, but Tully would have us drive out to collect just one piece. Only time I've seen a delivery is three items or more. This is odd, man."

Eoin let the chords snap free and sighed. "Odd, strange, whatever, it's easy work. Let's just get it inside already."

"Just saying. Old piece like this doesn't exactly look like it came from a mansion."

They each took an end and rolled it down the ramp to the footpath. They let it go with a *thump*. William shook out his frozen fingers, wishing he'd brought gloves. His wardrobe consisted of jeans, t-shirts, and jumpers, all in various tones of gray, blue and black. He made a mental note to change that.

The driver reappeared and zipped his jeans as he sighed. "All set, lads?"

"All good, man. Cheers."

The man saluted them before snapping up the ramp and closing up the truck. Then he took off with a honk of the horn in a bitter cloud towards the hills. William grabbed the back of the couch and pushed it inside as Eoin held open the doors.

"After you."

A morning DJ read incoming emails about the recent Halloween attractions across the country, some members of public writing about how much they enjoyed their time and how they'd like to see more events, while older listeners penned angry-fisted messages about Christ and tradition. Eoin snorted a laugh as they shoved the hulking piece of furniture to the back of the shop.

"Can still see my breath, look." Eoin blew air as thick as smoke before sniffling. "Think someone would get rid of a second-hand radiator or something soon. How can Tully expect us to work with our hands getting frostbite?"

They came to a stop by three other couches in various states of repair, including a leather-love seat that William thought would make a great addition to the new apartment. Then again, Tully didn't offer workers a discount, and the 300 price mark was purposely inflated. His two-seater brown leather would do for now, not that he had anyone to share it with.

With the couch set, William stepped back and blew hot breath into his cupped palms, relishing the heat. And—was that *fishy* smell clinging to his skin?

Jesus...

He grimaced. "It's on my hands now. Fucking disgusting."

Eoin leaned in and breathed a cushion, like a chef sniffing the broth, before back-peddling and slamming his fist to his face. "*Jeeeeesus*, did your man have marine life over to watch TV or something? Smells like SpongeBob used this thing to entertain a fish orgy. Feckin' trout's couch or something."

"It stinks."

William looked about the open space, wondering how long it would take for the smell to work its way into every fabric in the shop. The material rollers of samples behind the counter were easily susceptible to harsh smells. He'd once spilled petrol by the till after his car ran out and Eoin made a trip to the garage. The samples had been ruined. And after Tully screamed the building down, William worked overtime to dump the entire stock. The bastard made sure it came out of William's paycheck, of course, and then gave one hell of a pep-talk about responsibility to boot.

"We're gonna have to open the windows," William said, knowing Eoin's reaction before he even spoke.

His friend's shoulders fell lax. "Seriously? Will, we'll be like Jack Nicholson in the snow by the time a customer comes in. To be honest, I've always wanted to use a boxcutter on some arsehole with a big mouth."

"It's either that, or we get a right shouting from Tully and work overtime dumping stock. Which will come out of our pay, you know that."

"Bollocks."

"Bollocks is right."

"How about we just wheel the thing to the back door, prop the door open and clean it there?"

William scanned the street through the front glass— an empty road on a dull Monday morning. Customers usually came on their lunch hour, twelve till two being the busiest, and not much else until after five. "Fine," he said, and motioned for Eoin to grab the other end. Eoin's face lit up as he snatched the fabric and pulled, then his nose wrinkled. "It's moist...fucking hate that word, but that's it, isn't it? It's *moist*."

As they pushed, William had to agree. The material *was*...moist. The touch of damp suede lifted the small hairs on the back of his neck. Like a ceramic cup, he'd always hated the touch. With the couch in place, William pushed open the fire exit (never to be left open!) and sucked down fresh air while rubbing his hands together for warmth.

Eoin kicked the couch. "What do you think? A wash or a reupholster?"

William scanned it over. "Just some stains, the material itself is fine. I think a proper clean would do it, provided the frame is still holding up."

"Don't know why Tully accepted the piece of shit. Who's buying a green suede couch, for fuck sake? Do we even have any suede cleaner left?"

"White vinegar in a spray bottle or—"

"Rubbing alcohol," Eoin finished with a wave of the hand, recalling the training. "I know. Right, I have some bottles from the love seat last week. Hold on."

He returned with two Febreze bottles now containing homemade suede cleaner and handed one to William. They got to work, starting with a brown circular splotch on the straight-cushion about the size of a football. William used a cloth to dab at the sprayed mark. It came away dark and stinking.

Eoin balked. "Smells even worse when it's wet. What the fuck is this stuff?"

"I don't much care, man. If Tully accepted it, he wants it and he wants it clean. Come on."

They worked for a full hour, breaking only for fresh air in the alley when the odor got too much. William once found a tossed rainbow trout by the stream at his grandmother's when he was a child. The thing must've been in the sun for a day or two, and the smell from the couch now matched that stink note for note. Unbelievable. Still, they scrubbed until two cloths had been used, and when half-ten came, the stain was finally gone.

"Thank fuck," Eoin said, and wiped sweat from his forehead. "At least I'm not as cold anymore."

William agreed. The constant motion got his blood pumping and he no longer felt entirely like a human icicle.

"You going first, or am I?"

William couldn't help but smile. Two crumpled shopping bags sat by the repair couches, half-filled with trinkets and oddities discovered beneath the cushions and inside furniture. They'd both agreed not to take home their spoils until at least one bag was filled. So far, at a glance, they had just over forty euro in change, a TV remote, an unopened condom, countless scraps of paper, two children's toys, a dog leash, an Ethernet cable, a twenty pound note, and countless other knick-knacks.

"My favorite part, man," Eoin said with a smile. "Come on."

"Well, I got two buttons and three-fifty from the corner sofa last week, this one is all yours."

"You remember the rules," Eoin said, and he rolled up his sleeve. "Anything I find, I keep."

"And anything you miss is mine," William finished.

"From the stench of this yolk, I'll probably find a family of kelp. You can have them for dinner if I do."

"Funny, man."

Eoin laughed as he approached the sofa while shaking out his arms. When the work was mundane, you made the most of what you had. "I'm going in," he said, and slipped his fingers down the side of the armrest. He pushed all the way to his elbow as his tongue jutted from his lips.

"Might find a nice dress for Karen for Christmas, yeah? Oh, or a pair of shoes for the baby when he gets out, wouldn't that be lovely? Or, imagine if I found a—"

His smile disappeared. His brow wrinkled.

"What?" William asked.

"It's...hold on."

He withdrew his arm slowly as his sleeve fell back into place. Then he eased himself up and opened his palm.

"For real?" William asked.

"Well I hardly put it there myself, did I?"

The eyes of the small fish stared at nothing and everything—all six of them. Black scales ran the length of the body, tipped in white. Its belly looked more *red* than pink, and a minuscule dorsal fin sat raised along the spine.

"What is it?" Eoin poked the scales before flipping the monstrosity over. A black, *moist* fuzz covered its left side. "Ah, Jesus!"

He dropped the fish and shivered as he backed away. "That was on me fuckin' *skin*, man! What is it?"

He flipped his hand over and back, as if the fish had managed to hold on. William noticed the shine on Eoin's palm. "Wet?" he asked.

"Soaking in the bottom there. Disgustin'. Like someone spilled a bottle of water."

"Go get some rubbing alcohol and disinfect your hand, man. This thing isn't right."

As Eoin raced for the counter, William eyed the dead thing on the concrete. Six eyes, all open and glazed. He recalled an episode of *The Simpsons* in which a three-eyed beast got lifted from a toxic-river. As with the cartoon, he wondered if men in pressed suits would come and try cover up their findings. If he called the media, would Eoin garner the attention of being the first to discover a new type of marine life? He didn't know, and he didn't much care one way or another. Not to mention, Eoin could have any number of diseases from touching the thing.

Then the couch gurgled.

A moment passed.

William and Eoin shot each other a look as alcohol dripped from Eoin's fingers into the sink.

Drip...drip...

The creaking came again—an old ship at night.

"What is that?" William backed away. "You're hearing that, yeah?"

"Yes, I am."

They both froze. William's heartbeat drummed in his ears. And once a full minute had passed, he let out a sigh of relief. He hadn't realized he'd been holding his breath.

"The hell was that?" He spoke in hushed tones as Eoin joined him, rubbing his hands together. "Eoin, I'm calling Tully. It's—it's disgusting. It's not right. I mean, what? What are you doing?"

"Hands are *itching*." Eoin strained his voice as he clawed at his palm with his nails, the flesh turning red. "Like I got fiberglass on them or something."

"That's it. Tully's getting an ear full."

As William pulled his phone, Eoin stalked to the side of the couch and began pushing.

"What are you doing?"

"Moving...it...to..." Each word came with a grunt as the couch shifted. "The backroom. Ah." He shook out his hands. "Look, you call Tully, but if a customer comes in here and smells this shit, we're not going to hear the end of it. It's going in the back room."

"Good thinking," William said, and pushed the phone to his ear. The line buzzed once, twice...

"Tully, you there?"

A sniffle. "What is it, William? You better be at work."

William's fist tightened on the phone. "I am. Listen, we had a delivery this morning from some..." he pulled the invoice from his pocket. "Just says F.C. A green suede couch, looks as if it's—"

Tully cut him off. "No deliveries today. Not a deliveries until Wednesday. What are you talking about? Do I need to come down there again?"

Eoin yelled from the back room.

"Tully, I have to go."

William hung up and raced across the open floor before shouldering open the door. The backroom sat in darkness save for the glowing green exit sign overhead, and between the aisles of materials and tools, Eoin stood lax before the couch. The door swung shut behind William.

"What was that, what are you yelling about?"

Eoin turned slowly, his expression unreadable. "Will," he said, "Give me your phone for a moment, would you?"

"Yeah, sure."

William handed over the device without question, but when Eoin pocketed it and withdrew a boxcutter, his nerves exploded.

"Hey, man, what's up?" He raised his palms. His knees quivered. A cold fist clenched his guts.

"Just sit down for a minute, yeah?"

"Eoin, the hell are you doing, man?"

"Just...over there. By the deliveries. Come on."

William swallowed a lump in his throat but did as instructed. The boxcutter jittered, following his every move as if attracted by a magnet. When he reached the stacked boxes on the far side of the couch, Eoin finally lowered the weapon. "Good. Now stay."

William watched Eoin back from the room before the exit swung closed. He stood in green-lit gloom with that fishy stench seeping into the air. Slowly, he craned his neck and spied the camera in the top right corner. Memorizing the screen from the safe room, he was sure he was in frame. As was the couch. Everything that happened in here—*should something happen, don't freak out just yet*—was on tape. Eoin didn't have access to the safe room and only worked shifts with William. If he never looked up, he wouldn't even know the camera was there. Either way, Jesus Christ, what had gotten into him?

The fish. Something on it—*the mold?*—wasn't right. That had to be it. He recalled nature documentaries of spores on ants, parasites on marine life...they could drive a host crazy. Was it a fungus? Whatever it was, William needed to get Eoin to a hospital. For both their safety.

Then Eoin returned, still unreadable. His usual jolly demeanor was nowhere to be found, and this *stranger* caused William's heart to punch. The boxcutter made him want to vomit.

"Shop's closed," Eoin said. "Lights out."

"What are you talking about?"

"Just sit down a minute."

William did as instructed, and slid down the boxes onto the floor. His bladder stung, as if ready to let loose.

"Eoin, dude, we're cool, okay? We—" He swallowed, tried again. *The camera*, he remembered, *it's all on tape.* "We were just messing around ten minutes ago, yeah? You're my pal, man."

Eoin nodded in agreement, though the boxcutter remained clenched. "Remember the time we found a twenty pound note in Ford's couch?"

William said he did faster than intended.

"Was like Christmas, wasn't it? Always did like our discoveries, my favorite part of the job. What would we find down in the cushions..." He paused, raking fingernails deep across his palm as he hissed. "This is the best one yet. You're not going to take that from me."

"I—I don't intend to?" William laughed nervously. "Never said I did."

"But you heard it, didn't you?"

"In the couch? The groaning?"

Eoin mouthed the word 'groaning', and then added, "It was my name."

"It wasn't, Eoin, it was a groaning. Like a board creaking. Frame could've been expanding from the heat, it's been in the back of a freezing truck all morning. The wood expands."

"*It* called me. You didn't hear? Nicer than Karen's voice, too."

"What the fuck, man?" William ran a palm across his face, the building nerves too much. "Eoin, I'm starting to panic, I'm not going to lie. Come on, you're freaking me out now. What would Karen say, yeah?"

"Fuck Karen," Eoin said in a monotone. "Fuck the baby, too. Fuck them both. Let them rot in the Earth and let the worm have their eyes. How does that sound, buddy?"

"You've lost your fucking mind."

"No, I've found it." Eoin stalked to the couch, placed a tender hand on the armrest. "Found it in here."

The baritone *creak* came again, as if in response to his words. Eoin moaned, too.

The camera. Remember all is on camera, should he... oh, fuck.

Eoin stalked forward, and the boxcutter blade licked out with a flick of his thumb. Every muscle in William's body tightened, ready to *fucking go* and Eoin's family be damned. But the man dropped to his knees by the couch. He brought the blade forward and hacked at the backrest, slicing with surgeon-like precision. He made an 'X', and then slipped his hand inside. William spotted his chance and slowly rose.

"*Down*," Eoin yelled. "You stay. You watch."

"I don't know what you expect to find down there. But I want you to think about Karen and the kid for a moment." He thought of another angle to try. "You could have a fucking tumor, man, think about that? Explains your mood shift, your—"

"And what about the creature, you gobshite? And what about *this*."

He yanked his arm free with a cry of triumph as spindly threads of white clutched his forearm like mozzarella cheese. They made slopping, wet sounds. Threadworms, William realized, and each at least a meter long. They worked their way around Eoin skin like weedy cobras, glistening in the green glow of the exit light and collectively thick as a trunk. And as Eoin laughed—actually *laughed*—William bolted to his feet—*fuck it!*—and made for the door. He slammed his elbow against the wood and spilled out into the empty room. The backroom door swung shut, cutting off Eoin's cries of ecstasy, and William raced for the work phone.

With a shaking hand, he dialed Tully's number.

"Come on, come on..."

He hit wrong digits multiple times, and only on the third time did he get the number correct. The phone buzzed.

"What?" Tully answered. The echo told William he was in the car.

"Get down here. Right now. Bring the Gardaí with you. I don't know what the hell is—"

"I'm on my way, William."

And with that, Tully cut the line. William stared at the receiver a minute before placing the phone back into the cradle. The outdoors tempted him, a dull yet gloriously monotonous day separated by just a single pane of glass. But then he thought of Karen with her sizeable bump. Thought of nights at the table with her and Eoin when the young worker had just joined the crew. He couldn't abandon Eoin's family.

Or maybe it's getting into my head, too, he thought. *Calling me back and not letting me go—whatever* it is.

A smell like a damp construction site made William grimace and he turned to spy tendrils of smoke seeping from an oozing black puddle on the floor—the spot where the bizarre creature had been.

He yelled until something in his throat ripped. "What the fuck is this? What. The. Fuck!"

The floor began to rumble as if a freight train sped through the alley. William eyed the backroom door, frozen to the spot. Furniture polish toppled from the countertop as the groaning came again, loud enough that his arms broke out in gooseflesh. He grabbed a boxcutter of his own before it fell from the nearest shelf, then stepped towards the room.

"Eoin?" he yelled.

Only that hair-raising creak responded.

William took a deep breath, counted to three, then shoved the door. And screamed.

Two gargantuan spindly arms like living oak branches pulled Eoin's body into the crevice of the couch—limbs owned by something colossal and decayed. Eoin's torso, arms and head still remained visible, but that would soon not be the case. And, oh, how he laughed. Rickety fingers curled around his face, streaking his skin with brown mulch, then pulled and pulled, taking him down, down, down. The terrible groaning increased—like an oversized child enjoying a rare sugary treat. And soon there was

112

nothing left, nothing at all, save for brown stains on an old couch that dried in the glow of an exit light.

With the boxcutter raised, William charged the couch just as Eoin's head vanished. He spilled to his knees and shoved his arm inside the couch where his fingers grazed the greasy hair of his friend's scalp. He worked that hair into his fist but Eoin continued downward, and after a *rip!* William's hand came free clutching nothing but some black strands. He popped the boxcutter blade, threw aside the cushions, and stabbed at the canvas beneath. He ripped an 'X' before shoving his hand inside. His fist connected with the concrete floor beneath. Nothing lay inside. Nothing at all.

"Eoin!"

William sliced the back of the couch, tore and stabbed and screamed. He reached inside and found nothing but a wooden frame and stuffing. He yanked handfuls of the stuffing free before getting to his feet and kicking the frame. The wood *cracked* and splintered. He dropped the boxcutter and yanked the frame out, too, tossing it across the aisles and leaving nothing but a hunk of material. Still, nothing. After a few minutes of gutting the furniture and breaking more wood and reaching further and screaming and yelling—he soon found himself surrounded by broken wood and green suede, yellowed stuffing and shredded canvas. The couch was no more, and Eoin was nowhere to be found. And even as the front door of the shop opened, William barely noticed. Sweat dripped from his nose as he fished about in the remains for any sign of his missing friend.

"The hell is going on here?"

Tully stalked over, squeezing his keychain in one meaty fist. He knitted his bushy brow as he scanned the scattered materials. "Robbed? Were we robbed, William?"

William almost fucking laughed. Something as mundane as being robbed would be welcomed with a middle finger. He asked, "Do you smell it?"

Tully's nose wrinkled. "Like fishmongers. Where's Eoin?"

"I'm trying to find him."

"On the floor?" Tully plucked a shred of suede. "What's this?"

"I don't know."

"What do you mean you don't..." Tully let the material drop. "A couch? Did we get a delivery?"

William stood. "I was about to ask you the same thing."

"*No deliveries until Wednesday.* What is all this?"

"A green suede couch. At least, I thought it was."

"You're making not a lick of sense."

The cameras, William thought, and a great smile lifted his face. *Proof. Actual proof!*

"Watch the security footage, Tully, the CCTV!"

"The cameras don't *record*, William. Do you know how expensive it would be to fill up hard drive after hard drive with footage of material aisles? Who robs a second-hand furniture shop?"

The more Tully spoke, the further William's brain drifted. Like going down the couch, pulled by something rotting and ancient... "You cheap bastard," William managed, and Tully's reaction almost made him chuckle. What else could he do now? If not laugh, then...

"Go insane."

"Excuse me?"

"No footage, no nothing. Just a lingering smell of *fish*. It's almost...funny."

William left the backroom—*drifted*, in fact—to the three couches in various states of repair on the showroom floor. Each one was a possibility, right? Was that how it worked? He recalled the fish, the bizarre creature that had melted in an acidic puddle of goop. Did something *fish* us out? Are we the pond? If William tried the deli, could he bag some trout or mackerel and tempt the abomination out from his very own living room? He didn't even realize he was laughing.

As a squad car pulled up outside, a young officer stepped from the vehicle. His reddened face told William he was scared and cold, inexperienced, and without a guide. A possible robbery, it was written across his face. The bell tinkled as he entered.

"Tully's in the backroom," William said as they crossed paths. "No robbery, don't worry."

"Stay here," the officer demanded, and his nose wrinkled as he power-walked. He opened the backroom door, and William stepped out into the freezing morning. He should call Karen, of course he should, but what would he say? They'd lock him up. *A couch!* Everyone in the country had a couch...

And that meant a lot of possibilities.

He could start at home, yes, his two-seater leather sofa. A stop at the supermarket on the way home, some *bait*. Then try his parents if that didn't work. They had an L-shaped love seat, white, four cushions...

"Ridiculous," William spoke as he crossed the street in a town that no longer felt stable. More like a child's play set. "Like someone ripped out the support and broke the frame..."

He spied windows upon windows, each protecting living rooms full of happy families and couples, and couches and couches and couches. "Possibilities," William spoke aloud. "Thousands of possibilities. I'm losing my mind."

And the further he walked, the more his thoughts drifted down that dark, bottomless tunnel, slipping oh-so-easily into new and unknown territory.

He'd start with a trout. That seemed simple. Familiar. He could always graduate to bigger bait should that not work. He hadn't been fishing in a very long time. A chuckle escaped his lips as he thought of Karen, alone and clueless right now. She had a lovely piece of meat cooking in her oven, after all. One that would do just fine.

COMES WITH THE RAIN

"JESSIE!"

David leaned on the nearest tree and caught his breath. He wiped his brow and gritted his teeth, heart hammering from the run.

"Fucking cheap lead, goddamn it..."

Soon as he arrived home, a complaint would be on its way to the manufacturer. Second-hand or not, nylon shouldn't snap like degraded rope. The dog had to be close by.

Pushing himself from the trunk, David clutched the stitch biting his side and trudged deeper into the woods. He pulled his phone and squinted to the screen—a quarter to six. If he didn't find Jessie by sunset, the dog's little escape would turn into a full-fledged disappearance, just like the tourist he'd come looking for.

"Jessie! Come 'ere, girl!"

He strained his ears, but hissing wind in the trees muddled one noise from the next. He clicked his tongue and repeated the magical word *dinner* again and again. Still, nothing.

"Please, Jess, come on..."

After searching for signs of Alain Faure, this was the last thing he needed. Damn French backpacker had gotten himself lost in the hills—same story each summer.

Greyford's nearest police station sat ten miles away in Rathdubh, leaving mostly locals to comb the land since sunrise. The town could not do with bad publicity, not when they *depended* on hikers and hillwalkers like Alain for sustainability. The occasional broken ankle or sprained wrist from overachievers scaling harder mountains always drew concern, but injuries tended to be phoned in and kept out of the press. Mountain Rescue usually reached the scene within an hour, too. In the case of Alain Faure, however, nobody had heard a thing.

"Jessie!"

David's stomach roiled. He loved that damn dog. Jessie'd never ran so far ahead before, not even as a pup. Today she'd caught wind of something and shot off without warning, leaving David with a broken leash and an aching chest.

"Here, girl!"

He craned his neck and peered through the foliage to try and gauge the weather. Gray clouds, pregnant with rain, threatened to break at any time, same as yesterday. He didn't like the idea of Jessie being out for the night in such lousy weather.

The weather's one thing, he told himself, *but what about other animals? Protective deer, rabid foxes, badgers? Ireland doesn't do snakes or bears or wolves, at least. I can be grateful for–*

His shoulders slumped as a disturbed patch of soggy leaves came into view. In the center, lay a dead animal.

"No..."

As David jogged, he chucked the broken leash. So long to cheap shit. He fell to his knees and ignored the water seeping through his jeans as warm tears slipped down his cheeks. He wiped his face in his sleeve and reached out, stroking the matted fur. Then his breath caught.

The dog hadn't collapsed, hadn't caught itself in a fight with some rabid animal. The dog had been *drained*.

Ribs pushed against too-tight skin, each visible bone contouring on the flesh. The animal's sunken right socket housed a lifeless eye, the surrounding skin firm and dehydrated, reminding David of jerky. He caught sight of Jessie's tongue, lolling from non-existent lips, white and thin...

The dog looked like a misplaced museum exhibit.

David let out an involuntary sound as a wave of misery left his mind reeling. His teeth chattered, and not from cold air, but from fear. His skin prickled, the woods suddenly too dark and vast—a perfect setting for prowling predators.

"Who did this?" he asked, knowing the question would go unanswered, but needing the noise. "What the hell *did* this?"

He squeezed a handful of sludgy leaves, fists shaking. Then he sucked a deep breath as something tickled his palm. He flung the leaves aside and shuddered. They smacked the dead dog and burst to reveal a thick, jittering earthworm. The creature fell from the dog's thigh and splattered to the mud.

David grimaced as he wiped his dirty fist into his jeans. He needed to call the police, bring them here and show them the scene. Whatever had caused such a freak show still lurked in the trees, something that also had to do with Alain's disappearance, he bet. His heart raced at the idea.

It's nearby.

David hated the thought of Jessie's body in the middle of the woods, but couldn't justify sticking around when something—or *someone*—capable of such horrors stalked so close. He imagined a lunatic with a suction device strapped to his back, something like a mad scientist's version of a vacuum cleaner, able to siphon a body free of all liquid, leaving nothing but a dried-out husk. He shivered as he stood and held his breath, straining his ears. Wind sizzled through the branches—branches that looked all too much like the bobbing, fragile arms of dead men, but he heard nothing unordinary. That alone felt strange.

Unlocking his phone, he loaded the dial-pad as he moved. Harsh light forced him to squint, and he swiped away a handful of notifications.

Then something rustled from behind.

David spun, unable to find his breath. Branches bounced and swayed, hiding any number of possibilities, but out in the open, nothing stirred. The peach-fuzz on the back of his neck rose and his balls tightened.

Assert yourself, idiot. Speak. "Who the fuck is out there?"

He cringed at the crackle in his voice, but his nerves were shot. If a nearby animal heard, it would charge or run, either way telling him he'd overreacted. If it was human, however...

David stomped the ground, hoping to cause a jump. Nothing.

"Show yourself, now! I'm calling the police."

He back-peddled, locked in the direction the sound had come from.

Then came movement, followed by a sliver of a profile behind a mottled spruce trunk.

David stopped. "I can see you, asshole." Despite the insult, he swallowed a golfball-sized lump in his throat. "Come out."

But...did he *really* want whoever was hiding to show themselves? What if his *mad scientist with a suction device* theory came to pass? Then what would he do?

David scanned the immediate area and spied a fist-sized rock. After scooping it up, he readied himself for an attack. "I've got a weapon," he announced.

The silhouetted figure fell forward, feet dragging the marsh to a sound like ancient sandpaper. A backpack swayed from hunched shoulders.

"*Alain?*"

The figure paused, turned, and David gasped as something long and thin swayed from the man's head. At first, David thought Alain wore a dog collar, a loose leash hanging in some form of fashion, but as the man stumbled closer, attracted to David's voice, he realized that was not the case—whatever fell from the backpacker's head was attached to the roof of his mouth.

As Alain shuffled into a patch of unfiltered light, detail swam into focus, and David's legs threatened to buckle. He raised the rock and backed away. "What the hell is that thing?"

The appendage curled from the backpacker's cracked lips, pulling shapes and coiling around his midsection like an agitated snake. It looked as thick as two of David's fingers, glistening in the evening glow.

"A *worm?*" The creature kept Alain's mouth from closing, clamped to the roof of his mouth and impairing his voice. "*Ih mahhss 'eee huggry...*"

It took David a moment to realize what the man was saying—*It makes me hungry.*

Clumps of hair stuck to the backpacker's waxy forehead, caked in dirt and twigs. Dark, sagging skin surrounded his eyes looked sickly and malnourished, as if the parasite had sucked all its needed nutrients. A strand of saliva slipped from Alain's mouth and dribbled to his chest. Then came an agonizing wail that forced David's hair on end.

"It makes me so hungry...It needs to feed."

He lifted his head, squeezing his eyes shut as his shoulders hitched and the parasite wobbled. After staying that way a moment, as if steeling his nerves, the backpacker lurched forward. A look of determination manifested on his face.

David jabbed a finger. "Back. Stay where you are and let me call the police, man. People are *looking* for you. Whole town's been out since sun-up. We can get you help... You need a hospital. That *thing* has to come out."

Whatever the hell it is, David thought. *Jesus Christ...*

The hiker sobbed and emitted a raw cry. "It won't let you...it won't let you get close without...oh, God, it hurts... *it hurts*..." He fell forward again, and the worm poised like a strike-ready serpent. An opening appeared in the abomination that reminded David of a leech, pulsating around a collection of little yellowed nubs.

"I was in the mountains," Alain continued, his voice urgent, and David matched him step for step. "It got late and the rain came. I tried to take a shortcut back to town because I did not have a coat...then they bubbled from the ground, hundreds of them, up in the mountain..."

They? David's heart raced. *Hundreds of them?*

"They came with the rain," the hiker cried. "Oh, God, it hurts...my mouth hurts...it makes me so hungry..."

David took off.

Rocks and outcrops tried their best but David dodged each obstacle with adrenaline-fuelled reaction. A branch slapped him in the face and he dropped his phone, hardly noticing. Spotting an embankment to his left, he chanced a look back before easing down, the trunks making good brakes when his footing became erratic. At the bottom of the hill, he paused by a river separating the woodland from some farmer's property. A farmer who most likely sat at the fire watching the evening news, oblivious to David's predicament. Across the water, the whole town sat in peace, unaware of the dangers in the trees. And David began to panic.

Swim, he thought. *Cross the river and get to that farmer's house. He'll have a shotgun.*

David took a breath before stepping to the bank, hovering a foot above the rippling water just as something slithered below. Something long, pale and ugly.

"Oh, God, no..."

David backed from the river and gasped as Alain came to a skidding stop further down. The two locked eyes a moment as the backpacker let loose a pained moan. "It won't let me stop. I'm so sorry...it won't even let me sleep...I need to eat..."

David yelped as a large rock took his feet out. He landed with a wheeze and scuttled on his hands, the moist earth soaking his clothes. Alain bore down, an exhausted soldier taking commands from an unseen general. Only David knew that he *could* see the commander—an oily worm currently coiling for another strike.

I can't hit it, he thought. *It's too thin! Can't risk getting close...If I do, it might...*

He didn't complete the image, interrupted by a flash of Jessie's dehydrated corpse. He still held the rock, though, and as Alain lunged towards him, he gritted his teeth.

"I'm so sorry, man..."

David flung the stone with a grunt and watched as it zipped through the air in a vicious arc before cracking the backpacker square in the temple. Alain's head jerked, and the worm tensed before crashing down in a limp swing.

David searched for another weapon.

"Do it!" Alain shouted. "Please...I'm not bleeding enough. Put me down, already. An aneurism, a hemorrhage, anything, *please*! So hungry..."

David worked another stone free, his hands slipping on the wet surface as he wrenched it back and forth from the mud. He slipped his palms in the soil and scratched the dirt, raw fingers crying out in protest. The rock pulled free with a slopping sound, and something beneath slithered into the freshly exposed mud. David stumbled upright with the weapon now clutched to his heaving chest as a stitch gnawed his side. He wanted something smaller for throwing, something useful from a distance, but he had no right to be picky. He'd need to get close enough to bash the man's brains in.

"Stay where you are, Alain. Don't come any closer."

"I can't help it," he whined, staggering closer. "It's hungry. It makes me." The worm curled into a perfect *U*, circular mouth opening once again to reveal the horrible nubs within.

That thing drained my Jessie, David thought. *My goddamn dog, you sonofabitch.*

His arms quivered as he swung the rock. And then set it loose.

The worm struck out, its mouth connecting with the projectile midair, right before it smashed Alain square in the face. The hiker let out a slopping grunt before thumping to the mud, laying on his back as a wheeze escaped around the trashing worm and blood bubbled from his ruined lips.

David backed off, breath hitching as his pulse thrummed. His hands prickled and his legs threatened to buckle but he could not run. Not yet. "Die!" he shouted. "Goddamn it, die, you sick fuck! Just die! Leave the man alone!"

The worm slipped free of Alain's open mouth with a sickening *pop!* and wriggled into the earth by his side, presenting David a view of needle-sharp pincers. The appendages flexed, reminding David of an earwig, and then the monster slipped into the dirt. A thought hit like a punch—*It's still alive. It's somewhere beneath my feet.*

"No...no, no, no..."

David scrambled to the embankment and used the trees to hoist himself up, unable to shake the idea that the worm could be anywhere.

Hundreds of them...

Every few steps he glanced back to make sure Alain hadn't gotten to his feet, but the backpacker didn't even appear to be breathing. He lay by the riverside, a traveler breaking from an exhausting trip. A body to be found. The authorities would be the ones.

They're under my damn feet!

David crested the hill and jogged to the forest trail as aches settled inside his bones. He cried out for help but the words echoed uselessly throughout the thicket. Civilization felt a lifetime away, the woods a loop he'd never escape—a nightmare inhabited by deadly parasites capable of draining bodies clean in an instant.

"Jessie..."

In the light of the setting sun, the soggy earth glistened all around. Rain dripped from green leaves as fresh streams carried new rainwater to unseen places. Then the earth began to bubble.

Despite the pain, David picked up speed, *needing* to be out of the woods as the ground rumbled beneath his feet.

They're coming, he thought. *Oh, God, they're coming...*

Then the woods erupted.

Long white creatures, caked with mud, broke free to his left and right. Clumps of deep red soil rolled from segmented bodies. David let out a constant roar as he side-jumped one directly in his path. The worms seemed lazy and docile from their burrow, and they lurched half-heartedly as David avoided each attack with ease. To his right, a couch-sized worm ripped from the weeds and slapped the soil like a beached whale, a stench of month-old meat spoiling the air.

A clearing appeared ahead, one with the glow of a fading sun that promised to end the terror. With an involuntary grunt, he forced his legs faster, and spilled from the woods into the barren field sometimes used as a carpark. A young man jumped from fright, camera dangling from his neck. At first David thought it was a worm.

"Hey...what's happening?"

David slowed as his breath came in short wheezes. He clutched his chest and looked to the sky to avoid passing out. "In there...don't..."

He couldn't speak, hurting too much. Each syllable felt like a stab to the lungs. He recognized the young man's face from around town, a South-American with a bright smile, but couldn't place a name.

The photographer cocked his head and his brow knitted together. "It's okay, man, I have a hood. See? And a torch." He pulled the implement free of his jacket and clicked the 'on' switch to demonstrate. "I won't be out for too long, anyway. I only want to snap a few shots of the woods at night, test out this new lens...It's meant to rain pretty hard any minute now and...are you okay, man?"

David realized his legs had continued pushing him by their own accord, no longer able to stay so close to such horrors. Two phrases rotated like a carousel in his brain and he fell towards home, towards safety—*I'm in shock...I can't speak...I'm in shock...*

He jabbed a finger in the direction of the trees, unable to stay put. "Don't...please..." he managed, but the rest would not follow. As town lights twinkled in the distance, he lurched on, needing the embrace of civilization before ever stopping again. He kept his eyes trained on that warmth, that promise, and even as the young man screamed, he did not slow.

SHE SELLS SEASHELLS

WITH CIGARETTES, CAR keys, and his tablet, James stepped from his car into the salted air of Brittas Bay. The wind carried a whiff of greenery from the dunes shadowing the road, large mounds making for a cool vehicle. If the young woman by the roadside answered his questions quickly, he could get back to the office and write up his article before the sun cooked his Honda. A missing swimmer, athletic and in his twenties, with no body, and already a full week gone. Most likely James would be here a while. A forceful fishy stench scrunched his nose.

"Morning."

She turned and squinted, a slender arm raised against the glare. Pretty and tanned, the type of girl James would've caused trouble for a decade earlier. Now he sucked in a gut that bulged his shirt and forced a smile, hoping against hope his wrinkles weren't as deep as he imagined. He hadn't shaved this morning, and thought that at least might lend a touch of *cool*.

Goddamn it, I'm so lame...

The cause for not shaving tightened his chest, but he tossed the memory from his mind like a drunkard from a bar.

"Morning," the girl answered, and her voice sent a slender nail up his back. "Police?"

She eyed him up and down as heat flooded his face. "What, no? I'm...I'm a reporter. Doing a write up on David Buckley. The swimmer. I'm sure you've heard?"

The young woman nodded. "Sad story. He was what, early twenties?"

"Twenty-four. Trained, too. Still, nothing from the water." James flashed his tablet, recording software already running. "Mind if I ask you some questions? You from around here? Trying to get some local insight for my piece."

Her smile faltered, but only for a moment. "I'm just trying to make a little pocket money out here, I..." She shrugged, and David's chest lurched. Catching his reaction, she laughed. "No! I'm not doing *that*. I'm an artist. Coming into summer, we get lots of folks flooding the sands in the early hours. I usually pop out at six or so and grab a few shells, paint 'em, decorate 'em, try to flog a couple of souvenirs."

"So you live here?"

"That I do."

"And...Jesus, sorry, that stench is strong."

She cocked her head to the side. "The fish? Get used to it when you live here. Tide brings 'em in, sun cooks 'em, you smell 'em."

"Were you selling last week when...?"

"No." She made her way to the side of the road and eased herself to a cross-legged position by a corduroy bag on the sands. Behind her, the salty air blew inland along the crashing sea, messing her hair. "My mom's not doing well, so I try and get out as often as possible. I'm just trying to keep her taken care of. Making some pocket money, y'know? No work going in town."

"I'm sorry to hear." James rested the tablet on the dune beside her and also sat, hoping his legs wouldn't pop and

130

give him away as an old fuck. He hadn't slept well for days already on account of—*stop it*, he told himself. *Enough time has passed.*

The bag beside the girl bulged at odd angles, brimming with what he guessed were the decorative shells and rocks.

He fished his cigarettes. "Smoke?"

She shook her head. "But you do you. I don't mind. What've you got so far on David Buckley?"

James lit his cigarette and inhaled, the first hit of nicotine swimming to his head. "Lived in Wicklow Town, married, one kid, training to compete on a national level. Fit as they come, y'know? Strange stuff."

She looked out to sea then, where foam-topped waves crashed the sands before sizzling into the rocks and retreating. The sound captivated James, and he closed his eyes a moment, glad to be out of the office and out of his headspace, back in nature's open arms.

"It's beautiful, isn't it?"

"I haven't been to the beach since...Jesus, six years, maybe?"

"Should be mandatory for folks. Less fighting if we could just get some perspective once in a while."

Sure, James thought, *less fighting but still the odd dead body now and then...Nature's got teeth and a temper, too, don't forget.*

"You nervous?"

The question came from nowhere, and James choked his smoke, his eyes watering as he punched his chest. "What? No. I'm..."

"Nervous. You think you're too old, and being spotted with someone like me would lead folks to question."

"I...I never said that."

"You didn't and you did," she said. "What age do you think I am?"

James heartbeat quickened. He hadn't had a conversation with a woman he didn't know in God knows how long. Didn't know where to start. Still, he studied her pale skin, her tied brunette hair and bohemian-styled dress. "College student," he tried. "Twenty...three."

She broke into laughter and clapped her hands, eyes never leaving him. "Quite a compliment, thank you."

"Why? What age are you?"

Never ask a lady her age, jackass!

"Older than you think, man. Older than twenty-three, at least."

James chuckled, mesmerized. "What about me, then, huh?"

"Thirty-six," she said, not missing a beat. "Just over the youthful hump and full of apprehension."

James slowly exhaled smoke. "Damn you're good."

"I know. Apprehension and...sorrow, actually. Grief."

James' voice caught in his throat.

Questions! You're here to do a job, man. Don't think about it.

"You come here regularly, right? Selling shells? Just like the rhyme."

Her brow furrowed. "Don't know about a rhyme, but I'd say semi-regular here, sure. Most weekday mornings, weekends when Mom feels well enough to take care of herself."

He wanted to ask more about her family, get to know her, but he forced himself past, the possibility of no paycheck stronger. But just. "Can you remember anything about last week? Garda presence, anything?"

"Oh, they were out pretty much twenty-four hours after it happened. I can see the beach from my home. They taped up the main entrance, right where we're sitting, actually. And then the newscasters reported from six PM. Helicopter came about seven, did rounds until late into the night, then again the following morning. Locals combed the beach day after day, even some in dingy boats, out in the shallows, but after Sunday, so, like, five days now? Things died down. I'm sure some folks are still looking further down shore, out where the current goes, but that's all I saw."

James nodded and flicked his spent smoke. "Can I get a personal quote?"

"Tragic," she said, her eyes far away. "Just...tragic. No one to blame, you know? That's the worst part of things like this. People want closure, but when it's nature, you can't exactly yell 'fuck you' to the waves. Well, you could, but you'd look insane."

James smiled, forced. "I don't think I can print that, but thanks all the same."

His mind wandered, her words touching too close to home, and this time he allowed it. Silly, he knew, to be so hurt over a dog, but goddamn if that Labrador hadn't made his day. Heck, his whole previous *seven years*. He'd never given much thought to the day he'd lose her, and now that it'd come, he was completely unprepared. In his mind, he saw Holly bring him a stick, drenched in rainwater. Saw her curled up by the fire, lips flapping with snores. Saw her turn excited circles at the word 'walkey', and...God *fucking* damn *it*.

"Sorrow," the girl repeated. "I told you."

He sniffled and cleared his throat. "Yeah. Blocked up inside like bad plumbing. Comes surging up now and again."

"Like waves. It hits you in waves."

"Sure does."

"What happened?"

James steeled himself, the story passing his mouth too many times already for one week. "Bad genetics, man. Can you believe that? Poor girl just..."

"Tragic. No one to blame. You want to yell 'fuck you' at the ocean in Momma Nature's name? I won't judge."

James laughed and sniffled. "Nah, but...thank you. Rushed off to the vet but she'd already gone cold, and..."

"Hey." She reached across, prodded his shoulder. A jolt shocked his system, and a mess of butterflies burst about his stomach. "Tell you something off-record, all right? Just a chat. My dog—and I swear to God this is true—ran off a month ago. Never found him. Little Jack Russell named Buppa."

"No shit?"

"Absolutely zero poops...and afterwards, I stayed up long into the night, night after night, with this new fear of death implanted in my chest. Just *worrying* that my mom will go soon, and what then? She's sick, after all. Thoughts of cleaning out the room, boxing up her stuff. Her clothes, her thrift store trinkets and old letters. But then I remind myself that that day *will* come, sure, but it's what happens *now* that matters. That we enjoy the present, and take care of the ones we love. Hell, if that dead swimmer could tell you something from the grave, I'm sure it would be something similar."

"You're probably right." David tapped the recording software off, the urge to work already fizzled out. All he wanted now was to sit on his couch and let the current sad spell pass, process this unwanted crash of emotion. Fuck what anyone thought of a grown man missing his dog. That was his damn *Holly*, for God's sake.

"You okay?"

Her words broke through and James shook his head, squeezed the bridge of his nose. On his sleeve, a single dog hair blew with the breeze. "I'm fine. I think I should just go home, give this article to someone else. Ask to work on a fluff piece I can do without thinking. Thought I was ready to do some *real* work, but..."

"I understand." She studied him a moment longer, making him feel like a weird museum exhibit. "I didn't come out here to sell my shells a full week after Buppa. I totally get it."

"I'm still glad I came out, though. It's been nice to chat with someone...different."

Her cheeks lifted in a smirk. "I'm as different as they come, that's for sure."

"But thanks for the conversation. I really do appreciate it."

"No problem, um..." She shook her head, waiting.

"James," he said.

"James. No problem, James. I'm Elaine, by the way."

"Beautiful name." The words came by their own accord, and her blush made him happy they did.

"Thank you. Well, you take care of yourself, James. And tell your friends to come buy a shell sometime."

"Speaking of which, before I go..." James plucked his wallet and eased open the flap. "How much?"

"Just five a piece...I do try real hard on each one, though, and—"

"No, I mean the whole bag."

Her mouth opened in a comical 'O'. "Can't be serious? I've gotta have, like, twenty of 'em in there."

"Twenty, right? So that's one hundred. I'll take 'em."

"James..." She looked out to the water while suppressing a smile. "I can't do that, honestly. Besides, you'd be robbing all the potentially lucky customers I could get today. All those folks who'll have to go home without a souvenir. Don't be...shellfish."

The joke hit like a dead fish and James scrunched his face. "Okay, okay. Let me take one, then. How does this work?"

Her eyes widened with excitement and she scooped the bag, pulled the top. "Okay, so..." She rummaged

around. "I paint each one with water color and then seal
'em with a spray can. The water colors look really cool and
I'd always wanted to...hold on..." She plucked one free.
"Here, I always wanted to do one orange, and it came out
quite well, don't you think?"

James expected to fake excitement, but the bright
shell really was impressive. He cocked his head to the side,
studying the gradient effect she'd accomplished running
from tip to bell, curling with the shape of the shell itself.

"This is a listening one." She held it to her ear in
demonstration. "You ever do that as a kid? Hear the ocean
in a shell. Obviously not true, but nice to pretend."

She handed the shell to James and he took it gingerly,
turned it in his palm. She eyed him closely as he brought
the shell to his ear and listened, a thin hiss of white noise
filling his eardrum. He smiled, and she returned the
gesture, the act so childish yet the nostalgia welcomed.

"It's so strange. Bizarre hissing. It's..." He frowned.
"There's something else."

"Oh?"

"Something like..."

The bark came again, this time stronger.

"No..."

"What? What is it?"

James focused on the ocean behind the girl, the belly
of waves flopping on the sands. And, further out—*too far*
out—a dark shape kicking foam in a panic.

"A dog," he said, putting the shell down and getting to
his feet. "Jesus, is that your...?"

"Buppa!" The girl leaped up and brought a hand to her
chest. "James! Oh, God!"

He took off, the wind blowing him as if to keep him
away and the sand gripping his soles. When he reached
the rocks he skidded and almost went over, balancing at

the last moment before ripping off his shirt in preparation. He kicked off his shoes just as his right foot splashed the icy brine. Within seconds the water was up to his waist, slowing his movement like instant-glue. He slipped free of his second shoe, leaped, held his breath, and went under.

All went black.

James cursed his smoking then, wishing he'd stuck to giving up the previous month, but with Holly gone, so did the commitment. He kicked back to the surface and spat saltwater, sucking fresh air inside his lungs. The sun blinded him and he blinked frantically to clear them, relocating the dog before a wave pushed James back under. The world disappeared, replaced by tickling bubbles that popped in his ears. He pushed through the nothingness, using broad breast-strokes until his lungs burned for more air. Bursting topside, he sucked and got a mouthful of water. Spitting, he fought the panic that threatened to take over and scanned the waters once more. The dog had gone.

James shouted, a primal sound that came all by itself. He hadn't gone off course, hadn't been thrown in another direction by the slapping water, no. The dog had just disappeared.

James turned, the beach bobbing in the distance, and there stood the girl, waving to him, and *laughing?*

The sound carried above the roar of the ocean, subtle as the noise in the shell, but distinguishable. James' hair stood on end. She clutched his tablet in her right hand, the corduroy bag swung over her left shoulder. Another wave came and took the sight away, replacing it with darkness once more.

James' body cried for rest, needing a break, but his will refused and forced his limbs to continue moving as dread and confusion flooded his mind. Why on earth was she *laughing?* Why take his *things?*

My mother's sick, he heard her say. *I'm just trying to take care of her...*

Something grabbed his ankle.

Feed her...

James' breath blew out, rushing to the surface in a stream of bubbles. Through the churning waters, a gray and sickly arm worked its way around his leg. He kicked out, his head thumping and his chest screaming. Nails raked his skin as he wriggled from the grasp and pushed upward. He broke the surface and gulped oxygen, just as the thing took hold and ripped him back under.

James flailed his limbs. He tore from the grasp just as he caught sight of something that made him lose air once more. A woman floated there in the darkness, hair like a halo of splintered rope. Barnacles jutted from her bare and wrinkled midsection, her skin a flabby mess, bloated and waterlogged. Two black orbs sat sunken in her skull, glaring with all-consuming hunger. Below her midsection lay the stuff of fairytale.

I'm seeing things, his mind screamed. *I'm dying and I'm seeing things.*

The woman's mouth fell open as if paining her, revealing broken and yellowed shark-like teeth. Her lower portion—the aquatic mystery belonging to a storybook—propelled her. A missing chunk on her side seeped infection, slowing her movement.

She's sick...I need to take care of her.

James pushed himself topside again, saltwater stinging his eyes as he aimed in the direction of the beach. At least, what he *thought* was the direction of the beach.

Where the hell am I now? Oh, Jesus, oh, God...

He inhaled and a massive stitch bit his side. Above the crashing waves, land titled sideways and he kicked, blowing out brine that entered his mouth and nostrils.

He crashed his arms through the water, needing to stay surfaced, needing to keep track—but then white hot pain ripped through his body.

James screamed as he plunged back under, catching sight of the corpse-woman sinking gnarled teeth into his heel. Her eyes fluttered in ecstasy, and from nowhere—*and everywhere*—a voice filled the ocean.

So sweet...So good...

A school of fish shot by, their better instincts warning them of the monster in their wake. James whipped his leg free again as the creature's teeth shredded his ankle in a cloud of red. The creature's eyes widened, registering his unexpected fight, and she reached out in a panic, missing him by inches. James swam, churning the waters to a froth as a scream rose in his chest that threatened to shred his throat. He tried controlling himself, tried calming down, but his body had other plans.

Behind, something splashed the surface in a perfect staccato rhythm. Something gaining by the second.

He dared not look and instead focused on the dry land, the casual calls of seagulls overhead driving him crazy. Slender fingers tickled his shredded foot as he forced himself to quicken, survival kicking into gear. The whitewater around him flashed bright red, filling his vision. He was bleeding out something fierce.

So good, came the voice. *So...good...*

James yelped as needles punctured his calf, jolting him to a stop and tearing him under. Ice water filled his nose, shooting down his throat. He opened his eyes and pushed toward the blurry sun overhead as muted sounds of the underworld filled his head. A stream of red ran past his face from the warm current gushing from his ankle. His bladder let loose.

Get up! Get the hell up!

James reached down and worked his fingers into the arm of his captor. All the while, the surface slipped away. The arm slid in his palms, freezing to the touch like a hardened lump of slime. Pieces flaked free and drifted around his face, little dots clotting his vision.

I can't get a grip! Jesus!

No, the voice replied. *Too nice...no...*

He pulled as hard as he could as ancient skin slopped in his grasp.

My car keys!

James wrestled with his pocket, then yanked out the jagged metal and ran it through his knuckles. He caught the creature's arm with his free fist, and drove the key deep.

A scream filled his head, pressurizing his brain.

He worked the key back and forth, the wound jetting an ink-like substance. The nails jarred in his flesh slid free. James pushed the arm away and kicked back to the surface, dropping the key as his vision thumped in time with his chest. He splashed out, sucking down cold, *godlike* air, just as his alarmed senses registered a roar coming from behind. James filled his lungs fast. The wave crashed down and ripped him away as easy as a fly on Velcro, tossing him in the organic tumble dryer of the sea.

He stopped moving. His energy disappeared. In his mind's eye, he caught flashes of the girl, her laughter, his Holly, her dog, her...*mother*. He saw all this as the wave smashed him along, speeding like an invisible derby car. Wherever it took him now, he didn't care. All he needed was rest.

His mind dulled, registering nothing but turbulent liquid, like a mother's womb...

Soothing.

Sand scraped his back, soft at first, then pressing hard.

James hissed to a stop along the stony beach. The wave that carried him retracted back to the ocean, fizzling through the sands. His skin prickled in the freezing air and he rolled to his stomach, coughing and gagging. He gasped lungful after lungful of oxygen as his vision doubled and returned, doubled and returned. Heat bloomed around his ankle as blood slithered down into the stones to mix with the brine. He wheezed and blinked his eyes clear before falling onto his back and squinting at the ocean.

A flock of gulls batted inland, sensing the new danger lurking below. And out on the water, something dark appeared and disappeared, moving toward the horizon. Something undeniably human, but only just about. The sight tore a yell from his chest.

Cutting through the hissing waves, came another sound then. A siren, one that shocked him back to his own situation. James gritted his teeth, clamping his leg with his fist. Warmth pumped around his knuckles, the wound worse than he thought. A laugh filled the air, one James doubted anyone could hear but him.

She got inside my head...the dog...used me...

Stones crunched just before a hand gripped his back and eased him down flat. A face appeared overhead, blocking the sun.

"Sir, keep flat. That's it." The man tussled something on his lapel, a microphone, and muttered a jumble of words James couldn't quite distinguish.

Am I...dying?

The man peered down again, his eyes working about the wound. "Sir, we're taking you to the hospital, okay? I need you stay calm and breathe. Can you remember what happened?"

"The water." James' vision darkened, and he shook his head. His stomach roiled with the need to vomit. "Comes in waves."

"You've taken a bite. Can you remember what it was? A shark?"

"Mother Nature," James said, his words slurred. The answer *felt* right. "She's got teeth, too, don't forget."

"A shark," the medic said, getting to his feet. He ran a hand over his balding head and took a deep breath. "In Ireland of all places, Jesus, what the hell happened here?"

Someone yelled from the entrance of the beach, at least, what James *thought* was the entrance of the beach— he couldn't tell anymore. Something about a bag filled with shells.

"My tablet?" he tried, but doubted if the words passed his lips, or made sense. To his surprise, the medic told him to stay quiet and try to remain calm. Just a bag of shells.

Nausea surged from the pit of his stomach as someone lifted him. If he'd slipped out of consciousness, he couldn't tell. He bobbed and bounced, and then something covered him, something warm and soft. A blanket. Men spoke fast, their words too quick to catch. A door crashed shut before an engine rumbled his body. The rocking motion made his urge to puke worsen, and James groaned. The quiet and warmth soothed him, and he relaxed while taking deep, slow breaths.

From nowhere and everywhere, a voice filled his head. A voice meant only for him, and one the medics or anyone else would not hear.

One that said, "*So good...Too nice...*"

Before a churning darkness ripped him under.

I'D RATHER GO BLIND

*C**LICK.***

Checking if this thing even works. Give me a sec.

Whirr...Click.

All right, that's coming through nice enough. Sounds like a bad radio drama, but it'll do. You laughed at me when I grabbed this thing from the bargain bin, remember? Two euro. Who'd want a cassette recorder in this day and age, right? Well, who'd let it rot in here, I said. And you laughed.

If I'd known what I'd be using it for now, I'd have left it for some hipster with a dusty collection. But that day, out there with the sun beating down and the breeze kissing the waves...one of the best days this ol' bastard ever had. I hope you know that.

Give me a moment.

Click.

The baked goods turned this morning—can smell 'em from here. Weather changed for the better about an hour ago, the kinda day you like. The breeze from the window is a godsend, and I imagine outside looks pretty as a painting if I could see. But those baked goods...

Why is it everyone thinks cakes, scones, and muffins help with mourning, honey? Bakeries stink of death now, dough n' corpses going hand in hand, but it isn't their fault, I suppose. Just tryin' to balm the wound.

143

I could've eaten some, or thrown it away, but I haven't wanted to do jack-shit since...Give me a moment, sweetheart. Need to make sure this relic's still running.

Whirr...Click.

I'm surprised it's holding up. *Top stuff*, as you'd say, right? *Said*, I mean...Where was I? Right, the moldy food.

We bought muffins on the way to the second-hand shops the day I got this recorder, remember? God, I loved our *adventures*—that was your word for it. I called it an *outing* and you called me stuffy. Saving pocket money for a month just to have a day together, what were we like? Fifty cent here, twenty there. Just looking at our *day out* jar launched a butterfly battalion in my stomach.

Felt like Christmas waking up knowing we'd spend forty-odd euro on someone else's throwaways, but like your dad always said, one man's trash is another man's cat litter. He hasn't called me in days.

Click.

Dun Laoghaire Pier that day, what a sight. Took the DART at eight in the morning before the crowds festered, our bellies full of too-salty porridge because I never made it right. But you never complained. Dublin Bay splayed out before us as if it were a fairytale.

Cones for ninety-nine cent—*dipping into our jar before the day even started*, you said, so I bopped you on the nose with a dab of vanilla. Staring out at the twinkling ocean, yapping about the possible deals we'd snatch. A dress, you wanted, knee-high and red, good enough for Mark and Emer's dinner dance.

They came by yesterday, by the way.

Snuck the washing out and returned it clean, can you believe the cheek? They didn't mean anything by it, but they took more than the clothes. I grabbed the basket off them, kicked 'em out and slammed the door. Temper got the better of me, as usual. But they'll understand. Eventually, everyone will.

The fabric softener angered me just as much as a cashier's fake smile; you know my grudge with those people. The synthetic smell worked its way up my nostrils while I stood there holding the basket, making me wonder where your scent had drifted. Down the drain for some lucky rats? Possibly. Most likely gone forever and that hit me like a punch from McGregor.

I wanted to inhale those clothes as they were, a little change for this chump, y'know? But instead I closed my eyes and breathed fabricated lilac and lemon. And that's when the idea for all of this struck, right there while slipping down the wall with the basket held to my chest and the fake stink churning my stomach.

We listened to Etta an awful lot in those final days. She brought you to tears all the time, and you called me a damn *statue* for not reacting to the lyrics, but I did, sweetheart. I swear I did. I still do. Her voice floodin' the car on Sunday drives, remember? Trips up the Wicklow Mountains just to wait half the day in traffic as bad as the City Centre because of the weekend. But the world felt like a movie-set with us in the lead roles, sunshine or rain, windows rolled down and the breeze just right, lost in our own immortal romance. Something starring Doris Day or James Dean, I imagine. Those were the lies those songs gave.

It's a sensory thing, something learned from the movies, hearin' music and thinkin'—*really thinking*—it's a soundtrack to real life. Makes us believe we're the heroes of the tale, doesn't it? But heroes don't die. Only the rest of us do. We tend to forget that part, especially with Etta humming sweet nothings in our ears.

Click.

Where was I? After I managed to make those two toe-heads stop banging the door down by repeating I was fine, my eyes were puffed enough to scare a carnival regular. I dragged myself off the floor and collapsed in the bathroom.

You still lingered there, you see—just a bit.

Your hair-dryer lay on the floor from that morning, your toothbrush in the sink. I'd showered after you, and you would've strangled me if I hadn't unblocked the drain, but just once I wish I hadn't listened. I always listened, and in the corner still sat the open bottle of bleach you begged me to throw away because we lost the lid and you worried it'd spill all over. That's the one thing I put off doing that you asked, isn't that funny?

In the bedroom, I kept our sheets untouched.

I've been sleeping on the couch.

Click.

There in the bathroom I breathed you in, lost in a kaleidoscope of good times, even in the arguments, and just for a moment the world pretended to be all right. The stink of the baked goods drifted, and the open bleach became just an undertone. I was with you, honey. Everything came clear—the wrinkles around your eyes when you smiled, the ones you hated but always melted me. Spooning while watching a movie on the couch, knowing we were both up for work *in just a few hours* but we foolishly stayed put. And I'm glad now more than ever that we did. The fun times, the silly times, even the mundane, all right before my eyes.

When I got my bearings, I stumbled into our bedroom, rolled up the duvet. Each movement of the blanket gifted me another whiff of you. I rolled it like a giant worm—I'm not stupid, I know it's not shaped like you. You'd sever my bollocks if I said it did, but the illusion did the trick. I kicked off my boots and lay on the bed. Then I spooned it. Just how we did.

Do. Just how we *do.*

My cramping stomach couldn't faze me, not for the entire day, but eventually, my bladder did. The sun disappeared somewhere back in that bad world, and when I opened my eyes to shade; it all hit home again, just like that blasted truck.

Click.

Remember the roar of the horn?

Click.

Should ease your mind knowing he died, too. Fecking drunkard shouldn't've been out on the road, a danger to the world and not a care. He had a wife, and I imagine she's not doing much better than me. She even managed to send me a card, if you can believe that.

Anyway, I hobbled from the room and took a piss, grateful for the chance to close my eyes once more and return to the good place I'd created. Even called out to you in the other room to tell you I loved ya.

Pretended you were fast asleep with a little drool on your pillow like I used to make fun of you for. That helped. I swear, and don't laugh now, I swear I heard you say you loved me, too.

Click.

I opened my eyes and the nightmare returned. I steeled my nerves. When I shook the last drops (and, *yes*, wiped the toilet seat), I caught sight of your hairbrush and...well, there's no easy way to say this...that blasted bottle of bleach.

I took 'em both back to the bedroom and locked the door.

Click.

You think I'm crazy, don't you?

Honey, if only you knew what it was like to be 'the survivor'. Straight away, they all jumped down my throat with stories of how it wasn't my fault, of how I couldn't have changed a thing even if I'd wanted. As if any of it made a lick of difference. And you'd slap me sideways for being so remorse, I know you would, but I'm carrying enough sorrow for two large men with a Siamese twin.

You're alive, they all said, like it made a difference. They don't know their hands from their arseholes. Did they expect a moment of clarity and a "gee, you're right, thanks!" from me? They're throwing any old words, I suppose, hoping something'll stick, thinkin' it'll make me feel better.

Or maybe they're just trying to make themselves feel better, who knows.

But I went with you that night, and even though you don't want to hear it, I often thought about such things once you drifted before me in bed. Thinking I wouldn't last if something sinister ever happened. But then the daylight hit and dissolved those bad thoughts as if they were vampires. Just silly little thoughts.

See, the daytime blinded me as much as the music, all that same *fingers-crossed* promise of safety.

Click.

Etta's lullin' from the bedroom. She's calling me like a siren, that magical voice actin' as a shot of whiskey on my sour mood. Same effect she always had, just like those magical days. Making me feel like the hero of this tale once more. And, look, I know it isn't real, none of it, but humor me this one time, honey. Because I don't know what else to do.

They all sayin' I can go on, that you'd want me to get back to normal, blah, blah, fuckin' blah, but what about what I want? They don't get to decide. I do. And I can't envision life without you. I don't want to.

So I won't.

I'm out in the living room one last time, out in the bad world. Cleared a path because I know I'll need it. Spread the strands of hair from your brush on your pillow. I'm smellin' the spoiled goods one last time. They're turnin' my guts like our old washing machine. I'm burnin' a photo of you into my mind before the bleach takes the bad world away.

Then I'm going to the room to lay with you. To smell you. They say smell is the fastest route for memory, and without the other senses clogging the path like Sunday drivers; I should get there soon.

Etta said she'd rather go blind, honey. She meant that. And so do I.

Click.

DARK STAGE

LEATHER-CLAD ROCKERS milled about the open floor of the Shantyman with their voices raised to be heard above the juke. Sweat, smoke and aftershave collected in an invisible cloud, hot-boxing the venue for another night of sex and sin. In the morning, recollection of those smells would send a hot jet of puke into the bowl of many unfortunate drinkers, but for now, tomorrow stayed at arm's length. The night had just begun.

At the bar, Fred involuntarily spat beer as his bones burned like hot coals. He slammed his glass to the countertop before wincing and clutching his fist. Only Tuesday night, and already he'd experienced several flairs. Arthritis at forty-three. Man, sometimes life dealt a stinker.

Paul paused with a handful of empty glasses behind the bar and arched a bushy brow. "Another one?"

"Make it a whiskey."

"I meant your hands, man. Bad?"

Fred flexed his fists and lay them out on the countertop, ignoring the layer of sticky film. His digits visibly shook. Goddamn it.

Paul sighed and grabbed a bottle of Jack, untwisted the top. "Look, I'll make it a double and I'll make it free. Ain't gonna lie, this place won't be the same without you, man. You were the best sound guy I ever knew."

Fred gave a tight-lipped smile and watched the bartender pour, jealous of the smooth motion. He envied the majority of the population and their pain-free joints. "Much obliged, buddy."

Paul grunted and returned the bottle beside the others, most half empty even though they'd only restocked Sunday. Then he shouted for Justine to handle the clamor of drinkers who'd swarmed like the walking dead and stepped out from behind the bar. He pulled up a stool next to Fred, snorted. "Bossman due down soon?"

Fred eyed his whiskey, hands folded together while waiting for the tremors to pass. Pain thumped beneath his skin in rhythm to the music of the room's speakers. "He gets in at ten. Just enough time for me to catch the show tonight. Then I do what I got to do."

"He's not going to be happy about losing you, Fred. There's a reason he bought you out from the Fillmore. You know how to work a sound desk better than any man in all of San Fran."

"Don't I know it, babe." Fred reached for his whiskey and quickly scooped it to his lips before spilling too much. He gulped, returning the glass to the table with a hiss. The chore hurt more than he cared to admit. Hot liquor burned his chest and he relished the waxy air in his throat.

Paul shook his head. "Man, it's gotten bad, huh? Jesus."

"Looks like benefits for me until I find a job that doesn't involve my hands."

For a moment the thought twisted Fred's guts and he eyed the wall of signed memorabilia behind the bar to avoid overthinking. His future looked as grim as most the Shantyman's pint glasses—but he had the choice to drink from one or not. A stupid thought. As teeth grinding as his hands could be, pain wasn't going to stop him living. Or so he told himself.

A framed and signed Bile Lords t-shirt he'd received from the band caught his eye and the memory of the show lifted his lips into a grin. That had been a night of true rock 'n' roll.

Paul noticed his line of sight. "That'd been a *real* one, eh? True music, man. Heals the heart."

"If only it could heal my damn body."

Paul snorted a laugh. Then Justine's yelling made him cringe. "Shit, man. I gotta get back. Look, enjoy the show tonight, all right? I'll give you a ride home after you talk with the Bossman. Drinks on me. Shame your last show is an open mic, but what can you do."

"What?" Fred squinted to the chalked sign above the bar. *Tuesday Night: Open Mic.* "Oh, goddamn it."

Open mics at the Shantyman carried about the same merit as a fart joke. Half-baked acts—typically formed just weeks before—came onstage and tried their damnedest to rouse a laugh in what'd become Shantyman tradition. Occasionally a try-hard band attempted an acoustic set in the hopes of appearing "high class," but lately the San Francisco music scene plopped out nothing but overweight Bon Jovi wannabes bashing out ballads to their front-row girlfriends. To Fred, a lobotomy held more appeal.

With a swivel of his stool, he caught a glimpse of the sound console through the sea of drunks. The equipment had become an extension of his very being over the past five years, each fader and knob as familiar as a curve or limb of a lover. The idea of a new sound man getting his grubby fucking fingers all over the controls boiled his blood. Past the sound desk, the stage sat in darkness. The reputation of the open mic dictated no PA and no lighting. The less the patrons heard the blasted cat-wailing of bedroom rehearsed and tone-deaf Twisted Sisters, the better. 1992 had so far promised a bright future from the glitzy MTV butt-rock era, but Fred only hoped the direction maintained course and didn't nose-dive into dry cement.

Someone tapped his shoulder. He turned and came face to face with a ghoul.

The man stood over six feet tall, a long black coat cloaking his anemic frame. Greasy, gray-peppered hair strung across his face alongside a thick beard. The scent of tobacco smoke drifted from his body, but his eyes, nestled into dark pockets, burned with intent.

"Can I help you?"

The man nodded once, slowly. "Open mic?"

Fred now noticed the battered case alongside the stranger's leg. Worn leather like that spoke of many traveled highways and cities. Perhaps even continents.

"I used to run the desk," Fred said, "But tonight's a free-for-all. Go up now, if you like."

Shit, he wanted to add, by the looks of things, you're the only one who showed, anyway.

The stranger didn't blink, and his eyes burned a hole through Fred. "A man who throws caution to rules."

Fred expected a question but the statement hung in the air and an awkward silence descended.

"You're not a glam act, clearly," Fred observed, breaking the tension. He eyed the stranger up and down. "And I'm interested in what you've got. Come on, I'll listen to you play."

The stranger nodded with eyes closed, his jaw clasped. His alabaster skin hinted at an illness, and by his slow, calculated movements, Fred needed to ask, "Are you okay?"

"I will be," the stranger said. "Come and listen to me play."

With a wince, Fred hopped from the stool as a lick of pain ignited in his knees and ankles. He rubbed his legs before reaching for his drink and swigging the last of it. He saluted Paul before leading the stranger through the boozy maze of the Shantyman's open floor. The half-drunk crowd remained stationary and Fred elbowed his way through, each stumble and collision setting his teeth on edge with agony. The stranger followed his path like Moses through the parted sea.

Fred peeled from the audience and made his way to the dim stage, catching his breath by the coolers. Cold air breathed down from an overhead vent, installed to keep musical acts comfortable. Fred usually complained about the waste of energy that the constantly running coolers consumed but right now he was grateful. A second later, the stranger exited the crowd and crossed to his side.

"There's another act," the stranger said. He cocked his head to the right, where by the sound desk, a Lycra-wearing duo basked in the attention of a gaggle of awe-struck rockers. The chicks were undeniably beautiful, their hair-sprayed styles sexy yet dangerous, with leather jackets leaving a sliver of toned stomach visible above hip-cinched pants. Stiletto heels put them both at an inch or two taller than the lust numbed gatherers. None of them paid Fred or the stranger any attention.

Fred nodded. "You know, even if they didn't play music, if they simply went venue to a venue with guitar cases, they'd gather a better following than most starving bands these days. And fuck it, more power to 'em, they know how to catch attention."

The stranger didn't respond and instead lay his guitar case on the floor. He popped the locks to reveal a time beaten Gibson. Grabbing its neck, he lifted the instrument to his side and kicked the empty case to the stage. "Pay them no mind. I want you to hear me play."

That was all. A shiver crawled along Fred's skin. Something about the stranger—his demeanor, his words, his look—just felt...odd. Yet, like before, Fred *did* want to hear him play. A musician who attracted attention with presence alone, no frills, glitz or peacocking, was a musician Fred itched to hear. He'd grown weary of the recycled synth-fused 80's soundtrack and craved something raw. Something new. Something the stranger might offer.

Another wave of pain bloomed in his wrists and Fred fought the urge to groan. He motioned to the stage with a shaking finger as the agony bit, then hobbled to a nearby stool. His bones felt like brittle glass and he silently cursed an impartial God before gathering his nerves. "Stage is all yours, man. Knock 'em dead."

The stranger climbed aboard the plywood floor, clenched his jaw, and sat. Two chest-high stools sat to the side of the stage for acoustic acts, but the stranger paid them no notice, opting instead for his own rump. In the darkness and the coolers, his hair blew around his shadowed face. With one creeping hand, he formed a chord, waited a beat, and then closed his eyes. From where Fred sat, he saw the stranger's lids flutter like a man hitting REM sleep, and for a moment, he pondered the stranger's age. The man could be forty or sixty, and both seemed likely. But before Fred could come to a conclusion, the stranger began to play.

The atmospheric white noise of the Shantyman faded as if sucked through a vacuum, the silence settling like a teacher shushing a giddy classroom. Surroundings melted, the low light dimming, and within seconds, only Fred and the stranger remained. Fred craned his neck this way and that, but beyond a foot in each direction and the stage ahead, only darkness lay. A thick curtain of black concealed the world beyond the music and attention the stranger did demanded.

The man stroked his first chord, a jangling D, and Fred's skin sizzled in response. The light hair on his forearm tickled and rose. The next chord came, followed by a quick diminished lick, and brought with it the numbness of a dentist's anesthetic. Fred's breathing hitched.

The stranger swayed in place, legs folded beneath him, and then parted his lips. His head fell back. A voice like aged whiskey and boiling nails spilled forth—the voice of a road worn warrior. The sound injected the air with tangible warmth not unlike a hot bath, and Fred gasped.

As the stranger formed words, their sound lost to the offline thump of his brain, Fred understood their message all the same. Spoken in a language only known to music, the feeling promised the kiss of a lover on a lonely night and warmth in a storm. More than that, it promised no pain, and hot tears blurred Fred's vision as, suddenly, his agony dissolved. His fingers tingled and trembled, followed by his legs, and then it all faded to nothingness like a hit of H. A sound caught Fred's ear, other than the music, and he realized he was moaning, all along. He shivered involuntarily, and the stranger looked up, caught his eye—and the music fell silent.

The sounds of the Shantyman swelled from another dimension, people populated the darkness, forming all around, and the light increased until it reached its former state. The steady *thump-thump* of the juke slipped into being, giving life to the scene. A youthful heartbeat. All around, the chaotic noise and scent of cigarettes and hops returned.

Fred breathed heavily, sweat tickling his forehead. He ran a palm past his face before blinking his vision clear. The song—*could it even be called a song?*—still worked through his system like an opiate, but fainter now, and fizzling.

Only one thought occupied his brain. Just one.

Fred Williams was pain-free. And he cried.

One of the long-legged ladies crossed the room with a case in her hand and stood before him, her hip slanted in a conscious pose. She teased a cocktail stick between her cherry lips before giving him a once over.

"You runnin' this show?"

Fred looked up, sniffled. "Lady, I don't know who's running this show anymore."

She cocked an eyebrow. "So, we can play now?"

A cheer erupted from behind her, followed by stomping feet, clapping hands and wolf whistles. Fred watched it all through the lens of a dream, a dream which was still fading as he struggled to keep a hold. He never wanted to lose the aura of the stranger's song. With a pain-free hand, he motioned to the dark stage. "It's all yours."

Then his stomach sank. The stage stood empty. The battered guitar case on the floor had vanished. And so, too, had the stranger.

Fred pushed himself from the stool and frantically scanned the room, spotting the tail of a long black cloak slip into the audience. The woman went to ask another question, but Fred shook his head and jogged after the stranger, barging into the wall of people whose eyes were glued to the glitzy duo about to perform. A large man elbowed him aside and Fred, surprisingly, laughed. No pain. He continued to squeeze his way through the organic sea and popped free near the bar. Looking to the left, he spotted the black-coated man stalk toward the exit. Fred ran.

"Hey!"

He placed a hand on the stranger's shoulder and spun him. He gasped.

A fresh-faced young man grinned at him, his skin plump and youthful. Jet black hair reached to his shoulders, which he flicked out of his face. Those eyes, brilliant blue and full of life, were all too familiar.

"How?" he asked.

The stranger only nodded. "Places to be, my friend. People to meet. I hope you enjoyed the show."

Then he turned and left. Fred stood in shock as the exit doors swung on their hinges, his heart thumping and his mind reeling. The faint sound of the glamorous duo drifting from the stage—a bad Guns N' Roses knock-off—hardly registered. Someone tapped his shoulder.

Thomas Whitman, the Shantyman manager, smiled. Then his eyebrows came together in a sharp V. "Everything all right, Fred?"

Fred shivered, struggling to keep his brain on track. The walls of the building suddenly felt too close, too confining. He needed space.

"Come, Fred. Come." Thomas led him to a free stool by the bar and Fred sat like an obedient dog. Nothing seemed possible, solid or real. Once more, he couldn't get over the rosy-cheeked man before him, who'd, up until recently, looked as gaunt as the stranger after a long battle with cancer.

Thomas Whitman looked him in the eye. "Can I get you water? You look like you've seen a ghost."

Fred licked his lips, dry and cracked. "Yes, please. Water."

Thomas motioned to Paul and an ice-choked glass slid across the counter. Fred drank greedily.

Thomas's narrowed eyes followed the glass as Fred placed it back to the bar.

"Now, then. Better?"

Fred nodded. "Better."

A banshee scream erupted from the audience as the duo onstage finished their first number, something about sex and sports cars. Then their next song began, sounding the very same, and Thomas clicked his fingers. "Earth to Fred, you there?"

"Huh? Yeah, sorry, Tom. I'm just..."

Just what? Still processing a song that cured your pain? Getting over the fact you just came into contact with someone who was most definitely not human?

Thomas grinned, his chubby cheeks lifting. "We're not here to talk about your retirement from the world of music, are we, Fred?"

A ball of ice hit Fred's stomach. "You know?"

"Of course, I know. I only hoped he'd come. Strange fellow, huh? Curious..." Thomas laced his fingers together. "Caught him in Seattle two months back at another open mic. Again in Portland a week later. Always traveling, always alone. Always with a song to sing. No one paid him any attention apart from those who knew...knew he had that certain *something*. The open mic here was a...a bowl of milk for the cat. Get me? I gave him my card and told him about our venue. Prayed he'd show for you. This place has a long history of odd happenings, you know." He looked about the room, royalty surveying his kingdom. "These walls have seen more cures and curses than any place. And I wouldn't miss a day for the world. Your hands, pain free?"

"As good as in my twenties, Tom. I can't...I can't believe it. I can't believe any of this."

Thomas chuckled, his beach ball stomach jiggling. He gave Fred's shoulder a squeeze. "You're here for the long haul, boy. As are most of us. Like it or not."

Fred decided he did like it, even if he didn't understand it. He flexed his fingers and felt no pain whatsoever. The absurdity still failed to register. With a nervous chuckle, he reached for his water and took the glass to his lips. Then he paused.

The ice, half-melted, misted on the glass and trickled across his fingers. And Fred felt...*nothing*.

"Tom, I can't feel the cold..."

Thomas gave a knowing nod. "It's wonderful isn't it? The stranger took away my pain, too. No chemo for me, no needles or heartache. It's wonderful."

"It's not wonderful." Fred squeezed his thigh, digging his fingers deep into the flesh past his jeans. "Nothing. *I feel nothing.*"

"No pain, kid. No more."

"No pain?" Fred laughed without humor. "No pain, no heat, no cold, no nothing, Tom! I feel *nothing!*"

"And you owe it all to this place." Thomas stood and looked to his audience, his people, his building. Then he nodded to the door by the stage where stairs led to his second-floor office. "I've got much to do," he said. "But I'm glad you're not going anywhere. Happy to have this all ironed out. If I could feel happy..." He laughed then, the action never touching his eyes. "Sit a spell and then get some sleep. I'll see you back in work tomorrow. And the day after that, and the day after that. Hell, have a drink on me. Relax. Enjoy the show."

AN UNUSUAL PET

YOU'RE DESCRIBING A triceratops."

The old man scratched at a dry patch on his forehead and leaned against the door. He clicked his tongue. "Sure, if that's what it sounds like to you. I'm just tellin' ya about Gordon."

Sarah laughed. "You call it *Gordon*, are you serious?"

Stepping onto the porch, he motioned to the open door. "Look, are you coming in or not? I've got work to do and I'm sure you don't have all day, neither."

"Of course, I'm sorry."

Sarah followed the man inside, the smell of grease and stale air attacking her senses. Black and white photos, sepia-toned with age, lined the walls. Class photos from the fifties froze smiling students in lined rows. Stacks of broken bicycles parts lay heaped beneath a staircase to the left like metal spaghetti.

"What did you say your name was again?" The old man asked, leading the way to a door on the far end of the hall.

"I didn't," Sarah said. "It's Sarah. Sarah Burke."

"And you're with your school newspaper or something?"

Her eyebrow arched in response. "No, I'm with *The Dublin Times*. Just started, actually. I used to be with a local paper."

"So you're from Ballydubh, originally?"

"Next town over, but Ballydubh was the nearest place with a newspaper so I started out here."

The old man entered the kitchen and presented the room with a flap of his arm. "Not much here, but it's enough. You like the Jesus painting there? Danny Porter did that for me."

Sarah couldn't help but chuckle. The painting depicted Jesus Christ with two muscular folded arms and the text DON'T CROSS ME scrolled beneath. She looked about the rest of the room, trying to hide her discomfort. A dozen fly-catching strips seeped from the ceiling, each caked in little black dots. More littered the floor. A dirty metallic dog bowl sat by the foot of the breakfast table, emptied of its contents.

"That's Gordon's, I'm guessing?"

The old man smiled. "Yup. Gordy loves the Pedigree with chicken bits. Ever try it yourself?"

"Dog food?"

"Ah, come on. I think everyone's wondered, no? I used to try the new ones every time I got it for Gordon. Some of them weren't half bad."

Sarah folded her arms and eyed the old man. "Okay, now you're having me on. First, you describe a *triceratops*, for God's sake, and now tell me you're a connoisseur of canine grub."

The old man lowered to a seat by the table and sighed. He rubbed his hands together, making a sound like dry paper. "Why did you come here? Sit."

Sarah took the only other chair, a rickety looking thing, and removed her notepad and pen from her jacket pocket. "Rumors spread fast around this place, I'm sure you know. I still have a few friends in town and they told me you came across an *odd* pet. That's all they'd say. *Unusual*. Being where we are, I assumed it might be a deformed pig

164

or some kind of farm animal, and I thought..." Sarah took a moment. "Well, I only started with *The Times*, okay? So, if I could raise awareness of an animal with a birth defect, maybe some folks would want to make donations and the public could pay for a life-changing operation. And if it wasn't a deformed pig or something, then...well then I'd have a mighty good story, y'know?"

The old man lowered his eyes to slits, gauging her. "Why would you want to tell everyone about my Gordon, anyway? Even if he is a *tri-top* or whatever you call it?"

"A *triceratops*! A dinosaur!"

"That what it is? So why would you want to tell everyone?"

Sarah removed her smartphone and placed it on the center of the table. "You don't mind if I record this conversation, do you?"

The old man nodded to the phone. "What's that?"

"My smartphone."

"Jaysus. That's not a phone. It's only the size of me palm."

Sarah's response fell away like a missed pinball.

"If it were a phone, then how would you be *recording sound*? That's a dicta-thing, or whatever you call it, that does that. Where do you plug it in?"

"It has a battery. Lasts long. There's an app that allows me to record conversations, just like a Dictaphone."

"So it's actually a dicta-*phone*?" The old man asked, nodding to Sarah while a smile spread across his weathered face.

"Jaysus..." Sarah rubbed at her forehead, the joke setting in. "It's got a camera, too," she added.

The old man brought his hands down on the table hard enough to make Sarah jump. He laughed, a noise not unlike a donkey. "A feckin' camera, in that thing?

Now you're the one jokin' with me. What else does it do? Become a TV, as well?"

"Actually, yes...I suppose."

The old man's eyes widened. "Holy Mary...See, here you are, completely amazed that I might have a pet *three-tip* thing, and you're walking around with a Dictaphone, television, and camera in your phone that's the size of a chocolate bar. And let me ask you again, why do you want to tell so many people about Gordon?"

Gordon. The name still made Sarah shake her head. "If you've *honestly* got a living triceratops in your backyard, the world's going to want to know. They've got a right to know."

"Why?" The old man asked. "What will they do if my Gordon is some old dinosaur or something? They'll come and take him away, won't they? And then what? Perform some mad tests or something. I won't even be allowed to visit."

This is insane, Sarah thought. *He's probably got a Rottweiler with pencils taped to its head out there...*

"It would be a marvel of the modern scientific world," she stated.

The old man snorted. "He'd be a freak. That's what'd happen."

"But you don't mind telling locals about him? If you *really* had a triceratops, you'd either run straight to a museum or keep it a secret. You wouldn't keep it like a dog."

"And why not? I told Danny and James and a few others in town, they all know. Told them because they're me mates. What are they going to do?"

"How can you be sure that these so-called *mates* wouldn't go and report it?"

"To who? Danny, I said. And James. *My friends.* Why would they go and do a thing like that? If you don't trust *your* mates, then you've got bad friends."

Good point, she thought.

"And they know it's here?"

"Sure. James brings back scraps from the butcher's every other Sunday for him. Loves the scraps, he does."

How? Sarah wondered. *How could it be possible for so many people to know of a living triceratops and not make international news? How?*

She answered her own question—*Because we're in the middle of nowhere in Ireland and these folks don't care about the outside world. They're quite content in their own little bubble. This is crazy...*

Still, she found herself asking the all-important question. "Can I see him?"

"Of course. I wouldn't let you go without seeing him if it's that important to ya. Come on. Mind the bits around the floor, I have them where I need them."

Sarah eyed the sideways spray cans and rolls of tape littering the linoleum as she followed the old man to the back door in the kitchenette. As he unbolted the door, his hands shaky, she asked, "What is it you do here, exactly?"

"Spray cars and bikes. Fix bicycles on the side, too. Danny drives down the vehicles he's repaired, and if they're in need of a paint touch up, I do it here in the backyard. Bought the house back in the Celtic boom so I don't have much bills. The work keeps me ticking over and busy. Just about. Although Gordon likes to annoy the shite out of me when I'm trying to get it done. Loves the roar of the engines, he does. There we go."

The old man nudged the door with his shoulder, cracking it open and allowing a fresh breeze inside. "Gets stuck on the floor mold sometimes when the weather changes. Wood expands. Come on out."

Sarah stepped into the back garden—an acre of dead grass that led to the foot of the woodland in the distance. A worn Toyota sat out in the open like an animal carcass, the driver door glistening in a fresh coat of black paint and lacquer. The old man's nearest neighbor appeared to be about a mile to the left.

"That's Danny's place," he said, noticing Sarah staring. "Garage is out back. He only has to bring the cars down that little stretch of road for me."

"And the woods? You ever go out there?"

The old man placed his hands on his hips and chuckled. "Every day. I've explored every square foot of that place throughout the years. It's where I found Gordon."

Sarah looked about the yard, trying to spot the creature. "Where is he now?"

Despite not trusting the old man's tale, a quiver of excitement still tickled her belly.

"It's his nap time. I'd say he's asleep in his house. I'll wake him in a sec."

"His *house?*"

"Sure. Looks like a doghouse. It's around the side there. James and Danny helped me slap it together last summer when I found him."

"And where *did* you find him?"

"Out there in the woods one day." The old man took a seat on the porch, squinting out at the tree line. He removed a package of cigarettes from his jeans pocket and offered the box to Sarah. "Smoke?"

"Sure."

She took a cigarette and accepted the lighter, and once they both had their cigarettes lit, the old man continued.

"I was out there at about seven in the evening," he said, blowing smoke from his nostrils. "Trying to squeeze in a walk before dinner. There's an old creek that runs through, 'bout two miles in. Wanted to see it before heading home. Love the hidden rivers like that. Calm me, they do. So I'm walking through, and I start to hear these footsteps. *Clomp, clomp, clomp*, twigs snappin', leaves crunchin'. I'm not scared out there or anything, but I held me breath, stood still, thinkin' it might just be someone from town out for a walk, too. Then this *thing* just comes out of nowhere, starts coming towards me, about the size of a dog."

"Gordon?"

A broad smile lifted the man's weathered cheeks. "The little man hisself, lettin' out this squeaky wail of a sound. Falling forward on account of a gammy leg."

Sarah blew smoke. "*Gammy?*"

"Busted up," he explained. "Think he'd taken a fall or something. I clicked me tongue, like how you'd call a dog, y'know?" He demonstrated, then added, "And he plodded on over. Went right past me and drank from the creek. Didn't seem to mind me at all. I bent down and stroked his head with my finger, like this." He waggled his index finger in the air. "He stopped drinkin' for a sec, but then went on. While he got some water in him, I went over and pulled a wad of grass, came back, and he took it from my hand. Jesus, my heart nearly exploded. Thing was feckin' adorable. Wait till you see."

Sarah couldn't keep the smile from her face. The old man's story played clear as a movie in her mind. Even if he *was* lying, she found him amusing and no longer cared if *Gordon* existed or not. She could always find another item for the paper, after all. A fluff piece. At least she spent an entertaining Saturday afternoon with an amusing individual.

"And how long have you had him now?" she asked, a laugh in her gut.

"Going on nearly a year. He's gotten a little bigger. Not much, mind, but a little. He's only 'bout the size of a regular dog. Not a little *ankle-biter*, as I call 'em, I mean a *real* dog. Like a Lab or something. 'Bout to my knee, there."

A noise from around the corner of the house caused Sarah's chest to lurch. She planted her hands on the porch and got ready to stand.

The old man smiled. "There he is now. Think we must've woke him."

Sarah rose, her body tensing. Her mouth dried up. "He's not going to attack me, is he?" she asked. "Is he dangerous?"

The old man honked a laugh. "Jaysus, no! Sit down, ye mad thing. He's nice. Don't worry. That thing around his head, this, like, hard halo of a yolk, keeps banging off his door, that's all. Don't worry. Jaysus, you're jumpy as a tick."

Sarah spoke fast, her heart racing. "Tend to get that way around prehistoric creatures, yeah. Look, maybe I should go back inside and look out the window, see him from there?"

The old man flicked his finished cigarette butt into the yard and slowly got to his feet. "Ah would ye stop," he said. "Honestly, Gordon's grand. Look, here he is."

Sarah thought she'd pass out. She couldn't believe her eyes. Slinking towards them with a casual stride was a creature unlike anything she'd ever seen before. Except for illustrations. About the size of a dog, and with the skin of a lizard, Gordon yawned, its beak-like mouth quivering. Three tiny nubs jutted from its head, small, but with time, Sarah knew they'd eventually become horns. Horns sharp enough to pierce metal.

Sarah stared at the triceratops. And then her legs gave out.

She crashed to her rump on the porch and brought a shaking hand to her chest, trying to calm her erratic pulse. The dinosaur regarded her with sleepy glistening eyes, shook its head, then jogged forward. The jog became a trot, and the trot became a charge, head lowered.

"Gord!" The old man yelled. "None of that now!"

The dinosaur slowed, looking to them both frantically before raising to its hind legs and crashing back down. A low, mewling noise came from its mouth as a slim tongue slinked forth and licked its beak.

"He's just excited," the old man explained. "Happens when he meets someone new. He's getting better, though. Usually he'd piss all over the place. At least he's stopped that. Gordon, sit."

The dinosaur sat.

"This is insane," Sarah repeated before pushing herself from the porch. She crossed the yard cautiously, eyeing the creature with disbelief. "You've actually *domesticated* him." Glancing back at the old man, she asked, "Is it okay to pet him?"

"Of course." He rose with a grunt and crossed to her side. "Give him a good rub on the ol' head. Loves that."

Sarah got to one knee. The triceratops stared her in the eye but stayed put, barely. It squirmed as if full of electricity. She reached out with one hand and gingerly stroked the creature's head, the scaly skin bumpy beneath her fingers. "He likes it? This is amazing."

"It's just my Gordon. Loves the greens, too. Want to feed him a lettuce head?"

"Sure," Sarah said. She got to her feet. "Aren't triceratops herbivores?"

"Huh?"

"I mean, don't they eat only vegetables?"

The old man scratched his chin and squinted. "Say, maybe that's why he's been having stomach problems lately. The damn dog food...Gees, I'm sorry, lad. From now on I'll stick to the greens. Thanks, love. I'll be back in a moment."

"Sure..."

The old man returned to the house and rummaged about in the fridge. Sarah listened to him whistle. She stayed put and kept eye contact with the creature, still feeling as if in a dream. The possibility of exposing this discovery to the world refused to leave her mind. She thought of the seconds she had alone, looked back to the creature—and then eased her phone from her jeans. She gave a quick glance back towards the house before opening her camera app and snapping a couple of photos. Her hands shook too much at first, but with a breath, she got a clear and focused image. The dinosaur sat still, watching the object in her hand with something close to amusement. Satisfied with the final picture, she slipped the phone back into her pocket and clasped her hands behind her back.

"Here," the old man said, returning with a head of lettuce. "I'll let you do it."

Sarah took the vegetable and kept her expression neutral, hoping the old man didn't notice the sweat now beading from her pores. She then fed the creature, watching in amazement as it finished the snack within a few short mouthfuls. Finished, it squawked.

"No more now," the old man warned with a pointed finger. "Gotta keep from overfeeding you. Else you get as fat as a couch one day."

Sarah turned to him. "You know he's going to get bigger and bigger, right? Larger than a couch."

"Larger than a couch, you say?"

"You haven't thought about that? What the future will hold?"

The old man shook his head. "I just live in the moment. Don't see no point in worrying about the future. It might hold all sorts, but that doesn't concern me. I'm happy tinkering about here with Gord and the cars."

Sarah didn't have a response.

"Besides," the old man continued. "Dicta-phones and cameras and TVs all in one, all that email stuff, the internet in general...just makes my head spin. Hell, I'm happy with my VHS player for movies. I think all the best ones have been made, anyway. Haven't seen a good picture made past the seventies." He looked at Sarah closely. "Speaking of which, I wanted to get this car finished up and sent back to Danny so I can catch the end of a film. Is there anything else you wanted?"

Sarah shook her head. "No, I guess not...Thanks for having me over. And for introducing me to Gordon."

The old man smiled. "Our pleasure. Honestly. If you want to stop by and see him again, get in touch."

"I will."

"Can I ask you something?"

Sarah was caught off guard by the question. "Sure?" she said.

"After all you've told me, now I'm getting worried you'll do a write up about my Gordon and folks will come by to see him...folks I don't want to see him. Never thought about it much, but after all you've said, I'm worried they'll take him away. Please keep Gordon to yourself."

Sarah looked to the creature and back to the old man. "I will. You've got nothing to worry about."

"Thank you. Come back sometime soon, yeah? We can take him for a walk."

"I'd like that."

Sarah made her way back to the front of the house, the sound of the old man chatting to his pet fading in the distance. She slipped her key from her pocket and pressed the fob, unlocking her car. Once she climbed in and closed her door, she sighed.

Looking out the windshield, she eyed the old man's house. An unkempt bungalow like so many others she'd passed on the drive from Dublin—the kind of place she'd not give a second glance on an average day. She'd never have guessed that, out back, lived a creature capable of changing mankind's understanding of the world.

Grinning, she fished her phone from her pocket and opened the photo she'd snapped. The picture came out perfect, a high-resolution of Gordon sitting on the dead grass, his eyes trained on the camera. Her stomach fluttered as the image of revealing her discovery to her editor swam to the surface of her mind. She imaged the disappointment in the old man's face. Imagined Gordon stressed as he was subjected to needles and prodding and flashing cameras.

Cameras.

She thought of the device in her hands, another marvel of the world folks took for granted on a daily basis. Then the old man's *dicta-phone* joke made her smile.

The photos were undeniable, to show them to an expert would lead to an investigation, no doubt. And within a day, those same experts would bore down on the old man's house. Changing everything. They'd take Gordon away.

Her finger hovered above the delete button.

"We've got enough we don't appreciate," she muttered. "No use digging up the past."

Sarah took one final, close look at the picture before jabbing *delete*. Her stomach gave a lurch, her mind reeling with the possibility of having made a mistake.

Then the phone prompted, *are you sure?*

Sarah laughed. "Yes," she answered. "I'm sure."

She deleted the photo, put the car in gear, and reversed from the driveway, leaving the ancient past where it belonged.

IN THE PINES

PETER GRIPPED THE porch railing and squinted at the robin flopping in the snow-covered meadow. The tiny bird kicked up flecks, squeaking and leaving miniature trenches. "Poor bastard..."

From within the cabin, Jamie called out, "What was it, Dad? Someone throw a rock?"

A series of bleeps from the kid's Gameboy followed, and Peter decided not to ruin his son's fun. Rarely did they get time together, let alone a trip away for Christmas, and Peter would rather tell a lie than have Kelly know their son saw his first dead animal on his watch. That sight would lead to a *conversation*.

Peter muttered a swear as a pillar of air puffed from his lips. He cleared his throat. "Just the porch settling. Nothing to worry about."

"Is it Granddad? Playing a joke?"

The question caused a wave of worry and Peter sighed. Truth be told, he had no idea where his father was. "Not Granddad. Not yet. He should be home soon, though."

With a grunt, Peter descended the porch and slogged to the now-still bird. He scooped the animal in his palm and studied it—beak slightly parted, twig-like legs frozen straight out like a dead thing in a cartoon. He imagined a *boing!* sound effect accompanying the sudden rigor mortis. A rust colored, oil-like substance stained the bird's underbelly.

"Dad?"

Peter jumped at the voice. In the cabin doorway, Jamie adjusted his mitts and hat. With a smile, he jumped the porch steps and bounced to his father. "What is it? That a rock?"

Peter palmed the bird and put his hands behind his back like a magician doing a trick. "Yeah. Just found it out here. Why don't you head back inside and wait for Granddad? You know, I'd say he's getting you a present from town." *Sure*, he thought, *and he's buying me a car to make up for the lost time, too.*

Peter didn't *hate* his father—hate was too strong a word—but the old man's alcoholism and lack of enthusiasm meant that Peter didn't expect much anymore. Add the birthday card for Jamie that needed forging each year, and well…

But then again, when they came to the cabin, Peter found the home cleaned and warmed. Two fresh beds were made upstairs. Not a bottle in sight. Still, none of that answered the question—Where *was* his father?

Something caught Jamie's eye and the boy turned. With the distraction, Peter tossed the dead bird and braced himself, expecting the kid to hear the thump. Instead, the boy pointed to the woods bordering the field where they had just hiked to reach the house only that morning. "What's that over there, Dad?"

Hands on his knees, Peter's brow furrowed as he scanned the tree line, noting movement between snow-heavy branches. "A deer?" he said aloud, though he couldn't quite tell. "Granddad gets them all the time out here."

The young boy gasped in amazement. "Can we get up close so I can get a photo for Mom?"

The deer shimmied through the trees and into the meadow, sending a wave of snow hissing to the ground. It shook its head from side to side as if agitated by horseflies. The animal snorted and its fur-covered muscles seemed to twitch at the shoulders. Peter reached for his son's hand instinctively, gripping the boy's cold mitts.

"Is it sick?" Jamie asked. "Looks like it's acting kinda funny." The boy's voice fluttered as if he'd made a joke, but Peter knew the quaver came from fright. Hell, he felt it, too. A slow lick of alarm slipped across his belly. What if it was rabies or something?

"He *is* acting funny." Peter strained to sound assertive, but the tightness in his throat protested. "Cold weather, Jamie. They'll act funny if they're cold, hungry and cranky. Same as us."

A lame explanation, but it seemed to do the trick as Jamie chuckled. "It's Rudolph, isn't it, Daddy? You can't fool me. I'm smart."

"Rudolph?"

The boys head fell to the side as if his father was the stupidest man to ever live. "The red nose, Dad. See, he has a red nose."

Peter's stomach somersaulted as the deer's head quivered again, its snout catching the light and reflecting a wet, crimson stain on its face.

Jamie's voice swam into focus, as if coming from very far away. "...spruce branches so I can finish my decoration?"

"Huh?"

"Dad! I asked if we can collect. Spruce. Branches. So. I. Can. Finish. My. *Decoration*. You know, for Granddad."

Peter gave his son's hand a quick double-squeeze. "Sure, sure. Look, we'll go this way, though, okay? We don't want to bother old Rudolph there."

As they set off, Peter just about managed to tear his gaze from the animal. A carousel of possibilities played around his mind on the condition of both the robin and the deer—*An oil leak. Both creatures drank, desperately craving water. No, no, that didn't make sense. Woodland critters were smarter than that, and besides, oil was not crimson...Some berries in the forest had spoiled. Possible, but would a deer scoff down enough to stain its entire snout? Just some berries? Unlikely.*

The snow crunched beneath their heels as Jamie pulled Peter along, the boy giggling and trying to race ahead like an over-excited dog on a leash. As they reached the tree line, Jamie's laughter tapered out.

"It's dark in there," he said, his voice sobered. "Kinda scary."

Peter nodded, shaking away the puzzle in his brain. "It's safe. Just a forest, Jamie. Your dad's here, remember?"

The boy smiled with such sincerity that Peter's chest hurt in the best possible way. He squeezed his son's shoulder. "Come on. Let's get some tree boughs for Granddad."

Crunching through the small piles of snow, they overstepped a fallen log and walked into the thicket, the ashen sky blotted out by a canopy overhead. Shots of light peppered through, twinkling in the shadowed snow like untouched sugar. Nearby, a squirrel shot up a thick oak, chittering as it scurried out of sight.

Jamie chortled, seemingly relaxed. "The best stuff's gotta be here. We're in the trees' home."

As they trekked the foliage, two things occurred to Peter. First, besides the sound of that single squirrel, silence pressurized the woods. Second, markings lead to and from an open clearing ahead. Jamie seemed to notice the disturbed snow, too. "What's that, Dad?"

"Animal tracks," he said, noting the hoof prints and other, smaller markings. "Could be from our friend, the deer."

"Rudolph's not *my* friend," Jamie said. "I think he's sick...I wouldn't wanna hang out with him."

"Yeah, we don't want to hang out with him..." A sight in the middle of the clearing sent a sudden shock through him. Peter wanted to faint. "Hold on..."

"Dad? What?"

Peter got to one knee for a better angle, tilting his head to the side. Something lay ahead in the disturbed snow, something which all the animal trails led to and from.

"Jamie, stay by this tree. Don't move."

"No! Dad! Don't leave me!"

"I'm not leaving you. Hang on here for just a second." He leaped to his feet and slogged into the clearing like a man in a dream, visions of his father snoring and still stinking of booze as snow eased over him like a nighttime blanket for the big sleep.

His heart drummed in his ears and a single wish blared in his mind—*Don't be my dad, please, don't be my dad. Don't be my dad...*

The snow covered most the mess, but some flesh still remained visible. Black flesh. Spotting the teeth, a dizzy spell washed over Peter and he brought a hand to his forehead. Those teeth did not belong to anything human...long, yellowed appendages jutting from exposed gums over nonexistent lips, reaching to the chin and two slit-like nostrils. This was not a man, but a monster. The sight made Peter want to scream but he stifled the urge in order not to scare his son.

"Dad," he heard his son call. "Can we go back to the cabin now?"

Peter nodded, his eyes drifting further down the dead creature's emaciated body. Spotting shredded wings (how had he missed the wings?), the creature reminded him of a humanoid bat—like something from one of his childhood comics his father would've shredded if he'd found. Then an odor ghosted on the wind, sickly sweet and not at all unlike strawberries. Peter wrinkled his nose.

The source of the smell was clear. A jagged hole as big as a fist gaped open in the monster's abdomen, leaking a sap-like substance which pooled and turned the nearby snow to crimson slush.

He experienced a mixture of feelings—shock, dread, and relief. This *thing* couldn't be his father.

"Crimson," he muttered, getting to his feet. He didn't want to be near the lifeblood of that beast, not after seeing evidence of what it had done to the animals. "Let's get back to the house before we lose light."

Suddenly something rustled overhead, shaking loose a snowfall from the trees. Peter squinted and blocked his eyes from the glare of the sun.

A black dot sped towards his face and he gasped and moved aside just as it thumped to the snow. A jay. The tiny bird spasmed about, flipping itself from side to side with feeble chirps.

Walking backwards, Peter almost tripped over a hunched log. He reached his son and grabbed hold of the boy's hand. Then he decided better and lifted the kid into his arms.

"Going to get us back to Granddad's quicker, okay?"

The boy's voice bounced with each step. "Y-yeah. Ho-oh-kay."

Peter maneuvered the trees with ease, overstepping rocks and reaching branches. Ahead, the field came into view, a flat bed of pristine snow with only two tracks from the cabin. But something else still lurked in the field, and closer now, too.

"Shit."

Jamie pulled his face away from his father's coat. "What?"

"Just...Rudolph. Try to be quiet, okay?"

Peter eased into the field, a thirty-foot gap between him and the deer. The creature's head jerked frantically about, as if flies were crawling about its neck, but he knew the crimson goop on that shiny nose was the real root of the problem. In an instant that sent an ice chill through Peter's core, the deer locked eyes and lowered its head, giving him a clear view of two very solid antlers.

"Dad!" Jamie screamed. "Look out!"

The deer charged. Peter shot off, the snow pulling at his feet and bogging down his progress. He lugged his son, gripping him tightly in his arms. The cabin appeared to bob ahead, seeming to get no closer but he knew that was only his fevered brain in a panic. Behind, the heavy clomps of the deer's hoofs grew closer.

He lurched to the left, narrowly avoiding an antler in the spine. He gasped as the beast skidded to a halt and turned, regaining its bearings. It once again lowered its head and kicked snow with its front hoof, angling itself just right. Peter charged for the house. Behind, the deer took off.

Jamie was screaming in terror. Peter's breath came in quick stabs as he pumped his legs harder, still gripping his son. The snow felt like custard, each step an absolute mockery in torture. But then the porch steps were beneath his feet and Peter leaped them in one, catching his first break of the day—Jamie had left the front door open before they left.

Peter raced inside and lurched backwards, slamming the door shut with his shoulders. He landed on his ass and let go of Jamie, half throwing the boy off him to free up his hands. He slammed the deadbolt home and fell back onto his rump, pressing his back into the door for extra security. His breath came in wheezes as he tried to calm his racing heart.

Across the room, Jamie cupped his mouth and stared wide eyed. Peter braced.

The hit came like a battalion. The door shook on its hinges, and Peter's skull bucked back and cracked off the wood. He shook his head to clear his vision and readjusted himself for another hit. But another didn't come. Instead, after a handful of tense seconds, a dull thump rang out.

"I think it left," Peter said through gasping breaths, knowing Jamie didn't have an answer but still feeling the need to speak. "I think that's it, Jamie. I think it's done."

"You promise?" the boy asked, skipping about from foot to foot. Peter noticed the boy had wet himself.

"I promise, Jamie. I promise. Look, go upstairs and clean...and clean up, okay? Everything's all right now. Get into some fresh jeans and come back down. We'll go back to my house as soon as you're ready. We'll be safe. I promise."

The boy gave a curt nod, his face drained of color, and then he rushed up the staircase. In the silence, Peter took a moment to catch his breath, worried about how fast his heart rammed his ribcage.

Rammed, he thought. *Fitting.*

Then something caught his eye beneath the kitchen table. A square of paper. Peter grunted as he pushed himself forward and scooped up the note. He was hit by a memory of Jamie rushing inside and slamming his suitcase onto the table. The kid must've knocked the paper to the floor and not noticed. Peter recognized his old man's handwriting.

Buying Santa Claus suit. Back evening. Love you.

A tight ball caught in Peter's throat and he struggled to loosen it. In all his thirty-nine years, his father had never said the words *love you*. He'd also never cleaned since losing his wife, or spent a day without the bottle. Yet here it was, as good as a perfectly wrapped gift beneath the tree.

"Jesus Christ," Peter whispered, turning his head to the ceiling to stifle some of the hot tears. "You actually made a damn effort. I can't believe it."

Memories of the sweet-scented goop oozing from the creature zapped back to mind and Peter scowled. The creatures had clearly been attracted to the smell, touched it, perhaps. Tried to taste it. He imagined a parasite living in the liquid, disguising its scent to appeal to other hosts in order to spread and reach further. He imagined the humanoid nightmare fell from the sky because it got infected, too, not because it was necessarily a threat itself.

His musings were interrupted. "Dad!" Jamie yelped from upstairs. Peter jumped to his feet. "Dad, everything's going to be fine!"

"Jamie? Jamie, what are you talking about?"

Peter's head shot from left to right, left to right, scanning the room. Suddenly he saw his father's Winchester. He spotted the rifle by the fireside armchair and pulled it into his arms, checking the barrel. Loaded. Jesus, the old man might be able to clean a house, but he left a loaded rifle in reach of an eight-year-old.

"What's going on, Jamie? Talk to me."

"Santa's runnin' 'cross the field! He's coming to get us!"

Peter's stomach somersaulted for the second time that day. "Running? Jamie, you're sure he's running?"

"Fast as he can, Dad! Don't worry!"

"Jamie, you're to stay upstairs, you hear? Stay. Up. Stairs!"

With a silent prayer, Peter unbolted the front door and stepped onto the porch, booting aside the spent carcass of the deer. Ahead, Santa Claus barged through the snow, the faint sound of crazed yelps carrying on the wind. Peter made out the white trimmings of the suit, the red fabric, and most importantly the crimson smears, splotched all over the old man's face as if he'd gone insane and smashed it into his features.

"Dad!" Peter called, but his father only answered with another lunatic cry. "Dad, I want you to stop. Stop right now."

His father kept coming, eyes wild and face strained with tension. Peter raised the rifle.

The shot cracked out across the field, sending a murder of crows flapping to more quiet locations. A splatter of gore exploded from the back of the madman's head, spraying the snow behind him. He swayed a moment, the trademark holiday hat knocked crooked on the now ruined face, then toppled.

Peter lowered the gun and panted, hearing Jamie clamor down the stairs with his suitcase in hand. "Daddy! Daddy, what are you doing? What happened to Santa?"

"Santa had to go with Rudolph," Peter replied. He clutched his son when Jamie slammed into his leg and embraced him in a tight squeeze. "We need to go now. Stay close to me, okay? We've got the woods to tackle before we get to the car parked on the other side."

"What's that sound, Dad?"

Peter heard it, too, a garble of white noise from the direction his father had come. His brow furrowed as he scooped Jamie in one arm and started out across the field, back towards the woods where they'd make a break down the hillside to the car. Then his stomach lurched.

"It's the town..." Peter said, his legs moving faster now. "The entire town is coming! They followed your Granddad. Keep a hold of me, Jamie."

As Peter fought through the snow, the woodland offering both a place of hiding and a place of lurking animals, Jamie asked, "What do they want, Daddy?"

Peter left the question unanswered and just kept moving, the snow gripping at his boot heels.

The call for blood from the townsfolk grew louder and louder.

KNOCK, KNOCK

A **BUSINESSMAN OUTSIDE** the house at two in the morning made sense in the city, but William lived in the country, and that made the passerby ever so curious. William parted the curtains slowly, just enough to avoid attention, and breathed through his nose to lessen the condensation on the window. As the man passed the streetlamp, a purple tinge highlighted his suit, and his gait was that of an elderly man with the skin to match. Like a raisin wearing a dollar store three-piece once owned by a pimp.

The gentleman paused at the mailbox, and William held his breath, letting the blinds fall to a slit. And yet, the businessman (if he could be called such—William imagined that cheap-looking briefcase contained blank A4s and half-eaten apple cores opposed to actual documents and contracts) paused and stared at the house.

William cocked his head, frozen. If the man approached his home, should he rush out and meet him halfway, just in case? But *just in case* what? The odd timing and strange location surely weren't enough to justify thoughts of danger, were they? Besides, the man looked old enough to fall asleep standing up, never mind getting a punch to the face. Oh, *and that face*, like a peanut dropped and covered in fluff from the underbelly of a couch. Still, the gentleman stared at William's home, and as he did, his shriveled lips curled into a grin.

Gooseflesh crawled along William's arms.

Right. I gotta go out there and ask him what the hell's going on. He's not breaking any law, but this sure as shit violates the social contract, at least. Where the hell did he come from?

Beyond Venus or Mars, William had no answers. Then the letterbox clattered and William balked and released the blinds. He backed away while slapping a hand to his now-speeding heart.

"The fuck, man? The hell is this?"

He raced back to the window and scanned the drive for signs of the stranger, but beyond a bat zipping about below the streetlights, the neighborhood sat in total silence. William's brow creased as he pushed from the sill and crept to the hallway, peering around the corner to the front door as if expecting a mountain lion. A lilac envelope jutted from the mail slot like a cheeky tongue.

"Seriously?"

William plucked the letter and worked his nail along the seal, greeted by the subtle scent of perfume. He made his way back to the living room and fell onto the couch, throwing away the envelope as he shook out the paper.

Dearest William. I'd like to talk to you about our Lord and Savior—Philip. Seven AM, today. I'll see you shortly, and I should hope for decaf.

William re-read the note five times, each read only serving to increase the bizarreness ten-fold. First of all, how did this decrepit old bastard place the letter in the mail-slot without him noticing? Secondly, where had he gone and how did he know William's name? Thirdly (and unfortunately not strangest of all), who in the dear-name-of-fuck was *Philip*? William ran a hand across his face and blew a breath, unsurprised by the sweat glistening on his palm. And who asks for decaf?

Lisa's doing, he thought. This had to be her work. She snored from upstairs as loud as a foghorn, sleeping enough for both of them. But of course, she could afford to—she wasn't the one banished to the couch for the last two weeks. The break had been her idea, after all, not his, as if a part of some sinister scheme to make him leave. It didn't seem all that out of place. Not these days, at least. She called him *puppykins* and *doodlebug* once upon a time, now she only called him if she needed something from the store.

"Crazy asshole," Will muttered. "The hell's she playing at?"

As anger bubbled inside of him, William stood and pulled his bathrobe tight across his bulging belly. Did Lisa have a piece on the side, was that it? Someone with the know-how and connections to put something in place to make him lose his shit and come out looking bad? *Oh, what would the neighbors say?*

"Gotta be her. Just fucking gotta be."

He snarled as he paced the room. Their relationship had dwindled over the past three months, and his constant drinking hadn't helped matters, but her jabs at his expanding gut and flirtatious giggles with *Robby* from work didn't help the situation. Still, he'd paid for the house, and for that he deserved to stay. Let her deal with newspaper adverts and crooked salesmen.

Then an idea struck. Seven AM only left four hours to show time. If insomnia hadn't already claimed his brain in the name of stress, then he might as well pop on the coffee (decaf, sure thing, Peanut Man) and wait. He'd play their game, oh yes. And he'd do them one better—he'd be one step ahead.

With the coffee ready and a cup in hand, William returned to the couch and switched on the television, basking in the soundless glow as the clock counted away the night and infomercials pushed Bluetooth vacuum cleaners. And when the doorbell rang hours later, he smiled.

"Door!" Lisa yelled from upstairs. The sleep-slur of her voice grated his nerves. Just like every other trivial action he'd begun noticing—her labored breathing while she scanned her phone, her slopping lips as she shoveled down cereal, her beer farts that could kill a rodent. *Goddamn.*

He gave the staircase the finger as he plodded across the hall and undid the lock. Then he smiled broadly.

"It's for Philip, right?"

The businessman grinned. "Correct."

Up close and personal, the tiny man was stranger still. His off-colored skin bordered on baby blue as if he were being strangled by an invisible aggressor. His suit was indeed purple, not black, but only in the correct lighting. His red tie squeezed at his neck, wrinkling the skin that slopped over like half-baked dough. He matched Will blink for blink, like an alien entity learning to be human. William imagined he could rip away that face like mozzarella cheese, revealing a gloppy and grinning skull that would chatter its teeth and take a chunk from his—

"May I come inside? Decaf?"

"What? Oh, right. Sure, come on in."

That seals it, William thought, *only a damn alien would ask for decaf coffee.*

He stepped aside as the stranger pottered across the threshold while clutching his briefcase to his chest in both hands. William eased the door shut behind them and followed the man into the living room, the day feeling more like a dream now that the meeting had begun. He also found it odd following a newcomer to his own damn living room, as if the businessman lived here and not him.

After plucking the brewed coffee and pouring a steaming mug, he asked his first question.

"My name," he said, and placed the pot back. "Let's start there. How'd you know it?"

The stranger accepted the coffee with a grin and gave a nod before blowing his brew and taking a sip. "Ah. Delicious."

The fuck is going on?

"Phone directory," the man said and smacked his lips. "How else?"

William arched a brow as he settled into his recliner. "And last night, I saw you at the driveway."

"Not me, sir. An associate."

William pinched the bridge of his nose. His brain refused to believe his ears. Perhaps this was all a bizarre dream and he'd soon wake on the couch, still being pandered to by grinning panhandlers with warehouses full of knock-off toasters. A *shave-and-a-haircut* thumped from a neighbor's door, then another, followed by a barking dog. This was real.

Big question, William thought, and asked, "Just who the hell is Philip?"

The man's eyes widened with delight, and he placed aside his mug before rubbing his hands.

Like decade-old sandpaper, stop it!

"You get many callers around these parts?" the stranger said.

"You mean religious folk? Mormons, that sort?"

"Correct."

"No."

"And are you a believer?"

"I'm an individualist," William said with a sigh. He had no urge to discuss beliefs at this hour of the morning. "Whatever it is you're selling, I'm not buying. Any group that would have me as a member is a group I want no part of. Especially once they start wearing silly hats."

"Ah, hats always become a part of a movement, correct. Would you like to see ours?"

"Not necessarily."

"They're quite amazing, our hats. Made in *China!*" The man pronounced the word as if only recently learning of such a place. "Look."

He unbuckled his briefcase and plucked a yellow beanie, the name PHILIP embroidered in purple along the front. He pulled it down over his peanut head and smiled. "Eh?"

"Lovely," William said. "Don't look like a *Barney the Dinosaur* uber-fan or nothin'."

Another knock came from out on the street and William stood, peeking from the blinds.

"Something wrong?" the man asked.

"The hell's going on out there?" William turned from the window. The prospect of Lisa coordinating this effort seemed less likely by the minute. Still, he had to ask. "Look, did *she* put you up to this? Is this some plan to get me outta my own goddamn house? Because if it is, whatever she's payin', I can double. Fess up and we can get down to some real business. Because this is getting freaky, man, and I gotta get some sleep soon."

The stranger cocked his head like a dog viewing a card trick. "Why, I don't know what you mean?"

"Jesus Christ."

Another dog barked from outside, followed by a yell that rose the hair on William's arms. "Right, what the hell was that? What's going on here, do I need to call the police?"

Lisa yelled from upstairs. "What's all that noise? What in the name of *Christ* is going on?"

"I don't know!" William shook his head. "Look, what is this?"

"Philip's will," the man said with a smile. "We even have a song of our people, would you like to hear?"

As the man pulled a pan flute from his case, Lisa stumbled down the stairs and into the living room, her hair a bird's nest and her eyes full of fury. "Look. I've got work in three hours and I'm *trying* to catch some sleep. Who the hell are you, and what in the *world* is all that noise outside?"

William slapped his arms down. "Fucked if I know, I was going to ask you the very same question."

Lisa looked as if she'd just chewed a worm. "Excuse me?"

"I said I'm fucked if—"

"*Who* the hell are *you?*"

"I honestly have no idea," the Peanut Man replied. "He just showed up this morning wanting to sell me on some hu-du, hokey magic-man stuff and I've been trying to get him gone. I made decaf."

"Excuse me?" William looked between them as his mind reeled. "*Excuse me?*"

The little man stood and placed an arm around Lisa's waist, gave a squeeze. She reciprocated.

Despite the break, rage washed over William. "All right, buddy, that's fucking it. Get your hands offa her."

"Dennis," Lisa cried, "Who is this man?"

Dennis?

"I don't know, baby," said the stranger, "But I think it's high time we kicked him outta here. He sounds crazy. Sounds *dangerous*. Completely *loco*."

William laughed, unable to control himself. "All right, all right. What is this, a prank?"

"What's he talking about?" Lisa asked.

The Peanut Man shook his head. "Look, mister, you're scaring my girlfriend. Now I don't wanna have to call the cops but I will if you don't leave my property right away, understand?"

"Oh, fuck this noise."

William turned and snatched a photograph from the mantle. "Look. Right here. Look."

"Well, it wasn't my best day," said the stranger, "But I think I look just fine?"

William spun the photo and glared into the face of the elderly raisin man holding Lisa at a friend's wedding. His heart jackhammered. "No, no, no. This was Richard's wedding, I...I remember that day damn clear. He's *my* friend." William looked up. "How'd you do it, huh? How in the world are you making this happen?"

"Baby, get the gun," Lisa said, shaking now. "I'll call the cops and you get the gun."

William placed the picture back and raised his palms. "Look, I don't know what the hell is...just...look, I'll leave okay? Okay. I'm going. You two just don't come near me. I'm walking out that door now."

The Peanut Man tightened his grip around Lisa as she clutched his purple suit, the two back-peddling to the bottom of the stairs with Peanut Man's face clearly faking panic—just about suppressing a belly-laugh.

"I'll be back," William said. He pointed a finger. "Soon as I figure out just what the hell is going on here, I'll be back."

"Don't you come back any place near my house, mister," said Peanut Man, shaking his head. "I saw you at the driveway in the middle of the night, just *watching* the damn house. I'm on to you. Take your voodoo magic and shove it up your bum, do you hear?"

"*The fuck?* Look, I'm outta here."

William opened the door and stepped onto the front porch, squinting as the harsh morning light burned his eyes. His bare foot touched the concrete and he noticed he wore no shoes.

"Can I at least get my—"

"Out!" Lisa screamed.

"Right, all right. Fuck."

The door slammed and William winced, starting down the drive. The everyday normality of a passing car and birds overhead made the situation that much harder to comprehend, but when the body came into view, reality hit home.

"Harry?"

His neighbor lay sprawled on the lawn across the street, the sprinklers awake and spitting on his red pajamas. William jogged to his neighbor's unmoving form, noting now the commotion from behind other closed doors. Voices rose and things banged, and then came a gunshot. William shook his head and placed a shaking hand on his neighbor's back. Harry lived alone, a guitar-playing accountant who enjoyed weekend cards and a beer up at Duke's. Now he lay face-first in his prized petunias, soaked through and sickly pale. William flipped the body over.

"Jesus fucking Christ."

He brought a hand to his mouth as three stab wounds leaked across Harry's stomach—three stab wounds in the formation of a smiling face. Through the open door of Harry's home, William noted crimson streaking the walls. His dog yapped incessantly from the backyard.

Yelling for help, William's heart raced as doors opened all along the neighborhood. At first, he thought his cries were answered, that neighbors were coming to call an ambulance and get this situation under control, but then he stood in shock as another detail registered—only men were walking their drives, their faces iced-over with the same shock his had been. And in each of the doorways stood identical peanut-faced businessmen, their arms around scared partners.

"And don't come back!" one yelled. Fred, a thirty-year-old bartender, flipped the stranger the finger as he stumbled down his drive. It's all he could do, after all—the man had a shotgun trained on his back and Wanda in his arms.

"I'll be back," Fred yelled. "Just you wait, you shriveled fuck, just you wait!"

William ran to Fred. "The hell is going on?"

"Just keep walking," said Trevor Lewis as he reached the two. He kept his face trained on the road ahead, not stopping but motioning for them to follow and soon they fell in line. All three walked at an even clip, joining the other men in a single file. As both sides of the neighborhood filled with confused men, Trevor spoke but didn't turn.

"They're everywhere."

"What?" William scrunched his face in disbelief. "This is fucking idiotic, why hasn't someone called the police?"

"I have," Trevor replied. "They asked me if I had a minute to talk to their Lord and Savior. Plus, you should notice Jerry and Owen aren't here. I tried calling them both while that decrepit old bastard went to Laurie and got his arm around her."

"This is crazy. This is absolutely insane."

The grinning faces of the shriveled business-folk watched the men march from town, some nodding in delight, while others kissed their new partners on the head for reassurance. Another car passed, honked, and William's eyes widened as the purple-suited fuck flipped him the finger. In the backseat sat two frightened children.

"The news was on this morning," Trevor added. "I was flipping channels while waiting for this maniac to arrive. Guess who the anchors were."

"Bullshit."

"I was just awake," Fred said. "Had just opened that pink, stinking letter when that guy knocked the door, hadn't even read the note. He just came on in and put on a silly hat and started askin' for decaf."

Decaf, fucking decaf!

"Then Wanda came down and screamed. Thought she was confused about that nutcase but then she runs to him and asks who's the hippy in her living room! *The hippy!* Fucker goes and puts his arm around her and I went to punch him but he whips out this fuckin' knife and asks if I want to leave in a body bag or on foot."

"Mine just came to the door with a rifle," Bill Mayhew said. "Yelled howdy-doody and just waddled on inside to the coffee machine. Was gonna run but Rachel's upstairs so I couldn't leave. Asked me where do we keep the damn coffee."

William's mouth dried. "And...where are we going now, Trevor?"

"We're going on a long journey. That's what I was told." He sighed. "I think we're going to see Philip, guys."

BANGERS AND MASH

Author's note: This story originally appeared in *Clickers Forever: A Tribute to J.F. Gonzalez*. J.F. Gonzalez' *Clickers* was the first modern horror novel I picked up in my post-King days. In a lot of ways, that series of books shaped the very writer I am today. When Brian Keene first announced the tribute's open call, I originally penned an essay titled *Finding Jesus*. I ultimately felt it too personal and decided to shelf the piece. Instead, I thought what better way to honor the man than to bring his monstrosities to the shores of Ireland and let them run amok. Clickers was a *fun* read, after all, so I tried channeling that B movie feel I loved oh so much. My friend Cooper (from Northern Ireland) helped with the language on this one, and although both he and J.F. Gonzalez are no longer with us, I'd like to think they'd enjoy the finished tale. I hope you do, too.

"**D**ID I EVER tell you the one about the lad who got his lad stuck in a coke bottle?"

The old man sighed and lifted his face to the rain. Watching from behind, Quincy dropped the plastic container and flexed his arms, expecting the two to have come to blows much sooner.

"I swear to God," the old man said. "If you don't shut up..."

"If I don't shut up, what?" The young man plodded through the mud and stood before his senior, puffing his chest. "Or what, ye wee bollocks? Who says you're the leader here? Myself and Quincy were recruited just the same as you. Think because we're both half your age, that puts you in charge?"

The old man locked eyes with the kid, nostrils flaring. Quincy scooped the container and sighed, wishing one of the others would offer to carry it instead of bickering like cats in an alleyway. The contents sloshed inside. "Guys, can we just—"

"I think you've got something to prove," the old man said. "Even your name, come on, what did you say it was?"

"The Beast. Can just call me Beast, though."

"Beast," the old man repeated, slapping his arms down. "You honestly expect me to call you feckin' *Beast*? And Quincy, he's happy to follow, hasn't said a word since we met this morning. That right, Quince?"

Quincy gave a curt nod before turning his attention to the raging sea, wanting the confrontation finished. Dark waves smashed the hillside, occasionally coming high enough to peak and spill onto the walking trail, reducing the path to muck. Three miles south along the cliffside and shroud in fog, the Porter beach house sat in isolation, pea-sized lights twinkling from the kitchen and dining room windows. Quincy had come a long way to collect crabs for Henry Porter. The entrepreneur paid double what he'd earn at any gardening center in the country, despite the live-in position being so secluded. The specialists would arrive at the house any minute now, their Bentleys and Mustangs chewing up the drive, and if Quincy came back empty handed, their trip to the Emerald Isle would be for nothing. They needed the crabs.

"See?" the old man said. "You with a temper, Quincy with no care, I'm the only one who can get this job done right. Like Henry Porter wants. Now move, before I put a size ten in your arse."

The old man sidestepped but Beast grabbed his arm. "And why did he hire me, then, eh? I know County Antrim better than any man, that not count for somethin'?"

Quincy sighed. "Guys, for God's sake, can we just get going? Team's arriving soon. Porter needs me back there."

The old man ignored Quincy and gave Beast a tight smile. "Said it yourself. Ye know this place better than any man. Don't need to prove yourself to me, lad."

Whipping his arm free, the old man readjusted his shirtsleeve before trudging further up the beaten path, heading for the hilltop. Quincy followed, leaving Beast standing in the wind and rain.

"What's your name supposed to be, anyway?" Beast yelled from behind. A hissing wave and a cawing fulmar responded. "*The Fisherman.* You know we're collecting bastardin' crabs, right? No fishin' involved. Quincy's the right hand man of this fucker, I'm just the tour guide, why the hell does he have you here? And what's all the shit hooked to your hat?"

The old man chuckled. "Bits and pieces. Mementos."

Quincy studied the items; a piece of red cloth the size of a thumbnail next to a sliver of aged leather. A shred of lace waving in the wind. Other blackened lumps of God knows what. Quincy wondered the same question as Beast—Why *was* the Fisherman here? Henry Porter hadn't mentioned him.

"The sooner we're done here, the sooner we get home," the Fisherman said. "And then you won't ever have to worry about my name or business again. Now come on, move it, Sunshine."

Beast's mouth dropped in a comical 'O' and Quincy fought hard to hide a grin. He didn't much care for the Fisherman, but Beast downright boiled his blood.

The Fisherman yelled over his shoulder to be heard above the crashing waves. "You're an expert on this county, you said?"

"Aye," Beast replied, his answer lost in labored breathing. If he dropped at fifty, Quincy wouldn't be surprised. "Lived here my whole life. Both you are Dublin lads, aye? Can tell by your cunty attitudes."

"Born and bred," the Fisherman answered, unfazed by the comment.

Quincy nodded. "Moved here to work in Henry's garden, that's all. From Dublin, too."

"Garden? It's a fuckin' beach house."

Quincy gritted his teeth. "The *front* garden, on the opposite side, you plank."

As they neared the top of the hill, the Fisherman paused and caught his breath. "And just over here we have the Giant's Causeway. Can you tell me how it formed?"

Beast's lips curled into a grin, his face shining with rainwater. "I can, aye. What's this? A test?"

"Just asking the expert."

The young man cleared his throat before working his boots into the mud and clasping his hands behind his back. "The forty-thousand interlocking basalt columns were formed fifty to sixty million years ago by a volcanic eruption. It's the forth greatest natural wonder in the UK, and it became a world heritage site in 1968." He winked. "How'd I do, teacher? Do I get a sweetie?"

"Ah, you got most of it right."

Beast's smile vanished, replaced by a look of seething hatred. "You playin' with me, lad? I'll have you know, I'm the feckin' tour guide here, *Fisherman*. I'm getting sick of your shite. What age are you, anyway? Sixty, sixty-five? With the weather the way it is, you better hope you don't slip on the Causeway and get slammed into the waves...it happens, y'know. Wouldn't want to tell Henry Porter that he lost a man today, would we? 'Specially not when he has such important guests coming by."

"Let's hope it doesn't come to that, then."

Quincy grimaced as the rain picked up, slamming his face with tiny pellets and drenching him in seconds. From out over the sea, thunder clapped.

"Come on," he said. "Let's just get this over with."

They crested the hill in silence, boot heels sloshing in the slop. At the peak, a row of barricades with a *Do Not Cross* sign blocked the path to the rocks below. Quincy had never been to the Giant's Causeway before, had no interest in geology, but on a few occasions he had squinted across from Porter's private beach at the amazing formations. Being this close took his breath away.

The rocks grew at some points to the height of a house, others only the size of a bathroom sink. The field-sized area below them looked low enough to walk on, creeping into the sea on the far side like a staircase. Frothing water slithered through the interlocking pillars before slipping back into the Pacific. Another wave came and coated the rocks, repeating the process all over again.

The Fisherman ran his hand along a barrier. "Council put these up, Beast?"

"Can't have tourists slippin' on the rocks and crackin' their skulls, now can we?" He hocked a wad of spit. "Who else would have, ye gobshite?"

The Fisherman booted a stray stone and muttered. "Same folks who covered up Hurricane Floyd."

The Beast, cocking his head, looked as if he'd just smelt a bad fart. "You are a feckin' weird one, you know that? What'd you put in the container back in the carpark? Fuckin' rotten meat? Smell's wreckin' me nose."

The couple's bickering slipped away into meaningless babble as Quincy stared down at the Causeway. "You'd think it was manmade," he said. "Like thousands of teeth, molars, made of rock."

"Well, now ye've gone and lost *both* your heads!" Hoping the barrier one leg at a time, Beast started down the hill, his arms cartwheeling as his legs fought to keep upright. "Over ye go, lads! Come on!"

As Beast disappeared down the hillside, Quincy looked to the Fisherman. "What *did* you put in this thing earlier?" He gave the container a shake, the contents squelching.

"Just what Beast said. Rotten meat."

Quincy ignored the comment, hoping it to be a joke. "And why'd you say he got the history of this place *mostly* right?"

The Fisherman sighed, eyes trained on the raging sea. "You're an inquisitive one, Quince. Gardening your only aspiration in life?"

The question sent a pang of embarrassment through Quincy. "I wanted to be a journalist. Still do. Porter pays well. I'll leave when I build up enough money. Move back to Dublin and get into a college."

"Well," the Fisherman said. "You can start asking questions now and get a head start. Why do you think our container is made of plastic?"

"Just what Henry asked for," Quincy said with a shrug. "The crabs are dangerous. Can't touch them with your bare hands. Porter said to use the gloves he provided and be quick. And don't get one larger than your fist...as if they'd grow much bigger."

"And just how long have you known Porter?"

Quincy readjusted his grip on the container, wanting to move, his arms staining. "I'm his gardener five weeks now."

The Fisherman smiled. "But this isn't gardening. He trusts you. What we're doing is top secret."

Quincy wouldn't describe collecting an endangered crab as *top secret* (he reserved that phrase for spies and double-agents), but he did know what they were doing could not get out to the public. Henry explained that the work of his 'special team' meant the survival of this rare species, but animal rights activists would throw hissy-fits if they heard an infant specimen had been pulled from its mother.

"So how'd he come to trust you?" the Fisherman asked.

"Porter?" Quincy cleared his throat. "First week on the job, cleaner stole a fifty from the mantle. Saw her do it. Henry asked if I did, and I denied it. She got fired, anyway. Turns out he'd rigged the whole thing, hired her *because* she had light fingers. Knew I knew, wanted to see if I'd rat her out."

"And you didn't."

"And I didn't."

"That's why he hired you."

Quincy sighed. "And why'd he hire you, Fisherman? Never mentioned *you* being here. Have a problem with the scientists? You an animal rights activist going to sabotage the retrieval or something?"

"*Retrieval*," Fisherman repeated with a laugh. "'Scientists'...Jesus. What other bullshit did he fill your head with?"

Quincy's chest tightened. "What are you talking about?"

"Let me guess, these 'scientists' are providing their own chef this evening?"

"Yes?" Quincy couldn't believe Henry hired such a rude an individual as the Fisherman, couldn't find the words. "He's a top cook from Kentucky, if you must know," he said. "Specialist. Arriving with the scientists."

"They got specific gluten dietary needs, do you think, Quince? Or do these 'scientists' just like their crabs cooked so-so?"

Quincy scoffed. "Bullshit. You think they'd come all this way to eat a crab? Beast was right, y'know that? You *are* odd."

The Fisherman smiled. "And yet there's something else you want to ask me. I can see it in your confused little face. Come on, be a journalist."

Quincy dropped the container and faced the old man, his anger boiling. "Just what the hell is Hurricane Floyd?"

From the bottom of the hill, Beast whooped, his voice merging with the raging waves. "Move it, ye wankers! Crabs will be dead by the time find 'em!"

The Fisherman chuckled and eased himself over the barricade. "Just something that never happened."

Quincy grabbed the container and followed suit, jogging to Fisherman's side. "How'd you come to know about it then? If it never happened? Floyd?"

"Fella by the name of Livingston. Colonel Augustus Livingston."

Quincy sighed, his patience running short. "And who's *that*?"

"He's one of the ones responsible for making sure the truth never got out."

Dodging a stone, Quincy fought to keep an even pace with the senior. For a man of sixty-odd years, the Fisherman moved fast. "What's the truth? You think Porter's somehow mixed up in all this?"

"Let me ask ye, Quince, how'd Porter make his money?"

"I don't ask, don't care to know that."

"Well ye should. You'd look a lot less stupid today if ye did."

"You're a cunt, you know that?"

"I do," the Fisherman replied, a smirk on his face. "Look, Livingston and myself shared emails back in '06. I followed the case of a woman named Gayle Lee's after Floyd happened. Follow so far? Her name was in the papers. Decided to start there. I don't fish for sea life, kid. I fish for...oddities."

Another wave broke from down below, soaking the Causeway before sizzling back to the Pacific. Beast whooped out on the basalt like a child full of sugar, jumping to avoid a second salty spray.

"She had a brother in New England," the Fisherman continued. "In a town called Phillipsport. Plenty of bodies after the hurricane hit were found with guns on 'em...Now why would residents take up arms against a hurricane, Quince?"

Quincy frowned. "They wouldn't...unless it wasn't a hurricane they were trying to hit."

"Bingo."

They reached the bottom of the hill, skidding to a halt before the Causeway. Quincy's head reeled with questions. He lowered the container to the ground with a grunt and arched his back, surprised by a pop. On the rocks ahead, Beast clambered about with his ass jutting from his jeans, searching for the hidden crustaceans like a fox scrounging garbage.

"So why'd they all have guns?" Quincy asked, unable to hide his interest. "These people of Phillipsport?"

"To protect themselves from the very thing you've been sent here to find. Bangers."

"Bangers?" Quincy couldn't help but laugh. "As in *fireworks?* What the fuck are bangers?"

"What's this 'special chef' of yours serving up tonight, Quince? You must have some idea."

"Porter joked something about bangers and mash on the phone," Quincy said. "...We're not out here looking for sausages, are we?"

The Fisherman surprised him with a clap to the head. "Stop being a fuckin' tool. Bangers, another name for the crabs, ye bollocks. But they're not *really* crabs, at all."

"Now've you've completely lost me."

The Fisherman gnashed his teeth, his face turning a wine red. "That Porter is a sick man, Quincy! Why can't you see that? He has deep pockets, not much else. Likes to impress other snobby-nosed *wankers* and that's about it. Those folks who covered up the Phillipsport incident? That's who's over in the beach house, not fuckin 'scientists'." He punctuated the word with a wave of his hands. "Couple of journalists who were paid to spread that shit around, that's who's there, you'd like them, wouldn't you? Few high-ranking army heads, too, and a kitchen ghoul from Ken-flippin'-tucky...They think it's some sick joke. And I appreciate a good joke, but this..."

"You think they're eatin' bangers...as a joke?"

"Like a memorial toast to the war, man. A war they think they've won. Think they've got the *whole* situation under control. But let me tell ya, they don't have the slightest idea what's happening."

"And just how would you know that? How would you know what Porter knows?"

The Fisherman chewed his lip. "Because I'm the one who told him all he knows. Knowing a guilt-fuelled Colonel in the US army helps, and it turns out doctorin' some documents for a self-important fat-cat doesn't take much. His beach house being in the middle of nowhere with a million year old postman cinched the deal. Easy."

Quincy rubbed his forehead. "What would you plan to do here, then? Why so hung up on Porter's business?"

"Because he did a bad thing and it's not right. All those lives lost in Phillipsport while Porter and his friends circle jerk about what a fine clean up job they did. *It's not right*, Quincy."

"Why tell me?"

The Fisherman's gaze softened, his face relaxing. "Because you're a good kid. I see that. And he took you for a fool. You have the option to report me and keep on working for a corrupt scumbag, or set something right and blow the story wide open. You're still young. Do what's right...Just keep your back watched while you do it."

Quincy tried to control his shaking breath. "If these creatures are so dangerous then why didn't you stop Beast from going out there? He's diggin' about for one of those things, look."

The Fisherman barked a laugh. "These creatures survived because they've *adapted*! The guy out there sniffin' rocks hasn't. Kids who grow up thinking bleach looks tasty don't get to have kids of their own. Law of nature."

A flock of gulls swooped by just then, flying inland without formation. Quincy's stomach flipped at the sound of their squawking, his brain sending a warning signal to run, run and get away from this place.

He swallowed, his throat dry. "So, what are *bangers*, exactly?"

"That's what we call 'em here," the Fisherman said. "In the US, I've heard them referred to by another name...Clickers."

"Do I have to ask why?"

"Oh, it's not just the claws you've got to worry about, Quince. There's a reason you were asked to transport the species in plastic, trust me. Ceramic, metal, all useless."

Quincy grimaced. "Is it something to do with hydro...hyrda...?"

"Hydrofluoric acid...You're pretty damn close."

"Jesus." Quincy rubbed at his forehead, a sharp headache blooming behind his eyes. "You're tellin' me these *crabs* have hydrofluoric *acid* inside them?"

"And in *you*, if you're not careful. And not acid. Venom. Very few people can prepare such a meal, one of 'em happens to be your special chef. You said these rocks looked like molars to you. Erosion from the water didn't do that alone. You know this is a breeding ground, Quincy, right? Porter told you that much."

"He did. And I guess you told him."

"Right. Bangers *did* lay their eggs here once, a long time ago...and they're back to do it again. Porter knows. Few years back, that beach house was owned by a lawyer and her husband, but when greedy ol' Porter heard the tales of the Causeway...Well, he couldn't resist."

"How'd the species cross from New England?"

"Remember Lydia the Great White, couple years back? A *Great White*, Quincy. In *Ireland*. All thanks to the warming sea temperatures. This is the first time the conditions have been right for them to cross the Atlantic in a very long time."

Quincy ran a hand through his hair, his heart jackhammering his ribs. He couldn't believe his ears. "What did you put in the container, man? What are you planning on doing?"

"That'd be tellin', now wouldn't it?"

"Found one, lads!" Out on the rocks, Beast clamored to his feet and smiled as another wave slithered across his trainers. He cupped his hands to his mouth. "And you Dublin fucks can fuck right the fuck off! This one's mine! That's a grand in my pocket and nothin' in yours! Pass me out the bin, Quince!"

Quincy looked to the plastic container by his feet, wondering what secrets lay within, as a wave of nausea washed through his body.

"Ah, fuck ye both, then," Beast shouted as he batted a hand. "I'll carry the wee bastard back."

"Porter told us not to handle them," Quincy muttered, still looking to the container. "We're meant to scoop them using the box and gloves."

Getting to his knees, Beast dipped his hands inside the bowl of a pillar next to him. "Just hatched..." he said, working his hands deeper inside the rock. "...Thing's nearly the size of a lobster. Might get me *two*-grand for this. Wait 'til ye see the size of...aha!"

Jumping to his feet, Beast waggled the monstrosity before his face. Quincy gasped. The tiny critter gnashed glistening pincers at thin air, fighting to curl its segmented body towards its capture but unable to reach. Quincy thought, *a crab, mixed with a scorpion, mixed with a lobster...*

"It's fuckin' huge," Beast said with a laugh. "The size of me forearm...*Jaysus.*"

The Fisherman gave a slow nod. "Next comes the parents. We'll need to move fast. Augustus told me he'd seen some the size of—"

Click-click...Click-click...

"—a large dog."

The creature scuttling along the Causeway made Quincy's skin crawl. Its spider-like legs clacked the rocks as it rushed to its young, determined to sever the human's grasp. It paused about ten feet away from Beast, seeming to gauge the threat as it rose to its hind segment and clashing its claws together in a sound like crashing bone china.

"Ah!"

Beast dropped the infant clicker and cradled his hand. He shot Quincy a frightened look, his lower lip quivering. "It stung me...wee bastard...it..."

Beast's hand inflated like a water balloon. He screamed as the flesh sizzled and popped, dripping to the rocks of the Causeway in slopping ribbons. Quincy watched in horror as the tiny creature scuttled to the mess and began to eat.

"The mother," the Fisherman said, and the fascination in the man's voice made Quincy's hair stand on end. "Watch."

A stinger like that of a scorpion darted forth from the large clicker, harpooning Beast through the chest. He gagged, clasping the appendage as it plunged deeper, pulsing. Blood oozed from Beast's lips, his eyes rolling to clear whites as he spasmed like a victim of electrocution.

That's the venom, Quincy thought, frozen to the spot. *The Fisherman's right...*

Slowly, Beast began to liquefy.

Once, when Quincy had been about eight years old, he and a friend had taken a microscope to a toy soldier on a hot day. They'd laughed as the toy melted as easy as ice-cream, slopping in sizzling lumps to the scorched earth. The soldier's face had been reduced to popping bubbles of stinking oil, the toxic stench burning Quincy's nostrils and forcing him into a coughing fit. The boys had stopped when the smell got too much.

Now, Quincy watched as the real deal played out before him, but this time, the stench could not be stopped. It collected in the back of his throat, a horrid mixture of rancid meat with a chemical undertone that smelt strong enough to strip paint. He gagged.

The parent clicker dropped Beast's carcass to the rocks, just as another wave crashed in, washing some of the mess away.

"Come on," the Fisherman said. "We need to do this now. Before we get ambushed."

The Fisherman grabbed the canister and rushed towards a collection of boulders to the left by the ocean. Quincy followed suit, his brain on auto-pilot and his heart punching his chest. The stench of Beast's dissolving body still hung thick as soup in the air.

Once past the rocks, the Fisherman dropped the canister to the sand and waded knee deep into the water. He disappeared around an outcrop and Quincy scanned the hidden beach, watching for more creatures, the boulders blocking his view of the Causeway.

"*Shit, shit, shit...*"

The Fisherman reappeared, dragging a battered and motorized fishing boat with one hand, his face scrunched in exhaustion.

"Get the fuck in and bring the tub," he said, the words melded as one. "Hurry."

Quincy lifted the canister and eased himself inside the boat, holding the sides as the Fisherman hoisted himself up with a grunt. Once onboard, the Fisherman eased himself to the engine and revved the cord. The engine spluttered, once, twice...

"Take the lid off the damn container," the Fisherman ordered. "Now."

Click-click...Click-click...

The engine roared to life, threading water as Quincy popped the lid and gagged. He peered inside, staring down at bags and bags of dead rodents.

"Rotten meat," The Fisherman said, steering the spluttering boat out to sea. "I wasn't lyin'. Now open one of those bags and start throwin' the things. We need 'em to follow us."

"Are you *insane?*" A sudden wave forced Quincy to grip the side of the boat for support.

"Are you a *pussy?*" the Fisherman asked. "These things are only meant to come and nest, but I'm throwin' a spanner in the works for Porter and the bastards. And I'd appreciate it if you'd throw some rodents in the water."

They've come back, Quincy thought. *After all these years, they've come back...and I can break the story.*

Quincy reached inside one of the bags, his hand closing around something moist and warm. He grimaced as he pulled the carcass and flung it from the boat. "Payback," he yelled. "For Gayle Lee and all the others who lost their lives at Phillipsport."

"Exactly!" the Fisherman agreed. "Now do another. They're coming."

Quincy's breath caught as a dozen dark shells appeared in the wake of their boat, almost in formation. They cut the dark waters with ease, moving just as fast as the vehicle. Scooping another handful of dead things, Quincy tossed another wad of carrion overboard, flinching at the bubbling commotion that followed.

"They're still coming," he shouted, gripping another leaking rat. "Good. That's what we want. We're almost there, keep it up."

Quincy threw the last rodent and ripped the second bag open, ready to repeat the process. By the end of the stash, their pursuers had grown to at least three dozen in size. The large shells bobbed up and down in the sea like moving rocks, occasionally surfacing enough to reveal claws.

"Almost," the Fisherman muttered, charging for Henry Porter's private beach. As the sand raced towards them, Quincy braced. "Now!"

BANGERS AND MASH

The Fisherman leaped from the boat, sprawling in the sand and losing his hat. Quincy took the impact, shooting over the bow and landing on his side. Air whooshed from his lungs, leaving him winded and panting. Within seconds, the Fisherman gripped his armpits and dragged him along the beach. Quincy scooped the hat, too.

A light appeared in the kitchen, followed by a man stepping onto the balcony, silhouetted in the doorway.

"What's goin' on out here?" the man demanded in a thick Southern accent. "Good Lor' Jesus, what the hell *is* this?"

Quincy got to his own feet and followed the Fisherman around the side of the house, his breath returning. Together, they raced towards the main road past a maze of a dozen brand new cars. From behind, the steady click-click of giant claws grew to a spine-tingling symphony.

Panting, the Fisherman cupped his hands to his mouth and jogged backwards. "Hey, Henry!" he yelled towards the house. "Henry Porter! Your dinner's comin'!"

Soon after, the screaming began.

THE CONDUCTOR

KELLY BARGED THROUGH the students gathered in front of Bray DART station and elbowed a sixteen-year-old.

"Will you fucking *move*, please."

Coffee sloshed in her thermos as she fished out her train pass and jammed it inside the machine. The ticket disappeared with a mechanical whirr.

Come on, come on...

Her ticket popped topside and she ripped it from the slot before smashing through the turnstile and out onto the platform. The 6:15 to Dublin—*just feet away, no!*—hissed and belched fumes before jittering to a start. Kelly bolted to the cart and jammed her thumb against the *door open* button again and again. "Ah, come on!"

The train picked up speed as sleepy passengers slipped by in the windows. "Well I hope you're all fuckin' amused!"

Her shoulders fell lax. The train left with a honk of the horn. Cold air bit her now, and her red nose ran as she sniffled and wiped it with the back of her hand. A slow trickling caught her attention and she looked down to find her coffee spilling from her thermos.

"Ah, for fuck sake..."

She righted the thermos and pushed it to her lips before taking a deep swig. She sighed. The bitter brew only served to slam her heart faster but she *needed* the caffeine. George just *had* to keep her up until two in the morning to talk about their *issues*, didn't he? There were no *issues*. Her promotion to supervisor at OneWave meant more hours away and less time to talk, *but that was part of the deal*. There was no time for anything other than work right now, why couldn't he just accept that? 'Moving too fast,' he'd said, but there wasn't *time* to court or explore, he didn't *have* to accept her apartment key if he didn't want to. Hell, he didn't have to *be* with her if he didn't want to. *And at this point, do I actually care?*

A horn blurted and echoed across the platform. Kelly turned and squinted down the misty tracks where a beam sliced the fog. She glanced to the digitized timetable, reading: HOWTH 6:40—not another train due for twenty-five minutes. The idiot in charge of updating the system was probably half-asleep and forgot to add the train. What else was new? Her phone would tell her what's what. She fished about her pocket and...

"You're kidding me. This is an actual fucking joke, right?"

She grabbed her hair in a fist as she recalled placing her Samsung by the coffee machine in a hurry. "Oh, perfect. Lovely. You absolute *gobshite*."

Whatever. The seven o'clock meeting with Mr. Dawson *had* to go ahead either way. She couldn't even call to tell him she was running late. "Not that I would."

Kelly would rather leap onto the tracks than risk smearing her reputation at OneWave. The long hours were worth the lack of personal time if it meant securing a foothold in the booming Dublin tech industry. A supervising position at OneWave on the resume would catch the eye of Google, Apple, or any of the other corporate giants set up in the capital. If only

THE CONDUCTOR

George hadn't...*fuck it*. Not to worry now. She needed to focus on work, not him, and not herself. And the new train approached.

It hissed to a slow stop; an October orange caterpillar of chrome stinking of burned gas. Kelly glanced about the station but saw no other passengers stupid enough to have missed the 6:15. Even the ticket booth attendee was glued to his phone, his bubble jacket pressed tight to block the early chill. *You'll be on time at least, come on.*

She jabbed the cart's 'open' button and the automated doors split apart. Kelly stepped onboard. The doors hissed shut. And before she could take another step, the train jerked. She grabbed a nearby pole to steady herself. And cold wetness seeped into her palm.

"The *fuck?*"

She balked as she snapped her arm back. A white, foamy liquid glistened on her skin like saliva from a rabid dog. In fact, the entire pole shimmered with that same wetness. On second glance, *all* the poles were slathered. Gaudy pink seats dotted the open floor, some with crude patterns of fruits and vegetables etched into the decor. Others with penises. A neon green linoleum floor worked its way up the walls to a bar of advertisements running above the windows. And the windows—*God*—had this train been stored in an abandoned warehouse? Kelly's mouth fell open as she read the posters, each from the 1980s and 90s, not a single one modern. The kind of thing a hipster cafe would frame. Coca-Cola and Colgate, vintage.

The train picked up speed but Kelly avoided grabbing another pole—*ugh!*—and made her way to the nearest offensively pink seat before dropping. The material was *warm*, as if someone had recently sat. She placed a hand on the seat beside her and again felt that unnatural heat.

219

Not enough to come from a system, no, this felt like body temperature. *Unnatural.*

She looked for television cameras in genuine disbelief, imagining a Hollywood host leaping from behind a chair with a *gotcha!*

"What the fuck is this, seriously?"

A station blurred by the window, and a couple on a bench pointed to the bizarre carts as she shot past. Did they notice something odd? The image only lasted a nano-second as the engine chugged faster. Outside the yellowed windows to the right, she expected the ocean and the docks. She'd taken the DART at least once a week for the past decade, she knew that sight as well as her own apartment. But instead of rolling blue waves, the ocean was *green.*

Kelly thought the dust was playing tricks with the light, but as she hoisted herself up using her hands (the *warmth*, oh, God!), the sky remained a natural blue. The ocean, however, was green.

I'm still asleep. Slept in. It's just a nightmare. Missing the train to work, Kelly, it's as boring a nightmare as they come. A gaudy, badly decorated train from nowhere? Come on, now.

Yet the warmth beneath her jeans and the slick moisture on her palm *felt* real. The aftertaste of coffee on her tongue *tasted* real. She dug her nails into her palm and that sure *felt* real...

"But of course it would. That's what you'd think if you were asleep."

Something thumped from the cart ahead, loud enough to make her tense. Through the small window in the door, she watched the divider sway back and forth, expecting the door to burst open. As her breathing quickened, she instinctively grabbed for her phone, ready to call the Gardaí or at least record what was—

THE CONDUCTOR

"Ah, fuck!"

No phone, remember! She pushed to her feet and swayed as the train barreled through the next station. *Killiney.* Each color outside the window looked as if someone had jumbled them about for fun. The once red-bricked walls of the station were a duck-egg blue. The people on the platform were yellow, and their confused and frightened faces blurred by as the conductor refused to stop. A deep *hoooonk!* sounded.

Where was this train headed? Who the fuck was *driving* this thing? As the speed continued climbing, the carts blasted past strange and off-colored outdoors and Kelly hyperventilated. She dropped to her knees, wide-eyed, and blindspots danced in her vision as her breath refused to catch.

I need to get off, Jesus, I need to get off! Too fast!

Yet the engine chugged faster and faster. Then the train *jerked* and a jet of crimson splattered the window. Kelly screamed and covered her mouth as the red streak jittered sideways instead of down from the force of gravity.

What the fuck was that, a fox? Did we just hit an animal?

Dalkey whipped by, then Glenageary...

Kelly slammed her fist down and climbed to her feet. Fuck this. Whoever was driving this disaster had answers, and *godfuckingdamnit* did she demand them. Anger raged inside her as she gritted her teeth and took an unsteady step forward. The sheer force of speed made her feel as if she was walking against a Red Alert storm, but she got another foot ahead, and then another, and soon her hand reached the cart handle she yanked the door open. A nauseous stench blasted her in the face.

Kelly heaved as saliva coated her teeth. Her eyes watered and she covered her mouth as she stepped from the cart into the divider, reaching for the handle of the next cart. With a deep breath, she whipped open the door. And froze in the doorway.

Corpses sat propped in the gaudy seats, jostling from the seesaw motion. Some looked fresh, with frenzied worms jutting from their decaying skin like live wires. Others were no more than mummified remains, their dried husks flaked and browned. A loud shriek of feedback screeched from the overhead speakers and someone cleared their throat. Then a distorted voice spoke.

"*Attention* all passengers, *attention!*" A laugh lurked beneath those gravelly words, a voice like a clogged pipe. "Have your tickets ready for inspection. Tickets ready. The inspector is on his way. I repeat, *the inspector* is on his way."

That grating feedback sounded again before the speakers popped. Kelly stood paralyzed as the handle of the door ahead began to jitter. Then the train *whooshed* inside a tunnel, plunging her into darkness. She heard the door crash open.

Thud...thud...

In the low light, a lumbering giant with bulbous, misshapen features lurched into the cart. The train burst from the tunnel and Kelly screamed. Yellowed bandages covered the creatures massive head, one veined eye blinking beneath. Chains clanked, bound to either wrist—scrawny wrists no bigger than her own. It wore a formal suit, crinkled and tight around its broken and hunched body, and as it stepped towards a corpse, it spoke. "Tickets, please."

The corpse jittered from the train's movement, its jaws wobbling as if in laughter. The inspector reached forward with a gnarled hand that soon disappeared from sight. Kelly was unable to look away as a wet, mushy sound accompanied the giant's hand working about inside—*what*, the corpse's *chest*?

THE CONDUCTOR

The hand popped free clutching a rotten, dripping organ.

An involuntary scream exploded from Kelly's lungs and still the inspector paid her no mind. It reached inside its jacket and pocketed the heart before a black stain worked through the lapel. Then it lumbered to the other chairs and repeated the guttural phrase, "Tickets, please."

Kelly took a step back inside the divider, then another. Soon she was bolting down the train. She shot past the dripping poles and angry pink seats and into another cart of much the same. She raced to the back door and pulled the handle, but the door refused to budge. She smashed her elbow against it, screaming each time her bone hit hard metal, and then she crumpled against the wall in defeat.

Tears streamed her face as her entire body hitched and trembled. Her bladder threatened to let loose.

Oh, God, what is this place?

The voice bellowed from the cart ahead, still asking for *tickets, please...*

Get me out of here, I want off. It's moving too fast and I can't breathe and I just want to see George and–

The train lurched to a stop.

Kelly was flung forward and smacked against a chair. Air whooshed from her lungs and she was faintly aware of cold linoleum squishing against her cheek. A coppery liquid dribbled from her lips and something thumped in the cart ahead. Then the speaker squealed again. The conductor's voice filled the train.

"I have in on good authority that one of our passengers has not yet presented a ticket. This is no free ride. You move, you pay the price. And now my inspector is very upset..." A moment of silence, a deep breath, and then, "I guess I'll just have to get it myself."

Kelly pushed upright, spotting a red splatter on the floor. Her jaw throbbed as her tongue worked over a loose tooth. Through the open door ahead, she saw the inspector press his head against the wall, working his red-stained fingers around each other nervously. His low, rumbling cry echoed back to her as he thumped his bandaged head against the cart.

Thud...thud...The inspector is very upset...

The door crashed open, deafening in the silence. Kelly balked and scrambled upright, scanning her surroundings for a weapon. Nothing. A shadowy figure approached. It passed the corpses that were now strewn about two carts ahead like rag-dolls. There the figure paused, looked left and right, before giving a curt nod. It seemed pleased with what it saw, and continued forth.

A conductor's cap sat atop its head. A formal suit, just like the inspectors, fitted its slim build. It clasped its hands behind its back casually, as if just out on a stroll. For a moment, relief flooded Kelly—*actual relief!*—at the prospect of another human aboard this abomination. Then the conductor paused by the inspector and reached out. Not with a hand, but with a thousand wriggling worms spouting from its sleeve. The worms slapped and slithered the creature's back as the conductor shushed and rubbed.

"Shh...I'll get the ticket. I'll get it, I promise."

As one worm fell to the floor, the conductor overstepped it and started forward again. Here it raised its head, and below the cap appeared not a face but a fleshy canvas devoid of features. A slit appeared down the center before slowly creeping apart, then the face split wide open.

"Jesus fucking Christ!" Kelly ran to the window, the outdoors once again appearing normal now that the train had stopped. She expected Tara Street Station, or at least

THE CONDUCTOR

Howth, but instead an unfamiliar woodland waited on the opposite side of the glass.

I don't care, I need out!

She punched the window and angry pain shot up her forearm. The glass held. The conductor approached. A chitter like a thousand night bugs filled the cart.

"Come on!"

She jabbed again. And again.

The inspector roared, "Get my ticket!" and the conductor giggled, an otherworldly sound that sent razors up Kelly's spine.

She braced her elbow and, with a deep breath, flung her entire body forward. The glass exploded. A cool breeze whooshed in.

Something was close behind now, the presence raising the peach fuzz on the back of her neck.

Kelly grabbed the jagged window frame and hoisted herself out as she screamed. She fell and her stomach entered her throat just before she *smacked* yellowed grass. She rolled onto her back, peering back up at the face peering out at her—a face constructed of a ball of curling worms, one with a conductors cap still remaining atop its head.

Kelly scrambled away as the conductor dipped back inside the train. For a moment she'd expected him to leap out and grab her, pull her kicking and screaming back onboard as cold worms worked their way inside her mouth and her ears and wriggled down her throat...but the conductor simply disappeared.

The train coughed a stinging cloud before the wheels grated and began to roll. A fat cloud shot from above the carts, and soon, the train was gone, chugging down rusted tracks that Kelly did not recognize.

Wait.

She climbed to her feet and approached the rusted bars, noting the copper film on the metal. These tracks had not seen use in decades. Kelly turned in a circle, surrounded by thick pines and withered grass. Wicklow? Had the train somehow plowed into another county?

A nervous smile teased her lips all the same. *She'd escaped! She was free!* Her shoulders hitched as the first bouts of anxious laughter teased her system. She grabbed at her arms, assuring herself everything was all right now, and sharp pain bloomed in her hand. Beads of glass glittered on her skin as crimson oozed from her open palm. She'd need a doctor. Hell, she needed the *Gardaí*—the train was still somewhere in the country, pulling up to any number of stations to gather more unsuspecting passengers. But would anyone even believe her?

She stumbled towards the pines, where a main road waited on the far side. She'd hitch a ride to the nearest hospital. Call George from a payphone. Then she'd call OneWave and say...what, exactly? She didn't exactly know, but the hospital would be a place to start. She beat aside the lower branches and overstepped nettles and thistles and shoved her way out onto the path, wincing as her palm demanded attention.

Then a car slowed as it rounded a bend, and an orange blinking light accompanied the driver pulling to the curb. Kelly jogged over, cradling her damaged hand, and the window of the gaudy pink Honda whirred down. "Need a ride?" the driver asked, the voice like wet leaves. "I'll just need to see your ticket first. No one gets a free ride."

Kelly screamed as glistening worms slopped from the vehicle and the door opened.

MUTT

MAM MOVED US to Wexford in the summer of '92 with nothing more than a couple of suitcases and a black eye. Flat clouds the color of nicotine stains drifted across a plum sky, and I yawned as the six AM bus rocked me from side to side. I never fared well with travel but I put up a good front for her, even if my reflection made me look like a horror movie ghoul. Each breath made a frosty pillar escape my lips.

"Not much further," Ma said, and squeezed my shoulder. "You can get a nap when we're there."

"Is it nice?" I asked.

"Yeah, Tommy." She kept her voice low to avoid waking the handful of other dozing passengers. A woman snored from across the aisle, her hair tucked beneath a blue plastic cap. "Anywhere's nicer than with *him*."

The *him* in question was Barry Laughlin, a recovering alcoholic who fell off the wagon soon as Ma moved us into his two-bedroomed cottage. Came home reeking of booze and pissed himself before cracking her one across the face. Then he'd passed out. We left at three AM and hitched to the Dublin Bus Depot. At nine-years-old, I already had as many moves under my belt as I had birthdays.

"Is there other kids there, Ma?" I asked.

She sighed and lifted her face to the overhead. "I don't know, Tom. Maybe. Now it's not going to be like Sallynoggin, understand? There's no bus to the cinema or shopping centers, we're going to be a little out of the way, yeah? But it's only for a little while. Can you do this for me? Be a big lad and be strong until I sort us out?"

"I can, Ma," I said, and rested my head against her arm. Her perfume ghosted in the air, and my eyes fluttered shut as a soft comfort overcame me. Ma sniffled, but it came from a place far away as I slipped into a dreamless sleep. I awoke when the bus jerked to a stop.

"Tom? Tom, come on, we're here."

She pulled me to my feet and the woman with the hair net gave me a smile as if we shared some secret before I was led down the aisle. As we stepped off, the driver swiveled and threw Ma a curious glance. She raised a hand as if fixing her hair to hide her swollen eye and we climbed down into the morning chill. Ma pulled our cases from the luggage before the bus farted a gassy plume and rattled off toward Wexford, leaving us standing at a Post Office in need of a paint job. Across the street stood a cafe, a barber shop, a petrol station, and not much else. The icy air gave me a shiver and Ma hoisted our bags before starting down the country road. "Keep up, Tommy. Just down here."

Ten minutes later, we reached a sign reading: *Strawberry House*. The offensively pink building stood on an acre of strawberry fields, and just behind it, lay a beige caravan.

"No, Ma," I said, and stopped at the drive. "No, come on."

She dropped our suitcases and spun. "Tom? You said you'd be a big lad, didn't you? This is the best I can do, okay? It's not going to be forever. Just a little while. I promise."

My stomach tightened as I joined her at her side. I'd spent two Christmases in a caravan, both in Wicklow and Cavan, and I couldn't believe my luck when we finally moved to a real-life brick house. We even had a TV and radiators. This felt like five steps back, and my lips quivered the closer we got to the house.

The door swung open, and a woman not much older than my mother appeared. She had red hair that curled around her shoulders, red lips, and a fluffy green jumper that looked well-worn and cozy. As she approached, she opened her arms and embraced my mother soundlessly. They stayed that way for a long time, and Ma sniffled as she cried into the woman's shoulder. The lady shushed her and stroked her hair, then she brought her to arms-length and gave a weak smile. Embarrassed, I simply stared at the pebbles by my feet. "Just a little while, Angela," she said, "Yeah?"

My mother nodded and wiped her face.

"He was a bastard and he'll never—" She looked to me then as if only noting my presence, and smiled broadly. "You must be Tommy. I'm Grace, an old friend of your ma's. You're going to look after your mum like a big lad, aren't you? You don't have to worry here, Tommy. You're safe."

She gave me a false grin that looked pained. I hadn't questioned our safety, and it only truly hit me then that Ma was going through something I didn't understand. She didn't tell me her *true* fears, her pain, her worries. All I saw was a woman of action making good by her child. Right then, though, I caught a sliver of my *private* mother, a young woman named Angela fraught with terror and holding things together with nothing more than her will. Until that moment, I'd never known.

"Is it okay for him to head out to the caravan?" my mother asked as she wiped her face. "Can I make him something to eat in the kitchen?"

"Of course, of course." Grace rubbed Ma's shoulder and led her to the house. "Harry will grab the bags, just leave them there."

Ma looked to me with tears streaming her face. The dam she'd been building all night finally broke. "Go out and claim your bed, Tommy. I'll be out to you in a minute with some food."

I gave her a smile, wanting to apologize for being a fussy little shite, but instead started around back. I reminded myself it was only temporary, even as the harsh chill made my nose run. Barry was a bastard, but he was a bastard with a fireplace. I wondered if we even had heating here.

Rows and rows of fat-leafed shrubs stretched off into the distance behind the caravan, and a sweet scent teased my nose. I spotted fat, red fruit on the shrubs and shoved off the urge to pick some. The last thing Ma needed was me acting out, so instead I approached the caravan—my new home.

And then I heard a noise. Something stirring beneath the structure.

A low whine. An *animal*.

I crouched and squinted into the inky sliver between the cinder blocks. Two orbs glowed.

"Jesus..."

The thing whined louder as it shuffled about. I threw a look back to the house but I was alone. Through the kitchen window, I saw Ma and Grace potter about with their mouths moving a mile a minute. I clicked my tongue...

And the thing darted forth.

"Shite!"

I fell on my arse as a filthy pup no bigger than my forearm hobbled from the gloom. The tendons in my neck tightened the closer it got—could it have *mange?*—but as soon as it reached my boots, I placed a hand on its head and patted. An earthy aroma invaded my nostrils and my palm came away brown.

"Easy, easy..."

The dog continued whining, shaking like a faulty washing machine as it sniffed my soles. Pebbles and twigs stuck to its fur, and I wondered how long it'd been under the home. It licked my hand and I broke out in goosebumps.

"Hey!"

I giggled as I scratched its chin, the moist fur slicking my fingers, but I no longer cared about dirt. I'd never had a pup before.

Ribs jutted from its sides, skin tight around the bone. Ma could bring food and water and we could have breakfast together. I suddenly hoped it didn't have an owner. And for the first time that morning, I enjoyed the idea of living in the countryside. I didn't have a TV, but I had acres of sweet-smelling fields, maybe a dog, and who knows what other kids might live locally. We could have all kinds of adventures through the forests and mountains.

And that's when Harry appeared.

He stalked from the house with his hands in his pockets and a smile on his face. He was older than Ma, about forty, and his eyes widened as he spied the dog.

"Ah, you found the mutt."

"Sorry?"

"The mutt," he said, and nodded to the creature. "That dog's been in our fields for a few weeks, went missing two nights ago. Where'd you find him?"

The dog lapped at my fingers, and its tail worked back and forth. "He was under the caravan."

"Right, well that's good to see. He doesn't have an owner, you know. Just came here a while back. Grace and myself don't mind pets, so if you want to keep him, if it's all right with your ma, then that's grand."

"Really?" I chuckled. "That would be amazing. I've never had a dog."

"Well you might do now," he said and took a knee before scratching the animal's ear. "Jaysus, some stink off him, though. You'll have to pop him in the bathtub later. Think you can do that?"

I said I could, and Harry got to his feet, his knees popping on the way. "Like what you see here? Ever been to Wexford before?"

"No, sir," I said, but couldn't take my eyes from the poor animal. *My first pet.* "We used to live in Wicklow," I said. "For a while, then Dublin. Never been down the country this far."

"Well, you'll like it. See the fields there?" He nodded to where the sun rose above shrubs. "That's where your ma's going to work with us. Ever seen the fields before?"

"No, I haven't."

"Well, you can pop out with your mother and see how it all works if you like. We have three other people in the fields with us. Harvesting takes nearly a month, and in the offseason your ma is going to work at Olivia's cafe down the road. You see that place on the way in?"

"We did," I said, recalling the small business by the Post Office.

"Well, it's not Dublin, and thank the Gods for that I say, but you'll have plenty to do while you're here. And it's only for a little while, anyway."

"How long's a little while?"

"A tiny bit, that's all."

The dog turned in a circle before sitting at my shoe, then it gave a yawn. "How does Ma know you?"

"She knows Grace. The two of them have been friends for years and years. Met in Dublin one time. Your mother not tell you?"

"No, sir," I said, and was shocked to know my mother even *had* friends. Like watching her break down earlier, I felt as if I were being introduced to a woman I'd never met in my life.

"Well, come on. Head inside and have a look around. You need anything, you just give me a shout. Come in with the pup there when you're ready and I'll back you up with convincing your mother to let you keep it. Sound like a plan?"

"Yeah," I said, and fresh excitement teased my stomach. I started to think I'd enjoy it here. "Thank you."

He winked. "Not a bother. Right. I'm popping out to the fields to check the berries. I've put your bags in the hall. I'll carry them out for you when you two have had breakfast. Need anything else, no?"

"No, I'm grand. Thanks."

"Right."

He whistled as he took off and the sun made him a silhouette as he strolled through the shrubbery. I looked to my dog (my dog!) and patted his head before making for the back door. He followed close behind, and I couldn't wait to feed him. A name? I decided I liked what Harry said. Mutt.

I named him Mutt.

✗ ✗ ✗

That night, I lay awake on my bunk with stinging eyes. My body craved rest but I was exhilarated; curled at my side was a clean brown pup smelling of shampoo and with a belly full of food. Ma said yes to taking the dog without missing a beat (of *course* she did) and I instantly forgave her for bringing us here. My little pup stretched out beside me as if he'd never known such comfort, and I scratched his fluffy back as a smile split my face. My first pet. Mutt.

The caravan wasn't much, but my bunk had a curtain for privacy. The polyester was thin and smelled of soap and it made Mutt sneeze a couple of times. I'd never heard anything so cute. We had no TV, no microwave or any appliances (we were to use the Strawberry House for cooking), but we did have a generator-powered shower, a booth to sit at for eating, and a nice couch at the far side. All in all, our new home was snug, and I drifted off to Mutt's steady breathing, not missing Dublin one bit. It was the deepest sleep I ever had.

"Wake up, Tom."

Ma stroked my hair, her outline haloed by the dawn through the bleary window. A chill crept through me and I pulled the blanket to my neck. I tensed as I noticed a lack of weight by my side. "Mutt? Where is he?"

"Outside with Grace, don't worry." She chuckled, apparently amused by my fears. "Get up and have some breakfast. I made a fry over at the house, it's on the table. I gave Mutt a couple of sausages and Harry's getting us some dog food later in town. I have to head to the fields. It's my first day. You be a good boy and keep yourself busy here with Mutt, yeah? Play around, call me if you need anything."

"I will."

"And remember, it's only temporary."

I said I'd remember that, though right then I didn't care. And once she left, I climbed into the booth with a steaming plate of hash browns, sausages and eggs. Each bite tested my stomach as my excitement built to get outside and mess around with my pup. Just thinking of his little face made me squirm, and I wolfed down my food before grabbing my coat and slipping on my boots. Then I went out.

"Morning, little fella."

Harry stood in the drive with Mutt sniffing around his green wellies. As soon as the dog caught sight of me, he raced over with his tail batting like a live wire. He leaped and slapped his paws on my legs, tongue lolling from his open mouth.

"Much better today, he is," Harry said. "Doesn't even need a leash. But you have to keep an eye on him while we get our harvest, okay?"

"I will."

"Good lad," he said, and hummed a traditional tune as he sauntered to rows of red-dotted bushes. Four workers were busy snipping fruit into baskets, and I spotted Ma kneeling in the second row. She smiled and waved. "Morning, Ma!" I returned the gesture before taking off towards the thicket at the end of the property with my boots slapping the drive. I was ready to see what the woods had in store for me and my pet. In the dawn, yellow squares glowed in the distance as families awoke, ready to begin their day. Something was missing, and when I noted the lack of electric nervousness I was used to in the city, I smiled. Things ran slower here. And I liked that. With Mutt at my heels, we entered the forest.

✗ ✗ ✗

When I returned home, Ma had a cough.

✗ ✗ ✗

"I'll be fine, will ye stop worrying."

Ma sat at the booth wrapped in her blanket, dabbing tissues at her red nose. She'd spent the day in the fields, and after dinner, went on the phone with the Gardaí. I overheard something about a 'protection order' and a 'court date', but I was too young to understand what any of it meant. Grace reassured me that Barry was an arsehole again and again, but I didn't understand why at the time. I was too interested in playing with Mutt.

Ma winced as she wiped her nose and her skin flaked around her nostrils. She sighed and faced the ceiling. "Better stay away from me for the next couple of days, Tommy. Don't want you getting sick."

I stoked Mutt's belly. "Do ye need anything?"

She smiled and cocked her head. "I'm grand, but thank you. Have to do the fields tomorrow and Friday, then we'll have a couple of days together. We'll head into town and see what's what. Get us some new clothes. They're giving me a week's pay even though I'm only doing three days. We owe them, Tommy. They're good people."

I didn't doubt that, but I hoped Ma felt better in the morning.

She didn't.

And Mutt's wagging tail and happy little yaps suddenly didn't feel so good.

✗ ✗ ✗

"Go on and play, it's grand," Ma said. She slipped into the jacket she'd borrowed from Harry and wiped her nose with the back of her hand. Dark circles drooped beneath her eyes. "Just can't afford to have a flu is all. Go on, have fun."

Mutt yapped in agreement but I didn't feel right playing. Still, I did as told, and took Mutt out to the creek I'd found the day before. He splashed about and leaped like a rabbit, but to be honest, I barely noticed. I didn't *want* to enjoy myself. Instead, I let him play until my stomach grumbled and forced me to return to the Strawberry House. And that's when I found four people standing around something in the fields. I clicked my tongue for Mutt to follow. My walk turned to a jog.

Harry met me halfway, and he couldn't disguise the worry. He forced a smile. "Doing okay, Tommy? Everything's all right, it's just—"

"Ma..." I glanced behind him and noted feet jutting from the shrubs. Someone got in the way and blocked my view. "Ma? Is it Ma?"

He blew a breath and placed a hand on my shoulder. "Just overworked, Tom. Happens out here, on your feet all day, y'know? Really, it's nothing to worry about."

Mutt yapped and wagged his tail and at that moment I hated them both. Harry for giving a false sense of security, and Mutt for being too dumb to realize when things were bad. How could he wag his tail and act happy while Ma lay unconscious in a strawberry field? I gritted my teeth and stalked over.

"Here's Tommy," Grace said. She was on one knee by my mother, a hand placed behind Ma's head for support. Ma craned her neck as her bleary eyes found me. She blinked and forced a quivering smile, then she propped herself upright on her elbows. I heard one of the workers sigh in relief, but when he spotted me looking he just smiled.

"Hey, Tommy." The other workers moved aside to give us space. Mutt leaped onto her lap. She chuckled and patted his head while I fumed at the animal.

"You okay, Ma?"

She let out a shaking breath. "Fine, don't you be worrying. Just from being on my feet all day with the flu."

"Harry," Grace said, "Go get Angie some water from the kitchen. I'll bring her to the caravan."

"Don't want to be a hassle," Ma said, because of course she did. And as Harry stalked to the kitchen—*still whistling*—Mam stood with Grace's help. All the while, Mutt wagged his tail as if there weren't a problem on earth. I wanted to hurt them all.

Χ Χ Χ

That night, Ma found a lump on her breast.

Χ Χ Χ

The next two years blurred by. When I was twelve, I spent most days buried in the Game Boy Ma got me for Christmas. I went on autopilot when we traveled for her chemo in Dublin, and I ignored the fact she wore a bandana at all times. She never removed the headwear around me, and on days that the Gardaí came to chat about Barry Laughlin, she tired easily and retired to bed. Harry and Grace paid the medical bills, and Ma said we were forever in debt. They gave us the caravan free of charge, out of friendship, they said, and Mam cried at that. Grace and Harry didn't cry. In fact, Harry continued to whistle. And Mutt's tail kept wagging.

On the days I wasn't lost to games, Harry distracted me by teaching me to shoot. He had an old AyA No.2 that he said he *never used on animals*. I don't know why he made the distinction but I didn't much care. I just wanted to make something go boom. We fired into the woods to dissuade foxes and badgers and any other critters wanting to make a home of the property. I enjoyed the kickback against my shoulder and the loading of the cartridges, but mostly, I just enjoyed the escape.

MUTT

At this stage, you're probably wondering what happened to Mutt. Well, I don't know how to put this...

Mutt remained a puppy. His eyes remained clear. His tail continued to wag. He never grew an inch, never a gray hair, and he was always by my side. It took all of my willpower not to aim the gun at his head.

X X X

When I was fifteen, Mam passed. Her once-regressive tumor exploded with a vengeance and destroyed her over a two week period. Just two weeks. I spent each of those days at her bedside in the Strawberry House, pushing Mutt away as he brought toys to throw and demanded more ear scratches. Mam said not to blame him, he was only a dog, after all. Even when he nuzzled her head while she tried to fall asleep and yapped like he was the king of the fecking world. She never said a word about his lack of growth, but, then again, she didn't have to. I saw it in her eyes in those final days. The same look I imagined was etched on my own paled features.

Even at the funeral, Mutt's tail batted back and forth, back and forth, back and forth...

X X X

At eighteen, I was one year into working for the Post Office down the village. Grace and Harry had been my legal guardians for three years, and I slept in the very bed Ma died in. Just outside the door, Mutt had a doggie-bed. A small one. One for puppies. For Christmas, Grace and Harry bought the pup a squeaky bone that grated my teeth each time he chewed. *Yip! Yeeeep!* Saliva spilled from his youthful gums as he wrestled the treat and bound up and down the hall, nails clicking the floorboards. I found myself wondering if they gave him that toy to drive me insane. Mutt never went anywhere without it.

Three weeks after my nineteenth birthday, I found the first lump on my neck. It was hard to the touch, not painful in the least. Grace and Harry sympathized when I cried, told me it was probably nothing, and they'd take me to the hospital that Monday. And Harry whistled.

That's when I noticed something new.

Neither Grace nor Harry had a single strand of gray hair. Both looked exactly like they did when I'd arrived all those years ago. By then I'd even gotten some grays of my own, but those two? Well, they hadn't aged a day. Just like Mutt.

I spent a lot of time wondering about Grace and Ma's friendship. They'd met in a bar, and bonded over mutual interests, but the older I became, the more I suspected Grace of *choosing* my mother. But how could I have proven that? I couldn't exactly go to the Gardaí saying, "They never age, the dog doesn't age, and Ma and I got sick just being around them." I'd be locked up.

I needed a better plan.

Everyone Ma ever met drained her, and those good friends and happy pup were no different. She deserved better.

The shotgun was easy to get.

Harry and Grace never suspected a thing. Not even as I tiptoed out and creaked their bedroom door open. I still can't hear right from the shot, and I sure as hell can't clean up that mess. Looks the color of strawberries. Strawberry jam. I imagine everyone heard the blasts for three miles.

He's cowered beneath the bed as I write. Whining as they do. But I'm not buying it. I never did. I've got his squeaky bone right here next to me, and I'll continue to squeeze until he comes out. He can't resist that sound, he never could.

He's just a dog, after all.

SPREAD

SARAH TRACED A finger along the hardened substance coating her inner thigh. Her lips trembled as her index grazed the source of the welt-like anomaly, and she leaped from the toilet seat. "The fuck, the fuck, *what the actual fuck?*"

With her jeans around her ankles, her belt clanged against the tiles as she shuffled to the mirror. Those puffed eyes and pale skin told of two things: a hangover, and fear.

"Lance?" she called in a trembling voice. But then, she thought, *or was it Layne? Shit.* "Anyone? Hello? Fuck."

The sonofabitch had snuck out while she'd slept. After checking the living room and kitchen, she concluded the bastard didn't even have the courtesy to leave a note—*of course not.* Just an unexplained thing between her thighs. "Fuck!"

Sarah hobbled back to the bathroom and snatched her makeup mirror. She placed it on the floor before kicking off her jeans, squatting, and peering down. Her hair fell in front of her face. "Oh, sweet Jesus. It's a dream. Gotta be a dream."

The white ichor spread from her lips like cold candle wax, a Rochester splatter stained to both inner thighs. She tapped a nail against one lumpy section—*solid*—and

243

her guts knotted. She swiped a roll of paper and tore a piece before running it beneath the hot tap. And then she scrubbed. Water dribbled from her leg and pooled on the floor, but the strange stain remained. "Shit!"

Next she grabbed the puff-ball loofah from the shower and grated her flesh. No use. Her skin only reddened. She boiled water, biting her lip to distract herself from her raw thigh while tapping her foot. Once the kettle popped, she filled a mug with steaming water and returned to the bathroom. Then she dipped her toothbrush and raked the bristles along her bumpy flesh, only managing to draw blood. She screamed as she flung the brush across the room. She tried creams and waxing, her own fingernails and steel-wool. She stopped just shy of a kitchen knife.

With her burned thigh now screaming and bloody, she pulled on a dress—to keep the skin clear from rubbing off clothes, and for ease of access—hobbled to the couch, and collapsed. Her legs pulsated as steady as the ticking clock. Before her on the coffee table stood three open beer cans—more evidence of her mistake. She sniffled as she reached for one and her engagement ring clanged off the side. She gritted her teeth, squeezed her eyes shut.

David would call in an hour (like clockwork), making sure—and joking—that his *pumpkin* hadn't gotten cold feet while he was out celebrating the fast-approaching wedding. And, really, what could she tell him? *Oh, that little thing? I dunno, man. Guess a giant dipped his hand in a bucket of paint and slapped me in the privates! Love ya!*

She mumbled into her open palms. "At least paint comes off..."

Then she chewed her lip as a plan formed.

Think, Sarah, think!

The doctor. But Saturday meant a packed waiting-room and, well, *shame*. She scorned herself. A medical professional dealt with this kind of thing *all the time*.

Or did they?

What if they'd never seen anything quite like this before? Sarah sure as shit hadn't. What if her visit led to a long hospital stay with multiple tests and bad diagnosis? Pokes and prods, and even skin grafts? And, somehow worst of all, *David would know*. Doctors might even want to write medical papers about the unusual condition. The press could catch wind. Some undiscovered STD from an unfortunate part of the world now calling her body a home—and wasn't that how AIDs began?

An STD. That's what this was. The worst thing Sarah ever had was a mild case of thrush. Shit, she'd been with David since high school, she never had the opportunity to catch more than the common cold. Until last night. What had she been thinking? But there lay the problem— she hadn't been thinking. She'd downed three shots of tequila as thoughts of a white dress went on a carousel through her brain, and then *he'd* pulled up a stool. A younger guy, mid-twenties, with long blonde hair and an inviting smile. He sat alone, watched her drink, and asked if he could buy her a chaser of beer. Sarah indulged. She'd never done anything like that, never entertained a clear attempt at flirting, but the *idea* she could snatch him up? Well, *that* was a thrill, one aided by booze. And then the trill became a need. And the need became a hangover, regret, and something plastered on her inner thighs. What had she done?

Sarah pulled her phone and bit the plastic for relief. Strewn across the recliner (*David's* recliner) was her crumpled red underwear, David's favorite. Two cigarettes jutted from a saucer full of ash. The air reeked of remorse. And Lance (was that even his name?) hadn't bothered to pack away their Chinese takeout before disappearing like a cheap magician.

The hospital, she decided, would be a last resort. First, she needed to find Lance. Her phone buzzed and she balked. David.

"Hey, sweetie." She cringed at the rasp of her voice. "You okay?"

"Hey, pumpkin. Yeah. Doing alright?"

"All good here," she said, and faked a stretch. Casual. "How's Barry? Getting you into all sorts, I'm guessing?"

David chuckled. "Ah, you know Bar-Bar. Jen would slap him silly if he tried anything like a stripper or a club, you know her."

"Yeah."

A lighter flicked before David sucked a breath and then exhaled. Having his morning coffee and smoke. Like clockwork. "Nah, we just had a few beers at the hotel bar. Spent the evening by the pool but I didn't get in, too cold. Stunk of chlorine, too, like that place we went last year, what was it, um…"

"The Splash Room," Sarah finished.

"Right, just like there." As David spoke, the memory drifted into her mind, a light and easy weekend. Trouble free. *You fool! Fucking idiot!*

David continued. "They've got a ping-pong table, though, so that's eating a lot of our time. Bet Bar three to one, he almost chucked a paddle at my head."

A silence overcame the line. Just a week ago, Sarah found these pauses comforting, knowing neither one *had* to speak. Now the lack of noise swelled until she wanted to scream. "Babe," she spat, "Look, if you want to head to a strip club, you know, um, I would have no issue with it."

"What?" David choked on his cigarette before clearing his throat. "That's not why I mentioned it? I'm just saying Jen wouldn't like it, I'm not going to get Barry in trouble. And, anyway, you know I'm not into *that*. I'm marrying *you* for a reason, silly."

A laugh burst from Sarah's throat, though she found nothing funny. Nothing at all. She could almost feel her sanity slop from her head and out her ears. *I've fucked it up and I'm deflecting so I don't feel guilty! And this is the first phone call. What about when David comes home? No way can I keep this up! And when he wants to make love and runs his hands on my inner thigh...*

"Babe, I gotta go," she said, and struggled not to add, *I think I'm gonna throw up.*

"Sure, sure. Have a great day, pumpkin. I'll be back on Monday. Just two more sleeps. Hey, wanna binge something on Netflix Monday night?"

"Yeah. Sure."

"Awesome. I'll call you later, okay?"

"Okay."

"Love you."

Sarah's mouth opened, but no words came. She sniffled as she hung up the phone and cradled her face. "God-fucking-*damnit!*"

After she blew a deep breath, she wiped her eyes with the back of her arm, and rose from the couch. She needed a plan. She needed to find—

Sarah laughed. Her phone. Last night at the bar...

"Let me show you," Lance had said, and took her cell before tapping in a street name. Sarah wavered as she struggled to view the bright screen. "Right there. It's just a couple hundred a month, I share it with a few other people. Does for the moment, y'know?"

Sarah chuckled as the memory unfolded. "You dumb motherfucker. I have you."

She unlocked her screen and tapped the Internet browser. Sure enough, he'd left his address open on Google Maps. Just a few miles away, Downtown. Without traffic, she'd be there in a half-hour. She envisioned smacking the door with the business end of a baseball bat before cracking the asshole's confused face to a pulp. Then a sharp sting popped the fantasy and made her wince. Her fingers shot to the infection and she cried. "Fuck, it hurts."

Gotta move, girl. Now.

She swiped her keys, leaving the mess for later that day, and then locked up. The harsh sun ached her eyes, and a dull throbbing filled her skull as if minuscule dancers raved in her brain. She swallowed bile as she hobbled to the car and gunned the engine before backing out of the complex and into traffic. A morning radio DJ promoted skincare on the radio and she hastily snapped off his fake voice. Unwinding the window, she allowed the breeze to swipe back her hair. Then she fished for a cigarette and lit up. She could do this. David would never have to know. And she would *never* make the same mistake again.

The record stores and pawn shops on First Avenue gave way to industrial buildings and office outlets. She hooked a right at the command of her GPS, and entered a back alley behind a scaffold-heavy complex in mid-completion. She watched a crane hoist a load of plywood before turning her attention back to the road—just as a construction worker carrying a 4x4 stepped onto the street.

"Shit!"

Sarah slammed the brakes and the car jolted inches from the man's midsection. With his eyes wide as saucers, he placed a hand on her grill and blew a breath. "Jesus, lady, watch where you're goin', would ya? Fuckin' signs all over da place. Can't cha read?"

"I'm-I'm so sorry."

"Christ on a bike."

"Look, I'm looking for an address, but I don't think I'm in the right place. Mind helping me out?"

"Oh, honey," he said, "It's the least I could do for you almost killin' me."

"Shit, I'm sorry."

"Yeah, yeah." He slung the board from his shoulder and propped it against the construction site wall before flexing and returning to her window. "What cha lookin' for, sweetheart?"

"It's a, like, apartment complex, I think? Or a house down here. 15 Applewood Road, I am on Applewood, right?"

The man chuckled, jiggling his gut. He leaned against the open window and flashed a half-complete set of nicotine-stained choppers. "Lady, this a joke? *You* looking for number 15?"

"What's wrong with number 15?"

He cocked his head as if not hearing her correctly. "It's a squatter's dive. Buncha low-life, nocturnal leeches rottin' the place out. Got boarded up years ago, y'know? Some activists keep lightin' a fire under City Hall's ass anytime someone suggests getting them out. They've just let the place go to shit. About twenty of 'em coming and going once the sun goes down, all pasty-faced *bums*. What's a gal with a car and a nice smile goin' and doin' somethin' there?" His confusion cleared then, and he nodded. "Brotha, is it? Yeah, mine's a dickwad, too. Robbed my mom's place just last month, and the poor lady lives in a trailer! A trailer, I says. What's the world comin' to, huh?"

"Can't tell you," Sarah replied, and rubbed the wheel. "But you've been a lot of help. Thank you. Sorry for almost running you over."

"Eh, *say lah vee*, right?"

"Right."

"You be safe," he said, and tapped the door twice before lumbering back to the site. Sarah watched him re-shoulder the thick board before she leaned on the gas and eased the car further down the alley. The GPS told her, "At the next intersection, turn right. Your destination will be on your left," but she barely noticed the robotic voice as a sharp sting bloomed between her thighs. She gritted her teeth and braked outside an abandoned premise with soaped-up windows. A *To Let* sign curled away at one corner, and garbage lay strewn across the chipped lot. The front door stood open, revealing a sliver of a darkened hallway. She took a shuddering breath before killing the engine and stepping from the car.

Sarah pushed open the rusted gate, tarmac crunching beneath her feet. She kept an eye out for needles and dog shit and overstepped potholes big enough to snap an ankle. Once she climbed the porch, she pressed her fingers against the door and pushed it inward as it creaked on its hinges. The bastard was in here somewhere, and he had a lot of explaining to do. Someone muttered from the room on the right as she stepped inside the dingy quarters, and a smell like rotted fish invaded her nose. She breathed through her mouth as she passed stained walls and peeling wallpaper. She need not have worried about stealth—the frame on the right was missing a door completely. Someone poked their head out.

"Jesus!" She clutched her chest as the greasy-faced girl smiled, her unwashed hair waving down from her side-turned head. She couldn't have been over thirty, a pretty lady who looked on hard times. A dirty hand curled around the frame as she said, "Been long enough. Thought you'd be here hours ago."

"I'm sorry?" Sarah suddenly wished she'd brought something to protect herself. A kitchen knife or even some pepper spray. She usually had a can of that in her bag, but besides her cell, she'd left her belongings at home. "Do you know me?"

"I don't," the woman said. "And I don't particularly care to, neither. But *he* does." She said *he* as if the word left a sour taste. Then she dipped back into the room and Sarah followed.

"Hey, wait."

The soaped over windows painted the room with a yellow hue. The unfurnished dwellings contained no furniture, and the dust-covered floor was littered with candy wrappers and empty bottles. Surprisingly, Sarah spied no needles. In the corner, a young blonde woman, maybe twenty-years-old, sat with her knees drawn to her chin. Her jeans cried out for a wash, both legs torn to shreds. She raised her head, and her large, glistening eyes landed on Sarah.

"Another one?" she asked. Sarah noted the disgust in the woman's voice. "Seriously?"

"Well, what did you expect, Marie?" the first lady said, and planted her hands on her hips. "He's upstairs, by the way. Better go get yourself reacquainted."

"*Reacquainted?*" Sarah cocked her head. "Listen, lady, I don't know who you are or why you're all here, but that fucker is giving me some goddamn answers."

"Join the club, sweetheart. Join the damn club."

Sarah searched for a retort but instead turned on her heels. Fuck those tweakers. The sooner she got out of here, the better. That fishy scent was making her nauseous, anyway.

As soon as she left the room and started up the stairs, she heard the girls chatter in low tones. One of them giggled, and memories of high school returned with a vengeance. Sarah gritted her teeth as the stairs groaned, just as dust-ridden as the rest of the house. She hovered her palm an inch above the banisters. Who knows what she might catch if she spent too long here.

Like the lower floor, the soaped-over windows up here also allowed for little light. The oppressive gloom sent a shiver down her back as she stalked first to the right, making for the open door that stood at the far end of the hall. She peered inside.

A young man lay passed out on a filthy cot, his bloated stomach jutting from his tight t-shirt. One hand rested on his bulge, the other dangling off the side over a half-drained bottle of Gatorade. He snored suddenly and Sarah tensed before leaving and making for the next room. Like the room below, the frame itself was also missing a door, and Sarah poked her head inside. Her anger boiled as she spotted a blonde-haired boy laying atop a dirty cot in an otherwise empty room. He peered at her with one open eye, uncurled his hands from behind his head, and waved.

"Hey, Sarah. 'Bout time you made it."

That motherfucker!

Sarah rushed across the room and grabbed hold of his shirt. She flung him from the bed. The boy hit the floor and let out a grunt, but quickly bound to his feet before dusting himself off. He grinned.

"I get it, I get it. You're angry. Wanna, like, kick my ass and spit in my face. But I can't give you answers with a mouthful of blood and broken teeth, now can I?"

"Start talking, you fucking maniac. You know why I'm here."

Sarah's thigh burned as if in response and she winced.

"Not think every guy and gal in here did the exact same thing?"

"What are you talking about?" She balled her fists as her nails bit into her palms. Her nostrils flared. "What the *hell* have you given me? Talk!"

He cocked his head and opened his arms in surrender. "What did *I* give to *you*? Missy, I think you best rethink what happened last night, all right? Far as I recall, I offered to buy you a drink. You had a couple more, called me cute, and soon enough you were dragging me back to your place—by the way, nice house—and I didn't say no, but I didn't make nothin' happen either. That was all your idea."

The deflection hurt and only served to cook up more anger. But he was right—it *had* been her idea. Sarah stomped her foot. "What has that got to do with *anything*? Who cares if I started it? What did you do to me?"

"We fucked, per your request. Per all the people in my house's request. You all asked me."

"And *what* did you *give* me?"

"A child."

"What?" Sarah spat a laugh as the last synapse in her brain finally gave way. But the boy (*Lance? Layne?*) didn't smile, no. He remained stone-faced.

"Listen, I'm tired. We were up late. We can talk more this evening, all right? Go back downstairs, get comfortable. Get to know the girls. And the guys."

Sarah recalled the bloated man on the cot in the next room—*a child*—and her skin prickled. The thing between her thighs still burned.

"What's on my legs? Tell me what's on my damn legs."

"It's..." He rubbed the back of his neck, smirking. "It's disgusting, actually. It's seed."

Sarah's stomach churned. The wax-like matter on her legs continued its incessant throbbing. And in her belly, something roiled.

"Get to know everybody, Sarah. I think you'll like them. You won't be leaving anytime soon. And if you do, you'll be back before David comes home. Believe me."

She suddenly noted the boy was no longer a boy. Breasts pushed against his shirt, and his features softened. His hips expanded and his shoulders shrunk. "I have a date tonight," she said. "New guy. Just couldn't get enough of me. You believe me now?"

When something *kicked* inside Sarah's stomach, something hard enough to make her gasp, she suddenly did believe. She believed very well.

THE CALL OF
CHILDREN

THE **WARM BREEZE** drifting through the window irritated Danny. The shadowed living room was where he wanted to be. On the television, the PRESS START screen blinked, and the PLAYER TWO - JOIN! tugged at his heart. He squeezed the controller. Jason had even taken his video games. Just thinking the name knotted his stomach, third time that day, but better than the previous week. He'd overheard Officer Reynolds tell his mom the first 48 hours were the most important, and if that were true, Jason would never be found.

Danny switched off the console. Summer break promised fun, evenings spent by the creek with giggling friends, ice-cream, water balloon fights, and long nights. Not a missing brother. Not a mother transformed into a bedroom-dwelling witch.

A month had passed.

Danny's mind drifted, first to the angry place he so often went, where images of good times flashed. Then came the dark place—Jason crumpled in a ditch with maggots making a home of his flesh.

"Jesus Christ..." Danny pinched the bridge of his nose, much harder than he intended. Then someone knocked the door.

He sat there a moment, not wanting an interaction. Easier to shelter himself from the sideways glances of neighbors. They offered nothing but a reminder.

"Danny," came a muted voice. "Danny, come on, open up!"

Bang, bang, bang.

He drifted to the door on automatic, past dusted photographs and quiet rooms.

"What?"

The high noon sun made masks of Fred Matthews and Ben Adams' grinning faces. Fred leaned on the doorframe. "You gotta see this.'"

"I don't feel like going out."

"You will," Ben said. "Trust us, man."

Fred and Ben were *Jason's* friends—though Danny wouldn't crown them that. Jason often confided he hated them, but living in *Buttfuck, Nowhere* meant making do with the worst. And these two were Jason's only option if he wanted chums. Shit, if he wanted a church, he had three choices.

"Come on, it's one hell of a day."

"I don't feel like it."

Fred pursed his lips in the way that had earned him the nickname Fishy Freddy from Jason. "This is gonna change your whole summer, Dan. Scratch that. You're whole *life*."

The teen had picked up a lot of traits from his father, a car salesman. "What if I told you we found him."

Not a question, *a statement.*

Danny's body tensed as a high ringing in his skull replaced the chirping of the birds. "What did you say?"

Fred's smile widened. "You heard me. Now are you coming or are you not."

"I...this isn't funny, Fred."

"You're damn right it's not. Not meant to be."

Danny's heart sped. His fingers found the door handle and tightened there. "My—my mom's not home, she won't be for another hour."

"Screw your mom. Not like that. You know what I mean. Just come on already!"

Danny stepped from the house and blinked against the blinding sun. The last time he'd been outside was a distant memory. The foliage and the breeze *seemed* real enough, though Fred's words still snagged in his mind. They'd *found* Jason?

"Alive?" he asked.

Fred sneered. "Would I be smiling like an asshole if I'd found a body? Do you think that low of me, man?"

"I don't know what to think right now."

"Then don't think, stupid. Just follow us."

Ben shook his head, rolled his eyes. "Can we just get out of the sun before I fucking pass out?"

"Yeah, come on, Dan. Hurry it up."

Danny did as told, but he scanned the streets as they moved as if expecting neighbors to leap out from behind parked cars and break into laughter.

What an idiot! Kid thinks his brother was found!

It's been a month, dummy! Could you survive a month outdoors? Flies are bursting from his eyes and ears right now!

"Is he outside?" Danny asked. "Where is he?"

The more he asked, the more he sweated. Could it be true?

Fred placed a hand on the gate of Joe Miller's field. Ahead stretched an acre of green hill leading to the woodlands. "Remember the start of summer?" Fred asked, and grunted as he hopped the divide. "The Gray house?"

Danny's chest lurched. "Fuck off. The place out there?"

Ben sighed at that and leaped the gate next, landing in a patch of weeds. "What other place, dum-dum?" he said. "Can you just hurry it up already?"

"Right, sorry."

Danny took the gate next and followed as the teens started up the hill. The blazing sun and fresh green scent were at odds with the confused and blackened mess that swirled around his brain. "You're saying Jay has been out in the Gray House for a month straight? It's got no electricity or anything. The walls are almost rubble. What the hell would he even *do* out there? What's he been eating?"

As they approached the shadowed trail beneath the pines, Ben pulled a blindfold. "You remember the deal?"

Danny licked at his lips. "You can't be serious, guys. Can we just move it? You don't expect me to—"

"Jason made you do it, right? You've been here three times, Dan. You know how this works."

Danny looked them in turn, then decided better than to question. The sooner they stopped arguing, the sooner they set off. "Fine. Just hurry it up."

Ben flicked out the blindfold and Danny closed his eyes as the warm material licked around his face. Ben breathed through his mouth, too close to Danny's ear, as he tied off the knot and a pressure hit the back of Danny's skull. "Happy, asshole?"

Jason always tied it lightly, careful not to catch hairs or cause a headache.

"Happy."

A hand pressed into the center of his back and Danny reached out his arms. His fingers found a shirt.

Fred laughed. "Touching me? Little lower and you'll get my ass, that's what you really want a hold of."

The lack of answers and the teasing—and probably the heat—finally got to Danny. Tears stung his eyes. He was suddenly thankful for the blindfold. "Jason always let me hold onto his shirt." His watery voice made him cringe. "I'll fall if I don't know where I'm going."

As if on cue, his shoe scuffed a rock and Danny's guts entered his throat the ground rushed to meet him. He crashed on dry leaves as the air shot from his lungs. Fred barked laughter from somewhere on the other side of the blindfold.

"Shit, okay, okay. Here."

Danny reached out and grabbed only air.

"No, okay, *here*."

He grabbed again at nothing.

"Oh, that's too fucking funny. Here."

This time, a clammy hand wrapped around his wrist and yanked him upright. Danny planted his feet, swaying a moment. "This isn't funny, Fred. If Jason's out there, I need to see him. And if he's not out there, then you're in a lot of trouble."

"Think I'd waste my day pulling you out of the house if I didn't know where your brother was? Come on, grab a hold."

Danny's fingers once again found the shirt and he balled the material in a fist. His knuckles grazed a lump.

"Are you carrying a weapon?"

He imagined a gun tucked inside Fred's jeans, a Magnum like *Dirty Harry*.

"If I was gonna hurt you, I could do it with my bare hands, idiot."

And I'm blindfolded...idiot.

"Where would I get a gun from, anyway?"

"I don't know."

"Good." As Fred started forward, Danny stumbled until he found his pace. Ben snickered from behind.

"He wouldn't shut up about the Gray House, remember?" Fred said.

"I remember."

"Every time we were at the creek, '*Hey, can we hit the Gray place tomorrow?*' and we'd be, like, an hour just back. He's obsessed with the damn building. Should've thought of checking there sooner."

Danny recalled Jason returning home in early June with his hands shoved inside his hoodie. He'd called Danny to his room before revealing his hidden treasure. A chunk of rock from the Gray House wall. Just a brick smothered in concrete and moss. When Danny asked him why he'd taken it home, Jason simply replied, "Because it's cool?"

Obsessed. Fred had a point.

"Mind, now," Ben said, and Danny grunted as his foot expected ground and found a drop. Fred pressed forward and Danny was pulled, his arms stretching. "Slow it down, man. I can't see a thing."

"That's how it's meant to be. Now quit whining."

The blindfolding had started day one, once Jason returned smiling like he'd won the lottery. "I've found a special place," he'd said. "Danny, you cannot tell Mom, all right? No one can know where it is unless I say so. I want you to see it tomorrow with the guys. But you're wearing a blindfold. You cannot go there without me. Understood?"

Danny said he understood very well, and so the summer month went. He'd forgotten about the Gray House when Jason stopped taking him, just another cool spot in the forest lost to time. They'd found many through the years, and each lost their spell with a couple of visits.

"We'd checked the entire woods," Danny said. "The *army* were out here combing the forest for days. You're telling me they missed the Gray House?"

"The Gray House is special, Dan. You know that. Just keep moving."

And so, Danny did. And with each step, his excitement swelled. What did Jason look like after spending a month in the woods? Had his downy lip hair sprouted into a full beard? Did he have tick bites all over a now-anemic body? Danny's thoughts continued along that path for countless minutes, only interrupted when Fred called, "We're here."

He hit against Fred's back. Ben chuckled. "He said we're here, dummy. That means stop walking."

Then the blindfold was whipped from his face and Danny's eyes burned in the white sun. He squeezed the bridge of his nose as the blurry and shadowed forest filtered into focus. Before him stood the Gray House.

The building looked to be a home at one time, although who would live way out here was beyond Danny. The mottled roof only covered half the rooms and fell away to the right, touching the weed-infested and exposed concrete floor of what may have once been a dining-room. A table stood in the corner, the wood now green and sprouting foliage. Above it, on the half-collapsed wall, was the infamously spray-painted words **GRAY HOUSE**. The boys had speculated for days what it meant, and when Jason suggested it was perhaps the surname of the folks who used to live there, the gang accepted the answer as the most likely, not giving it any more thought. Besides, the answer made for a good story, and they'd spent their travels through the woods coming up with tales of where the Grays now lived.

And then there was the door leading to the room beneath the roof, the frame still sturdy despite the harsh environment. A special door, Jason called it. It'd survived along with the roof even when the rest of the house had fallen. For that, no one was to vandalize what still stood. It was to be respected.

Fat, mossy pines guarded the building for miles, and if left alone, Danny imagined he'd never find his way back.

"He's in there," Fred said, and stood back, folding his arms.

Danny started forward as the sun strobed through the thick overhang. Ahead lay a moss-covered empty window frame, the glass long gone. With each step, Danny's heart punched. His shaking hands found the frame and he peered inside, waiting for his eyes to adjust to the gloom. A sharp scent, like fermented fruit, hit his nose, and in a small voice he called, "Jay?"

Something stirred in the darkness. Danny licked his dry lips. "Jay, are you in here? It's me."

Within the inky confines, a shadow rose—the silhouette of a young boy with shoulder-length hair. The shape approached from the gloom. And Danny's chest tightened.

"Hey there," Jason said with a smile, and though his skin looked a little dirty, his clothes unwashed, he appeared healthy and in no danger. Even his scent—*yes!*— the too-thick aftershave that Danny always hated, now flooded him with delight. "Coming in?"

And with that, hot tears spilled down Danny's cheeks. His chin quivered as he laughed and laughed and couldn't stop. His heart felt like it might explode. He let his head fall back as an involuntary cry ripped from his throat, a primal roar full of gratitude. Then Jason asked again, "D, are you coming inside or what?"

"Yes!"

Danny raced from the window and leaped across the knee-high brick wall of the dining-room. He reached the door, but before turning the handle, he looked to Fred and Ben and said, "Thank you. Just...*thank you.*"

They were grade-A assholes, could win an academy for how they played their parents, but right then and there, Danny thought them heroes. He pulled the handle and stepped inside the walls of the Gray House.

At first, the fermented stench was almost too strong, like old vinegar, then it began to clear as Danny's eyes adjusted. Jason stood against the far wall, a smile on his dirt-smeared face.

"Jay, how in the world have you been staying—"

The door slammed behind Danny and he yelped. He spun and tried the handle but it held tight. Fred cackled.

"Not fucking funny, guys! Stop it."

Then he remembered the open window and his fears melted. Besides, Jason was here now. He'd kick both their asses to high heaven and back.

"Dan, not gonna give me a hug?"

Danny turned and faced his brother, a moment he'd dreamed of every day for a month. A moment that kept sleep at bay and ached his heart worse than any broken bone. He glided across the floor on weak and shaking legs. Then his brother's arms engulfed him and that familiar aftershave filled the air and the soft fabric of his clothes and—

"I've missed you so much."

Danny tightened his grip around his brother, tighter than he'd ever held a person, as if Jason could float away as easily as a balloon any second and never return. As if—

"What are you doing?"

Danny pulled back as his fingers grazed a lump. His brother laughed. "What?"

"What is that?" Danny laughed, too, but a tickle of fear teased his stomach. He suddenly didn't want to be holding his brother.

"What was what, man?"

"You...I don't know, you've got something on your back?"

"Homo!" Jason released him—*thank Christ...*–and stepped back, but not before slapping Danny's shoulder. "The hell's the matter with you?"

"The matter with me? Jay, you've been out here for a month. We all thought you were *dead*! Do you not understand what you've put me through? Put Mom through?"

A sudden anger boiled inside him, quick and sturdy as a highway truck. He balled his fists. "What the hell were you thinking, staying out here?"

"Gotta move away sometime, Dan. Don't be such a buzzkill."

Danny shook his head, his arms falling to his sides. "A buzzki...Jesus, Jay."

"Hey, hey." He stepped forward. "Come here. Stop that."

And then Danny was in his arms again and the anger disappeared as easily as a magician's trick. But again, his hand found the lump. Danny broke free of the embrace. He walked backward towards the door, stepping on broken glass and chunks of rock.

"What is that? On your back?"

Jason cocked his head, an eyebrow arched. "I don't know what you're talking about, D."

"I felt one on Fred, too. Are you carrying a gun? What are you guys planning?"

Danny wanted to be home with his mom. He wished he'd never come to the Gray House. His back connected with the door—*locked, it's locked!*–as his eyes fell to the empty window frame. The sunny outdoors teased him here in the gloom, and the curdled stench bloomed once again in the air. Jason followed Danny's line of sight.

"Go on," his brother said. "Try it."

"Why are you doing this to me?" Danny blubbered as tears flooded his eyes. But, despite his confusion, he put his right foot forward. "I'm getting Mom."

"I dare ya."

Danny broke for the window as Jason pushed from the wall. He leaped at the empty frame and his stomach crashed against hard concrete. He worked his fingers into warm moss and pulled himself up, half-out the Gray House now. Then Jason grabbed his legs, pulled himself forward, and rough hands pressed into the small of Danny's back, crushing his gut against the window frame. Razors of pain ripped through his abdomen.

"Jay, stop it!"

Then a new sensation—something cold and gelatinous slipping up the back of his shirt...and a sharp *prick*.

"Ah!" Danny kicked out blindly and his foot connected with his brother's chest. Whatever was pressed to the small of his back slipped free, leaving a slimy trail. Danny fell back inside the Gray House as his chin exploded on the window frame before he crashed to the ground and blindspots erupted in his vision. The taste of old pennies filled his mouth.

Danny rolled over, facing his brother and the gloom, and spat. More hot liquid filled his mouth.

Jason clutched a pulsating lump in his right fist. Something that glistened with two stalks meandering like spellbound snakes. A pale slug. The largest slug Danny had ever seen.

"What the fuck is that?" Danny screamed, and scrambled to his feet. He spat again, and hot crimson spittle splattered down his quaking chin.

"It needs a home," Jason said with a laugh. "Jesus, Danny, it's not the end of the world. Stop freaking out."

"Help!" Danny screamed until his throat ripped, and then he screamed again. "Somebody, anyone!"

"Oh. My. God. Will you calm down?" Jason stepped forward and Danny scrambled to get his fists raised. He stood like a boxer, shaking as if being electrocuted. "Don't you dare come near me."

"It's fine, Danny, really. Like getting a shot at the hospital, just a little sting."

"I want to go home."

Genuine confusion overcame Jason's face as he said, "But we are home, Danny?"

Then his brother started forward and Danny threw a punch as Jason's head snapped sideways with a satisfying *crack*.

"Little fucker!"

Jason's knee whooshed up and Danny balked as the air shot from his lungs—*oh, God!*—and searing pain exploded in his gut. He collapsed to his knees, gasping.

"It's. Just. A. Fucking. Prick. Danny."

Through his blurred vision, something glistened on the floor. The hunk of window looked like a glass shark tooth.

"Now lift your shirt and do as I say."

Danny leaped forward, snatched the glass, and swung like a baseball hit in reverse. A wet *pop* accompanied his palm slicing up the slick blade. Danny whipped his hand back and skittered along the dirty floor as Jason screamed. He watched his brother arch his back and drop the slug, the glass jutting from the bottom of his shirt. A dark stain bloomed instantly, and he reached around, grabbed hold of the jagged glass, and pulled it free.

"Gah!" He dropped the shard and it clattered on the floor, then brought his open palm before his face. "What have you done, Danny? Why?"

Danny opened and closed his mouth like a fish out of water, but no words would come. His palm throbbed and he was faintly aware of a hot and sticky wetness leaking between his fingers, just like his brother's hand. But what was more was the thing jittering beneath Jason's shirt. It slopped from its hiding place and hit the floor and squirmed. Another slug. This one oozing black ichor on the dusty concrete.

"Danny, how could you?" Jason's face was full of genuine hurt as he stumbled around. He hit the wall beside the window and slid down, knocking a cloud of dust. His eyes fluttered and he shook his head, but soon, they closed, and he fell still. His chest rose and fell with slow and even breaths, but soon that too ceased. His pink skin paled to white—and didn't stop. It grayed. And shrunk. Until all that remained was no more than a mummified teenager. One slunk in a gloomy and hollow home with a slug wriggling by its feet.

But none of that mattered to Danny anymore. No tears came. He didn't even care where the other slug had gone, the one Jason had clutched in his fist in what seemed like eons ago. He still had brothers, yes, many brothers. A new family. And the stinging in his lower back had morphed to a pleasant *sucking*, as gentle and warm as a mother's touch. He rose to his feet with some effort, but soon found the door handle and stepped out into the hot sun. He had others to tell of Gray House. Not just his mother, no, but the whole town. He needed everyone to know. It was a special place, after all.

And as Danny stepped through into the forest, he had no doubt he'd find his way back to the village. He knew the path like the back of his hand.

He'd find his way home again, too. For home was such a special place.

FATHER'S DAY

VOMIT BURNED DAVID'S throat. He rubbed his forehead, eyes stinging, as he moved aside on the mattress to avoid the spreading mess seeping through the duvet. An acidic burp made him wince, and he eased aside the covers before climbing from the bed. Harsh light from the open window forced him to squint. The calendar on Julie's dresser read July. He frowned.

"It's March."

The stench from the bed attacked his nostrils, and with some effort, he calmed his stomach. On the nightstand sat a half-empty glass of water which he scooped and drained. Smacking his lips, he returned the glass and tried to recall the night before. If Julie hadn't woken him, hadn't kissed his forehead, whatever he did had to be bad.

A hazy image of Kenny's Bar swam to the swollen surface of his brain. There sat Charlie, laughing at some joke David couldn't recall. Following that scene came a shameful memory of pissing against the wall of a sheltered alleyway. Then another bar, and another. A woman was in the mix somewhere, too, a redhead with long legs and buckteeth. Jesus.

David held no recollection of engaging in anything more than a kiss with the girl, but that didn't mean nothing else had happened. In time, his jittered memory would catch, and when it did, he'd do his best to appear normal as a truck ton of shame sloshed inside his head.

Soon enough, even shame would disappear. It always did.

"Jules?"

The feeble sound sizzled his throat like used oil. Rubbing his Adam's apple, he waited for the pain to subside and checked the alarm. 10:21 AM. At this point, Julie was most likely tending her roses in the backyard. In the next room, April, their daughter, would have dolls spread across the floor, playing until either he or Julie forced her to get dressed. He'd start with April, getting her ready before cooking breakfast and attempting to smooth things over with Julie. All after changing the bed sheets, of course.

"What the hell?"

David stalked to Julie's full-length mirror on the far wall. The sight forced a gasp. He wore his Sunday suit. Raising his arms, he wriggled his torso, allowing the material to rub against his flesh, reassuring himself that, yes, the suit was indeed there. He hadn't removed the suit from its plastic zip bag in well over a year, not since the last job interview, and—as far as he could remember—he hadn't worn it out last night, either.

Had he come home and decided to try it on? Such an idiotic act would surely cause Julie to become as pissed as a feral cat. Understandably so. He could see himself now, stumbling about in the dark, opening and closing doors, hushing inanimate objects while Julie glared from bed.

How in the world has she put up with me for this long?

David didn't have the answer, and the thought made his hangover worse. After losing his job as a copy writer in IT, he went with Charlie on job hunts to the city. They'd stop at a bar on the first day and snagged a quick pint or two over lunch. Within a week, those drinks increased to three or four, and then, after no responses from their inquiries, they began to simply meet at the bar. That way just seemed easier.

Change the sheets, David thought. *Do it quietly, do it fast, then grab a shower and get April fixed for food. Take her and Jules out for lunch...if you have any money left.*

Shit. Did he have *anything* left? David patted his pockets, felt only loose material and lint. He always left his wallet by the alarm clock on the bedside table—*always*. Only a book and a glass of water there now. No wallet.

I'm in deep shit this time, man...Hell, maybe that's a good thing...

Perhaps he needed Julie's scorning—*wanted* her to do it—so that he could smack his ass into gear and get his life back on track. He only worried his problems had already stooped too low. Each time he thought of spending the day in town with Charlie, drinking and picking up chicks, excitement coursed through his being. Another day of being in the pits with Jules, worrying about the next bill, keeping April happy, maintaining their degrading marriage...Well, it made him want to scream. He didn't *want* to feel that way, but he couldn't deny facts.

"Fuck..."

David sniffed back tears as he folded the soggy duvet. He crossed each corner, keeping the vomit to a central location, then lifted. Thankfully, no puke had soaked through and reached the mattress yet. With the blanket in-hand, he tiptoed to the doorway and eyed the hall for any signs of his wife or daughter before stepping from the room. Other than a slumped toy near the living room door, he was in the clear.

David took the hallway in two strides and jumped inside the utility-room. He fed the sheets into the washing machine and switched it on. When the machine hummed to life, he scooped a fresh duvet from the countertop and made his way back to the bedroom. Then he stepped on a toy.

"Fuck!"

Pain throbbed through his heel as he bounced on one foot, hoping his *bad word* hadn't invaded his daughter's room. Breathing through his nose, he limped back to the bedroom and made up the bed as quickly as possible. With that finished, he shook his head. There had not been a toy in middle of the hall when he'd first checked. He left to inspect.

"What in the...?"

Two more toys now surrounded the first, each one *almost* identical to the last besides minor variations. Round heads, crudely shaped, sat on cone-like bodies David supposed were dresses but contained no detail. Only solid white plastic. Two circular feet popped from the bottom of what passed for clothing, and long sausage-like arms sat disproportionately to either side of the figurines. Strange-shaped eyes stared back at him.

April did this, he thought.

She'd heard him rush to the utility room and had arranged her toys for him to find. New toys she'd picked up while out with Julie. Had to be the case.

"April?" he called. His voice became stronger now he had a theory. "Baby? You awake?"

His daughter squealed with delight from her bedroom, raising a smile on David's face. At least *she* wasn't angry.

Her voice came from the other side of the door. "Are they out there, Daddy?"

David smiled. "The dolls? Yeah."

Another giggle. "I'm so *happy!*"

David laughed as he gathered the toys and entered the room. "Morning, Sunshine."

The blinds were pulled, blocking any external light and coating the room with dim shadows. April sat on the floor, pages and pages of sketches littered about her like squares of snow. Each one depicted a strange doll, same as the ones he held now, perfect down to the last detail.

David kissed his daughter's forehead, smelling shampoo from her tussled hair. "How you doing?"

He placed the dolls by her side and pointed to the pictures. "Those are really good, honey. Look exactly like the toys."

"They *are* the toys, Silly-head. My perfect dollies."

A smile twitched his lips. "Well, nobody's perfect."

April didn't like that joke. Her lips quivered as her eyes glistened. "Baby." David got to one knee and rubbed her back. "I'm only kidding. Don't worry. They're really cool dolls. Honest."

"I know..." His daughter's voice wavered like a warped cassette. "I just missed you is all."

David chuckled. "I slept in, honey. It's okay. I'm up now."

"No, you've been gone for *ages*."

"Ages? How long have I been gone, sweetheart?"

"Like a month or something, I don't know."

Cocking his head to the side, David arched an eyebrow. "Now that's a *slight* exaggeration. Look, I'm awake. Want me to fix you jammy toast?"

Jammy toast, David knew, would sweeten any of April's moods.

His daughter clapped her hands and smiled. "Yes! Can I show you something first, though?"

"'Course. What's up?"

"I got really good at this. Like, *really, really* good. Watch."

April pulled a blank sheet in front of her and eyed her coloring pencils a moment. Her fingers flexed comically as she decided on a color, tongue jutting from her mouth. She gave a light gasp before plucking the green, clearly happy with her choice.

"Now," she announced, straightening her back to try and appear what she called 'official'. "You like goblins. This is correct, is it not?"

David laughed. "Yes. This is correct. I do like me some goblins."

"Well, this is good. I'm going to make you one. It being Daddy's Day, and you being my daddy."

"It's Father's Day?"

Too late, David realized he'd spoken aloud, but April busied herself in her illustration, tongue still jutted from concentration. He eased back onto his rump and frowned. Julie hadn't woken him. For the last five years, each Father's Day, she'd made him a breakfast in bed. The idea that—if today *was* Father's Day—she instead went to the garden, left him a little sick. She had to be more annoyed than ever for that to happen.

David shoved the thought from his mind and watched his daughter scribble. She began by first sketching the goblin's head, a crude circle with two triangles for ears. Next, she filled in the features—long nose, bushy eyebrows, slits for eyes, and a broad mouth containing two more triangles for teeth. She rushed the body, doodling a simple matchstick form comically out of proportion to the head. Finished, she smiled up to David and squeezed her eyes shut.

"Done!" she announced.

David gave her shoulder a light squeeze. "It's perfect. Thank you, Pumpkin. Can I hang it on the fridge with a magnet?"

"No, Silly!" April grabbed the page and gave it a shake. "*This* is just the idea. The goblin's outside."

A cold chill crawled up David's spine. He thought of the toys. "What...what are you talking about, April?"

"Go check. I made you a goblin because you love them so much. Go!"

David stood on shaky legs and made his way into the hall, his pulse quickening. He eased open the door, and froze.

"Oh, my God..."

The goblin doll sat in the very spot that the others had. And just like the others, it was perfect, down to the last detail. David scooped the oddity before turning it over in his hands.

"This is unbelievable. This is insane." He faced his daughter who had come to watch. Despite himself, he found that he feared her. "April, how did you do this?"

She looked to the floor and pouted. "I just wished really hard. Like, *really, really* hard...did I do something bad?"

"No, baby, no." David rubbed her back. "You didn't. Honest. I just need to...I...need to see Mommy. Is she in the garden?"

"Of course she is. She seems happier now, though. Have you seen your cards yet? I don't think I like them."

"You guys got me cards?"

"*Everyone* got you cards. And flowers, too."

David ignored the 'happier' comment, and asked, "Why would *everyone* get me a card? I'm *your* father, sweetie. Not everyone's."

"I don't know."

"I'm going to see Mommy, okay?" He tried keeping his voice level but struggled. "You wait here."

"Okay, Daddy. Then you make me jammy toast."

"Then I make you jammy toast."

I'm panicking, he thought. He hadn't had an attack in years, but the tightness in his chest became all too familiar.

He crossed the hall on legs struggling to support him, mind spinning with possibilities. The air felt too thick and he found it hard to breathe. Had his daughter just *sketched* a figurine into existence? He'd watched many episodes of *The Twilight Zone* in his youth, but never expected to find himself actually *starring* in one.

Unless, He thought, *Julie's in on this, too...A Father's Day prank of some sort?* Julie did have a wicked sense of humor.

In the doorway, his mouth dried. He felt the room dip as he clutched the frame for support. Cards sat neatly on the fireplace mantle, only, they weren't Father's Day cards. They were sympathy cards.

David read them from left to right: *Sorry for your loss. Condolences. Thinking of you. Praying for you in this difficult time...*

Have you seen your cards yet? She seems happier now...

David floated to the mantle and plucked a card. He knocked three others in the process but didn't care. Reading the text inside caused an involuntary moan.

I just can't believe it, Jules...I wish there was something I could say or do to turn back time and make it all better. Please call me, okay? Please. I loved him as much as anyone. Yours, Charlie.

"No..."

David let the card slip from his fingers and looked about the room. The photographs over the breakfast table were missing, leaving rectangular spots of dust-free paint. Those were supposed to be spots where his and Julie's anniversary photos sat, one for each year.

Repeating the word *no* beneath his breath, something caught his eye—The contents of a fallen card by his foot.

Inside was printed: *Please accept our condolences, Julie. And reach out if you need us. We've dealt with many alcohol-related troubles in our time. Don't be afraid to get in touch. Thinking of you during this very sad time—Your friends, the DAO.*

"Dublin Alcoholics Outreach?"

A shadow drifted across the back window and David jumped. He eased to the kitchen and peered outside as Julie, watering can in-hand, made her way up the garden. The morning sun bathed her in a warm glow. She walked slower than usual—lumbering—as if lost. Beneath the brim of her gardening hat, gray hair peppered her brown locks, another change David hadn't seen before. She'd also lost weight.

David's chest ached. Pulling his gaze from the window, he wiped his eyes with the back of his hand. Then he dropped two slices of bread into the toaster and took the jam from the cupboard. He buttered the toast when it popped free and spread the jam, cutting the slices into triangles, just as April liked.

With the toast made, he made his way back to his daughter's bedroom, sparing one last glance out the window. Julie had her back turned as she spilled water onto her blooming roses. He watched a moment longer, wanting to go out there, needing to hold her, but knowing he could not. More important matters needed tending.

In the hallway, he scooped a foot-long caterpillar toy from the floor. Like both of the dolls and the goblin, it was devoid of all nuance expect for a wonky grin. David entered his daughter's bedroom like a zombie—colorless and wide-eyed. His daughter's reaction only confirmed his thought. She held up a plush-toy, a heart, and just like the other creations, the heart contained neither color nor detail.

"You're mad, aren't you?" she asked, holding out the toy for him to take. David eased himself beside her, then gave the heart a squeeze and clutched it to his chest before looking her in the eye. "April, I don't know how you did it, but I know you meant well."

"*I just missed you so much...*"

Her words descended into blubbering, lower lip quivering. David placed an arm around her and pulled her close.

"I know you did. I know...I'd do the same for you."

Her head bobbed in understanding.

"Your mother..." The word died in David's throat but he forced himself to continue. "She...she seems happier lately?"

"She said she's *getting better*. She talks to me about that kind of thing but I don't like it, even though she said she wants us to be 'open' with each other. I can't do that. *I can't.* I want you back."

"I know..." David gave her a smile that quickly collapsed. "But your mom is a very smart person, April. She's even stronger than Daddy. Believe me."

April's eyes shone like the surface of a lake. "She is?"

"Yup. She knows what's best, trust me on that. She's not happy right now, but she's *happier*, and that's because she's *tough*. Like a rock. She'll keep getting happier and stronger, too, and so will you."

"Promise?"

"I promise, sweetheart." David swallowed the lump in his throat, unable to look his daughter in the eye. "Pinky promise."

He scanned the papers on the floor, spotting the three dolls, the goblin, the caterpillar, and the heart. Another piece of paper jutted from beneath the doll pictures, and David had a sinking feeling of what it contained.

He nodded to it. "That one me?"

"Yes."

"I made you jammy toast. You want to go eat?"

April kept her eyes on the floor, complexion drained. "Yes," she said, then added, "I just missed you so much..."

"I know, baby. I know. Go on. Eat your breakfast."

April rose from the ground, her golden hair clinging to her wet cheeks and forehead. "The eraser is with the pencils," she said. And in that moment, David had never been more proud of her.

Just like her mother, he thought.

He took the eraser and then the illustration, flattening out the paper before him and working free the crinkles. A smiling matchstick man adorned the page. A happy sun loomed overhead with the word DADDY beneath the man's stick-legs. David looked to his daughter as a smile lifted his cheeks. Warm tears spilled down his face.

"What?" April asked.

"Nothing, baby."

As his daughter opened the door, David pressed the eraser to the page. And told April he loved her very much.

MATT HAYWARD is a Bram Stoker Award-nominated author and musician from Wicklow, Ireland. His books include *Brain Dead Blues*, *What Do Monsters Fear?*, *Practitioners* (with Patrick Lacey), *The Faithful*, *A Penny For Your Thoughts* (with Robert Ford), and *Various States Of Decay*. He compiled the award-winning anthology *Welcome To The Show*, and wrote the comic book *This Is How It Ends* (now a music video) for the band Walking Papers. He received a nomination for Irish Short Story of the Year from Penguin Books in 2017, and is represented by Lane Heymont of the Tobias Literary Agency. He can be found on Twitter @MattHaywardIRE or at his website www.sundancecrow.com

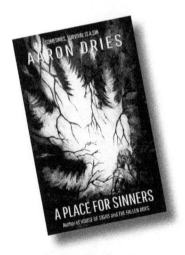